OUT FOR REVENGE

Thrilling crime fiction with a big twist

TONY BASSETT

Published by The Book Folks

London, 2022

© Tony Bassett

ISBN 978-1-80462-040-3

www.thebookfolks.com

Out for Revenge is the fourth standalone mystery in the Detectives Roy and Roscoe crime fiction series by Tony Bassett.

The full list of books is as follows:

MURDER ON OXFORD LANE
THE CROSSBOW STALKER
MURDER OF A DOCTOR
OUT FOR REVENGE

Details about these books can be found at the back of this one.

Prologue

The passenger unclasped his safety belt as the car drew to a halt in the quiet suburban street.

'Looks like I'll be having a row with my son's headteacher tomorrow,' he said.

'How's that?' asked the driver.

'He says my son's got to lose his ponytail. When the lad tried to argue, he said, "No. That's my final word. Lop it off."'

'Sounds like the name of a Russian general,' said the driver, a tall man in blue clothing. 'Do you know, this is what I like about you? Scratch the surface and you're basically just a kind-hearted, family man. Anyway, let's leave the car here and walk the rest.'

Ahead of them, drab-looking and unwelcoming, lay the main part of Albion Road with its rows of Victorian terraced and semi-detached houses. That section of the cold, narrow street in the Warwickshire town of Sedgeworth was clogged with parked cars, and free spaces were hard to come by.

A few minutes later, the two men reached the dingy terraced house where landscape artist Brendan O'Sullivan lived.

Their heavy footsteps echoed down the side alley. Then the driver knocked hard on the half-glazed front door.

Brendan had not been expecting visitors. He roused himself from his couch and turned off the television.

He glanced at his watch. It had just turned two o'clock.

He edged his way through the hall until he could see a dark silhouette behind the glass.

'Who is it?' he asked nervously.

'I've got a package,' said the caller.

All the grey-haired painter could see through the obscured glass was a tall man standing impatiently outside.

He opened the door a fraction and was immediately pushed aside as the car driver barged past him into the house, followed by his shorter accomplice.

'We've come to collect the money you owe,' said the driver, who was quietly spoken and from a Jamaican background.

'I haven't got it,' Brendan spluttered as he walked to the middle of the room. 'You'll have to give me a couple more weeks.'

'You've had enough time,' said the second man, who had been skulking in the alley.

The tall man strode across the living-room, decorated with paintings of country scenes, and pulled all three drawers out of the sideboard. They went crashing onto the floor.

'Have you hidden your money in here, Brendan?' he demanded.

Brendan insisted, 'No.'

He knocked over a flower vase before opening a cupboard beside the brick fireplace and strewing its contents down.

'Or in here?' he asked.

The middle-aged artist scrambled onto the carpet and picked up some of his prized ornaments, books and magazines that had tumbled out.

'I haven't got any money,' he protested. 'I wouldn't hide it from you.'

The tall man, who had close-cropped hair, stood still.

'No more last chances, Brendan,' he said. 'We've been very fair with you. You've owed us five grand since October. You knew today was payday.'

'You've had enough warnings,' said his associate, an Asian man with short, dark hair and dark clothing.

'Just two more weeks,' pleaded Brendan.

The tall man pulled a Beretta pistol from his pocket and fired it into the ceiling.

'No,' the man insisted. 'We know you've got the money and we want it now.'

'Why have you come here with a gun?' he asked.

'That was just a warning shot. Where's your money?'

The homeowner, fearful on seeing the gun, darted towards the hall in a bid to escape, but the second man blocked his way. So he dashed up the stairs, stumbling as he went, in a clumsy effort to elude them.

'Get after him,' the tall man ordered.

Both men rushed up the stairs and cornered their victim near the bathroom door. They punched him repeatedly in the head and stomach until, splattered with blood, Brendan slumped to the carpet. Then they kicked him and stamped on his face.

The tall man drew out his gun and pumped four bullets into Brendan's body before kicking open the bathroom door. Then, with the gunman grasping Brendan by the shoulders and his associate taking hold of his legs, they dumped his lifeless corpse in the bath.

The pair, both aged around thirty, then ran down the stairs and slipped out of the front door.

'You didn't need to use the shooter,' the car passenger complained as they sprinted along the alley and entered the street. 'I'm sure he got the message. You didn't have to go and kill him.'

'That's just the point,' said his driver. 'We did have to. Customers have to know the consequences if they don't pay for their stash.'

Curtains twitched behind windows in neighbouring houses as the two attackers ceased arguing and ran back towards their car.

Chapter 1

Two years later

The ginger-haired customs officer squinted suspiciously over his glasses at the holidaymaker standing before him at Birmingham Airport.

'Would you step over here, please, sir?' he demanded as he inspected the man's British passport.

Tadeusz Filipowski was led, cursing his luck, to a table at the side of the customs hall, where they were joined by a female officer. He hoisted his two blue cases onto the tabletop.

'The reason we've stopped you today, Mr Robinson, is you seemed to be in a particular hurry,' he said.

'Well, of course,' said the passenger, indignantly. 'I've been on the bloody plane for more than three hours and I want to get home.'

'Everybody coming through here wants to get home, sir. Have you got any cigarettes?'

'Two hundred cigarettes, five bottles of wine and five six-packs of lager,' he said without taking his eyes off the man.

'I'll just open your bags and check.'

Filipowski scowled as both his cases were opened. Shirts and white underwear began to spill out.

'Do I look like someone stupid enough to try and smuggle something?' he asked.

'You'd be surprised what people will do,' the customs man replied. 'You've been away for the whole of Christmas and New Year, sir?'

'Yes, just visiting friends.'

The two uniformed officials spent a few minutes rummaging around in both cases before the ginger-haired man adopted a look of resignation.

'You see? I told you.'

The official gave a weak smile. 'You're free to go,' he said. 'Enjoy the rest of your day.'

The traveller zipped up both cases and stomped off, privately relieved that neither the customs officers nor the Border Force staff he passed earlier had taken a close look at his forged passport.

Within a few minutes, after finding a trolley, he reached the bustling arrivals hall and scanned the rows of expectant faces for his associate.

By now, Filipowski was out of breath. His face, lightly tanned from the glow of the Spanish sun, was glistening with perspiration. He was glad to be back in the Midlands, but irritated by the loudspeaker announcements, the squeaking escalators and the hubbub of conversation.

He was exhausted after his flight from Malaga. All he wanted was to find the house his cousin had arranged for him, put his feet up and have a cup of British tea.

He felt a tap on the shoulder. He spun round and was greeted by the smiling face of his minder, Tyrone Blake, a giant of a man from a West Indian background.

'Good flight, my friend?' Blake asked.

Filipowski frowned. 'Flight was all right, but this bloody place with its bloody officials makes me depressed. Come on. Let's get out of here.'

Blake took the handles of the trolley and they set off through two sets of glass doors. Filipowski shivered as he felt the cold English midday air on his skin.

'Where's your motor?' he asked.

'In the drop-off car park. It's only a short distance. So you got through all right?' said Blake. At thirty, he was more than twenty years younger than his Polish boss.

Filipowski grinned for the first time since leaving Spain.

'Load of jerks work in passport control these days, Tyrone. Guy barely looked at my picture. Suppose it shows old Inky Taylor hasn't lost his touch.'

'You've been so lucky over the past few weeks,' said the younger man as they crossed the road.

'I know. I couldn't believe it when they let me out of the Winson Green happy farm last month.'

'They got you confused with another Polish guy?'

'Yes. A guy called Filipowicz. I wasn't going to argue, was I? Couldn't believe it when the door opened, and I stepped into Winson Green Road. Of course, I jumped on the first plane to the Costas.'

'Don't know why you didn't stay there. The cops will be on the look-out for you.'

'Business is business, Tyrone. You know, my heart was in my bloody mouth when that guy searched my cases.'

'You didn't try and bring anything through?'

'Nothing sizeable. Just some speed for my cousin in the heels of some cheap beach shoes.'

Blake inhaled sharply. 'Lucky guy,' he murmured.

They wove past dozens of cars on the ground floor of the car park until they reached a black Mercedes saloon. Blake pressed the remote.

'Like your style, Tyrone.'

Blake shrugged. 'It's a good runner. You know I love a Touareg, but I just couldn't get one. Rather than hang around, I picked this one up.'

'Where did you—'

'Don't ask, my friend,' he said, raising the boot and placing the suitcases inside. 'Let's just say it was a reliable source and the cops aren't looking for it. But I still reckon you can't beat a Touareg. They give a nice smooth ride – like my girlfriend.'

'You still with that girl? She must've the makings of a saint. Come on. Let's go.'

'Where we heading, boss?'

'My cousin's got a place for me in Balsall Common till the manor house is completely finished. It's a shame we can't go back to the Badminton Road house. I liked it there. Any news about Jake?'

'The cops had him put down after he bit one of their officers.'

'I thought that might happen. You couldn't trust him with strangers. Still he was a bloody good guard dog.'

'Don't know Balsall Common,' said Blake.

'Nice village,' said Filipowski as he climbed into the back of the car. 'It's only fifteen minutes down the road. I'll explain how to get there.'

'Don't worry. I've got me satnav.'

'I forgot to ask,' said Filipowski, as he searched around for his seatbelt. 'Have you spoken to Tahir?'

'Yes, and the trade's going well. Lots of people wanted a bit extra for Christmas. He reckons we're easily going to hit December's target. And the accountant's very pleased with the figures.'

'That's good news,' he mumbled as the car lurched forward and left the car park.

They had only travelled a short distance along the airport exit road when a blue Audi R8 sports car came hurtling out of a turning on the left like a bullet train. Blake was forced to pull up sharply and both men were thrust forward in their seats.

'What a bastard!' screamed Filipowski. 'Is he blind? Isn't he seeing us?'

Blake frowned. 'Don't know, boss.' He sounded his horn for several seconds.

At once the Audi driver slowed down in the middle of the road and made a two-fingered gesture from his open window. Filipowski began cursing and screaming before the fair-haired driver made off at speed.

'Get after him!' he ordered and Blake lowered his right foot to the floor.

Filipowski, who was known among acquaintances for his fearsome temper, was incandescent with rage as the two vehicles sped along the dual carriageway towards the Coventry Road.

'Ram him,' he demanded.

'Boss, are you sure?' asked Blake. 'Is this goon worth it? He just made a stupid mistake.'

'Has made a very stupid mistake, messing with us. Ram him.'

As the vehicles were travelling at more than sixty miles an hour, the C-Class Mercedes lurched forward until its front end was just feet from the Audi. Then Blake gave the pedal one final push, and their Mercedes struck the rear of the blue car.

Immediately after the impact, the driver glared at his pursuers in his rear-view mirror with angry eyes and his vehicle carried on along the road, making a clunking noise.

By the time he reached a roundabout on the outskirts of Meriden, a village renowned for centuries as marking the centre of England, he was finding it hard to drive.

He slowed the car and steered it into a deserted side lane in this secluded countryside location before coming to a halt on a grass verge.

The pursuing driver spotted the damaged sports car crawl into the lane.

'Pull up behind him,' barked Filipowski, 'and bring your new toy.'

Blake stopped his car on the verge a few metres behind the Audi. Then he reached into the glove compartment and grasped his Beretta APX Centurion before the two men leaped out.

The other driver was still inspecting the damage to the rear of his car. Then he glared at the two men – both much taller than him.

'Look what you've done,' he exclaimed before eyeing the pistol in Blake's right hand. 'Now hold on a minute…'

Red-faced Filipowski shouted, 'You cut us up, you bastard. Then you give us two fingers.'

'Look, I'm sorry,' the man pleaded. 'I shouldn't have pulled out.'

'Too right,' said Filipowski. He punched the man in the stomach and then ordered, 'Shoot his tyres.'

'No,' the man screamed as he clutched his stomach and glanced in fear at the weapon. 'Look, I'm really sorry. Forget about the damage to my car. I can sort that out. Just leave my tyres alone.'

But, as he was trying to reason with them, Blake strolled round the sports car and systematically shot all four tyres.

'Maybe you're following the Highway Code a little more conscientiously in future,' muttered Filipowski as he climbed back into the Mercedes.

Chapter 2

Sunita Roy was in a state of panic. She was at risk of being late for work and couldn't find her car keys.

She ran from room to room in her flat near Warwick Racecourse, searching, and finally found them on the dining room table. She grabbed them and dashed out of her front door, slamming it as she went.

She had only managed to take a few steps along her garden path towards her white Peugeot 208 on this cold, grey day when her mobile phone rang. She glanced at the screen. It was one of her close friends.

'Hi, Rupa,' she said. 'We'll have to make this quick because I'm a bit rushed.'

'I was just wondering how your date went?'

Sunita shook her head. 'It hasn't happened yet. I had to delay it because of work.'

A computer technician called Samir had called the young detective sergeant on New Year's Eve to invite her out for a meal.

'Where's he taking you?'

'We're going to an expensive seafood restaurant in Coventry, which he's heard good reports about.'

'Sounds cool.'

'I'll let you know how it goes.'

'Oh, I was just curious. I was meant to be meeting a guy myself on Saturday, but the swine never showed.'

'It's so annoying when that happens. Look, I'd better go. I don't want to annoy the boss.'

Half an hour later, Sunita drew into the car park at St James Street police headquarters, and she ran up the stairs to the CID office, swinging her small, brown handbag.

She was only ten minutes late, but as she greeted her colleagues and switched on her computer, she continually glanced at the chief inspector's door in case her poor timekeeping had been noticed.

Her colleague, DC Omar Khalid, grinned as he caught her attention.

'You're all right, Sarge,' he said. 'He hasn't been asking for you.'

Sunita, who was slim with dark, flowing hair and large, attractive eyes, smiled back at him.

'That makes a change,' she murmured.

'Did you hear about the shooting yesterday?' asked Khalid, sipping tea from a cardboard cup.

'No. Anyone hurt?'

'No. It was a strange one,' he said. 'Could be road rage. A guy called in from Meriden, complaining two thugs in a Mercedes tried to ram him off the road and then shot his tyres. The guvnor's got hold of some CCTV and he's also looking at a photo the driver took of the Mercedes as it sped off.'

A few minutes later, DCI Gavin Roscoe appeared at his door and called for her in his rich Birmingham accent, 'Sergeant, can you spare me five minutes?'

She joined him in his room – one of four private offices partitioned off at the side of the open-plan department.

'Come and have a look at this,' he urged her, turning his computer screen round before settling himself down in his executive chair. 'It's CCTV from the Kenilworth Road near Meriden – one of six new cameras paid for by the parish council.'

At first, all Sunita could see was footage of two cars, a blue Audi sports car and a black Mercedes, pulling over onto the grass verge along a narrow country lane with hedges on either side.

Then she saw a fair-haired man getting out of the sports car and examining his rear bumper. The driver berated the two men emerging from the Mercedes before his manner changed.

The older man punched the angry driver while the taller man fired his gun at the sports car's wheels.

'Don't you recognise them?' said Roscoe, gazing up at his sergeant. 'It's the drug baron Tadeusz Filipowski that we had in custody for a short time last year, and his side-kick Tyrone Blake.'

At first she was confused. Then a glimmer of recognition flickered across her face.

'Oh my God,' she exclaimed, putting her hand to her mouth and sitting down on a chair by the door.

Her mind sprang back to the moment when DI Tom Vickers, her ex-boyfriend, was gunned down at a house in the town of Sedgeworth and surgeons waged a battle to save his life. He had been lured there by an anonymous phone call while investigating a murder.

'They're the men in the frame for shooting Tom,' she said.

Roscoe, who was a little taller than her and with his grey hair reminded her of an agitated uncle, nodded as he collected two sheets of paper from his nearby printer and handed them to her.

'Exactly,' he said. 'They're back in Britain and we've got to do our damnedest to track them down and make them pay for what they did to Tom. Now have a look at these.'

She glanced at the printouts, which showed photographs and descriptions of the two criminals.

'After the shots are fired, the Polish guy glances down the lane towards the roundabout in the distance where he's spotted another vehicle. You can clearly see his small eyes and slightly pinched face.'

'Oh, it's definitely Filipowski, sir,' she said. 'And the guy with the gun definitely resembles Blake.'

He returned to his chair and spun the computer back until it faced him.

'This was a serious road rage incident,' he said. 'The victim made a full report to Warwick police and he's got my full support and sympathy. He was lucky not to be killed by these maniacs and he's been left with a horrific bill for bodywork repairs and new tyres. You can see the number plate clearly. I want you to trace this Mercedes as a matter of urgency. Get Omar to give you a hand if need be. We need to find these guys quickly.'

Chapter 3

Chief Superintendent Nicola Norris was sitting at her oak desk with the door wide open.

'Is that you, Gavin?' she asked as heavy footsteps echoed round the stairwell outside her second-floor office.

'Yes, ma'am,' he replied as he reached the landing, straightening his tie. He strode into her office, closing the door behind him.

'Pull up a seat,' she said, stroking her grey hair absentmindedly. 'By the way, how's your son, George?'

'He was fine the last time I spoke to him, ma'am. He's still learning the ropes, doing basic police training over in Warwick.'

'Good,' she said. 'Look, Gavin, I've called you up here because, I'm afraid, I've received a worrying report about one of our detectives.'

Norris, who had been badly injured in a horse-riding accident a few years before, manoeuvred her wheelchair closer to her desk.

'Disgraceful, but no big surprise. We had an inkling, didn't we, ma'am?' he said while sitting down on a small chair.

'Yes,' she said, peering over her reading glasses. 'You don't need reminding that some of the information I'm going to share with you must remain strictly between us.'

'Of course.'

'Your suspicions towards the end of last year have proved correct that one of our detectives has gone rogue. But it's only this week we've received clear evidence of this.'

'From a reliable source?'

'A very reliable source. From my own goddaughter, who works on the support staff with Summerstoke police. We now know we're dealing with a serious case of police corruption.'

He shrugged. 'Unfortunately, there's always been an element of it.'

'Yes, I know, and whenever it rears its head, we take swift action. But this isn't a case of a traffic officer turning a blind eye to his cousin's driving offence or a constable taking a backhander from a pimp. This concerns a detective inspector at Summerstoke who, for all intents and purposes, is involved in running an OCG linked to the drugs trade.'

Roscoe folded his arms. The suggestion that an officer might be closely linked to an organised crime group was an abomination to him. 'Deplorable, ma'am,' he remarked.

'Previously, as you know, Tom Vickers was examining whether Summerstoke CID had properly investigated the "body in the bath" murder case concerning the death of the artist Brendan O'Sullivan.'

'Yes, ma'am.'

'That's right. Things have moved on since then and we need to focus totally on this bad apple. What I'm proposing, after consultation with the Assistant Chief Constable, is that we set up a new taskforce – codenamed Operation Temple. Earlier today, I had a quiet word with Tom. He's been kicking his heels since he came back to work, and this is a role suited to him.'

She leaned back in her chair before continuing, 'I'm proposing to put Tom in charge of the day-to-day running of this unit and he'll, of course, be liaising with you.'

'That all sounds fine, ma'am. May I ask the name of the suspected officer in question?'

'Strictly between us, DI Seymour Trent. Do you know him at all?'

'I vaguely remember meeting him once. Isn't his number two at Summerstoke DS Philip Bains?'

'That's correct. Tom has told me he and Trent don't know each other, so he sounds like an ideal candidate.'

'Excellent choice, ma'am.'

'Anyway, keep all that under your hat for now.'

Roscoe raised an eyebrow. 'Ma'am, if DI Trent's gone down a wrong turning, there's a chance Bains has joined him on that journey.'

Norris shook her head. 'No suggestion of that for the moment.'

Roscoe continued, 'Tom formed the view last year that the police investigation mounted by Summerstoke CID had led to a miscarriage of justice in the O'Sullivan case.'

She frowned. 'We simply don't know for certain at present whether Trent's investigation was skewed against those two defendants. That will continue to form part of Tom's inquiries.'

'Ma'am, with respect, Bains failed abysmally to catch the two suspects who injured Tom in November. There are rumours both suspects were tipped off in advance about the police raid on their premises in Coventry that took place in November.'

Norris shook her head. 'You should never listen to rumours, Gavin. I've known Phil Bains for years and he's a good, honest copper. It's Trent alone we're concentrating on.'

Roscoe felt uncomfortable. He was never certain how much stock she took of his opinions. He harboured doubts about Bains' integrity. He suspected the man was as crooked as a country lane. They had clashed over police operations in the past, but Roscoe said nothing more.

'Have you had a chance to read through my memo about the road rage case?' he asked.

'Yes, I was coming to that. I see you've assigned DS Roy to trace the car. That's fine, but as soon as she gets a result, I want that information passed to the CID team at Summerstoke.'

'But, ma'am…' he protested.

'That's my final word on the matter. Operation Temple must take priority for the moment. Look, if your team were to take over inquiries into Tom's shooting, I'd have to present Summerstoke CID with a good reason why. Trent would no doubt complain, and my change of direction might put him on his guard. So, for the moment, we leave things as they are.'

Roscoe nodded. 'I hear what you're saying,' he muttered.

'The assistant chief constable decided this wasn't a case the professional standards department should handle for confidential reasons. So we're relying on you and Tom Vickers.'

'Very well, ma'am. I'll keep you informed,' he said, rising from his seat. He stepped towards the door, stroking his chin. Then he turned to face her again.

'I've just had a thought, ma'am. If Seymour Trent is dabbling in the drugs world, he could be in league with Filipowski and his drugs gang, the 101 Crew. After all, Trent absolved two 101 men of involvement in the "body in the bath" murder and charged rival gang members instead.'

She shook her head. 'There's no suggestion of him being linked with Filipowski at the moment, Gavin. Please let me know as soon as you and Tom make any progress. In my fifteen years here, we've prided ourselves on running a force with impeccable standards. Let's not allow one rotten copper to tarnish that reputation.'

* * *

The chief inspector was relieved when he finally approached his home on the outskirts of the market town of Queensbridge just after six o'clock.

It had been a long, tiring day. He had fought an inner battle to control his temper during his briefing from the chief superintendent.

His car passed several fields, which lay bleak and barren on that cold January evening. Then he turned into his narrow, unmade lane where a row of ash and beech stood like sentinels.

His daughter, Melody, greeted him as he parked in the garage.

'You're looking pleased with yourself,' he said as he collected some documents from the back seat and locked the garage doors.

'Oh, Dad, I've found out what's wrong with Starlight,' she said, crossing the lawn still in her brown jacket and fawn jodhpurs. 'It was a hoof problem.'

Her father smiled at his twenty-one-year-old daughter, who had been complaining for several weeks that the horse she rode regularly at nearby stables had developed 'temper tantrums'.

'Oh, Dad. It's so sad,' she said, close to tears. 'Starlight's only thirteen and the vet says she's only going to be suitable for light riding for a couple more years.'

'I'm very sorry,' he said. 'That's always been your favourite horse, hasn't it?'

'Yes.'

'Come on. Let's go inside and find your mother.'

Helen, smiling and wearing an apron, greeted them both in the hallway of the 1930s detached house.

'Ah, here you are,' she remarked, giving her husband a peck on the cheek.

'What sort of day, darling?' she asked as Melody strolled into the living-room and switched on the TV.

'Came close to losing my temper with the chief super,' he admitted, putting his folder of papers on the hall table. 'She's letting that prize idiot Philip Bains continue to look into Tom's shooting when the man's got nowhere with it in seven weeks.'

'Never mind. I'll make you a nice cup of tea and we've got roast chicken for supper.'

'That's good. Shall I give you a hand with the vegetables?'

'No, you're fine. Go and watch the news.'

He stepped into the living-room and settled on the leather settee beside his daughter.

An item of television news about a potential breakthrough in cancer detection caught his attention for a few minutes before Helen brought in two steaming hot cups of tea.

'Forgot to mention,' she said. 'We've finally agreed a date for Dad's retirement party.'

He turned the volume down with the TV remote. 'OK. When is it?'

'Monday, 11 February at the tearooms.'

'So they've finally given up the idea of the Crown and Sceptre?'

'Yes, and do you know what? Because they didn't want me to be scurrying to and from the kitchen all night, we've decided to let Amelia do the catering.'

'Oh good.'

'Have I got to go?' asked Melody.

'Of course,' said her mother.

'It'll be so boring. All those old people.'

'They won't all be old. I'll be there,' said Roscoe with a grin.

'Very funny, Dad,' she murmured.

'Listen,' he said, 'it's important you and your brother should be there. Your grandparents would expect it.'

Then his mobile phone rang. He walked across to the patio doors at the far end of the room to answer it.

'Roscoe.'

He could detect the excitement in his sergeant's voice as she spoke.

'Sir, cameras have picked up the Mercedes that was used in the Meriden shooting. It's parked outside a disused warehouse in Erdington.'

Chapter 4

The well-built man with closely cropped light-brown hair wandered totally naked across the bedroom carpet.

After making a visit to the ensuite bathroom he returned to his bare-breasted companion – an attractive blonde woman who was lying spread-eagled on the king-size bed. She was wearing just a black lace cupless Basque and matching thong.

'That was great,' she whispered as the off-duty detective, Seymour Trent, bent over her for a kiss. 'We must book this hotel again. I'd give it a score of ten.'

'What – the hotel or the sex?' he asked.

She giggled. 'Both.'

The woman, Polly Cook, looked around the room with its white walls, a grey carpet and long grey curtains draped around a large sash window. Above the bed were nine framed black-and-white photographs of Birmingham canal scenes from the 1920s.

'We'll get a room with a view next time,' he asserted in his flat Lincolnshire accent. 'All we can see from here is bloody cars coming in and out of the car park and the bloody boom barrier being raised all the time.'

'Some booms are almost permanently up!' She giggled as she glanced at him.

They both laughed. He moved away from the bed, taking care not to knock the untouched bottle of Chablis and its ice bucket from the bedside cabinet. He waddled towards his suitcase, on the floor beneath the window.

'Talking of scoring, I fancy a line. Do you?' he asked, searching in the bottom of his case for a small plastic bag containing cocaine. After a few seconds, his hand chanced upon the drug. It was next to his police warrant card.

He brought the bag over to the bed and deftly sprinkled the white powder in a neat line on her chest, just above her breasts. He rolled up a five-pound note and snorted it.

'It's good stuff. Really moist and soft,' he said. 'You can have a line in a minute. It's part of a new consignment that Filipowski's brought in.'

'Is that the guy you call Tiff?' Polly asked.

'That's right,' he said, wiping his nose with the back of his hand and then snorting the residue into his left nostril. 'Yes, Tadeusz Yanis Filipowski, to give him his full name. Everyone calls him Tiff. I thought it was because of his initials when I first got introduced to him. But it's not that. It's because he's got a temper like a deranged fishwife.

'I'll give you an example. His number two, Tyrone Blake, who runs a team of dealers, was meant to hand him five thousand pounds last September. But when he counted it, the money was ten-pounds short. He went mental. I was there and saw it all. I had to hold him back from hitting him.'

He continued, 'Tiff's all right but you've got to watch his temper. One day last year, he was walking along a Birmingham street after heavy rain and a bus drove through a puddle, splashing him. He ran after the bus and, when it stopped, hauled the driver out of his cab and beat him up. He battered his barber for cutting his hair too short and once threw a traffic warden over a wall.'

'Bloody hell. Sounds like he's got a massive anger management problem.'

Polly took the rolled-up note from him, formed a line of the white powder on the top of the bedside cabinet and began to snort it.

'I'm so glad I transferred over to Heart of England,' she said between breaths. 'I was so lonely back in Lincolnshire after you left.'

'I'm glad you followed me over,' he said. 'There's a lot more going on. Lincoln's such a sleepy city. I find Birmingham and the West Midlands is a much more switched-on place. There's a chance to make some real money here from selling stuff – particularly with all the young folk around. Did you know there's something like twelve universities in the West Midlands?'

'That's a good market for you,' she said. 'Won't take you long to make a fortune.'

'My plan's to retire by the time I'm fifty in eight years' time and then go and live in southern Spain. You can come too.'

'I don't know. What about Mark and the children? I'd have to see.'

'You told me you didn't want to be with Mark anymore.'

'I don't really think I do, but I feel sorry for the children. They love their daddy. Anyway, a lot can happen in eight years,' she said, touching his hand. 'You're great. You and me have got something special and Mark is such a prat. We'll have to see. I want to see my children grow up. What about your wife? Would you take her to Spain?'

'No way. I'd leave the stupid bitch here.' He paused for a moment. A sudden thought occurred to him. 'Your children could come too. I love children.'

'As I say, we'll have to see.'

'Wow, I'm really feeling good. Let me lie next to you,' he said.

Polly, ten years younger, shuffled to the edge of the bed to make space for her lover as he slumped down beside her. The bed creaked.

'Careful! You'll break the bloody bed,' she yelled. 'Then we'll be in trouble.' She started giggling again.

'The hotel staff would never know,' he replied. 'They're dozy bastards. Oh, my God! This is such good stuff. I'm so glad you came over from Lincoln. We're going to make so much money together.'

'Aren't you worried the brass are going to suss what's going on?'

'They don't have a clue. They've got their heads stuck up their own backsides. Oh, we're careful, me and the lads. We never discuss business while we're at work. We don't text. We only meet at the Old Guildhall. That's the only place we touch on business. Do you know I made nearly two hundred grand in the past six months, which I'm investing in property in the Canary Isles?'

'Is that where you're going to buy a villa?'

'No, I'm planning to go to the mainland. Too many bloody holidaymakers in the Canaries. I want to live in some remote spot on the Spanish coast and take up fishing again.'

'You'd be bored in five minutes.'

'No, I wouldn't. I'd have a home gym and I'd keep busy with DIY, photography and tinkering with classic cars. I'd be in my element. Plus I'd have plenty of sex.'

'Oh, that goes without saying!'

They lay together, smiling and chatting for a few minutes. Then the inspector looked her in the eyes and they began to kiss passionately.

Chapter 5

'George!' The sergeant's voice boomed out around Warwick police station at around lunchtime two days later.

Within minutes, fresh-faced constable George Roscoe was standing in the sergeant's office, clutching a half-eaten cheese and tomato sandwich.

'I was just having my lunch, Sarge,' he said, between mouthfuls.

'I can see that, son. But it'll have to wait.'

George brushed his fair hair out of his eyes as the sergeant announced, 'I want you to head down to the Crown Court building in Leamington. The sergeant down there's a bit short-staffed and there's a load of troublemakers getting worked up for a protest demo, so get yourself down there, son. As quick as you can. Might be a few arrests.'

George, who was still unable to drive, walked briskly to the town's railway station. After a short wait, he hopped on a train for the ten-minute journey to Leamington Spa.

There he faced a further ten-minute walk to Warwick Crown Court – a huge, white, contemporary building. But he was relieved to find he was not faced with dozens of banner-waving protesters seeking to battle their way into the building and cause mayhem. There were just eight protesters, and five police officers had already gathered outside the impressive, glass-fronted entrance to contain them.

Although small in number, the demonstrators were making a lot of noise. They were shouting, 'What do we want? Justice! When do we want it? Now!'

A few court officials could be seen peering from the windows towards the crowd on the pavement.

George stopped on the other side of the road for a moment, trying to recognise the sergeant he had been told to report to. As he stared across, a young black man with dreadlocks thrust a leaflet into his hand, headed, 'Free the Sedgeworth Two'.

He then remembered the case and that a detective was rumoured to have falsified evidence. An artist named Brendan O'Sullivan had been found dead at his Sedgeworth home, a victim of what the press had called the 'body in the bath' murder. Two men had been convicted last year, but they had strenuously denied their involvement and a well-known criminal justice lawyer was now campaigning for a retrial amid claims that 'corrupt police' had arrested the wrong men.

George glanced at the leaflet which read:

> *Last year, two innocent men were arrested and charged with the murder of an artist. Winston Stevens, twenty-seven, is a hard-working husband and father of two children from Coventry. He's been jailed for thirty-two years. Raj Kumar is a married man from Sedgeworth who's aged twenty-eight. He's been jailed for twenty-eight years.*
>
> *Both men can prove they weren't in Sedgeworth on the afternoon of the murder. Winston was shopping in the Bullring in Birmingham with family, while Raj had a dentist appointment in Summerstoke. We're calling on the police and Crown Prosecution Service to reopen the case. A gross miscarriage of justice has taken place.*
>
> *Clarence Stevens, aged fifty-two, Winston's father, said, 'We're hoping to find fresh evidence so we can launch an appeal. These two men have been framed. Somebody in Sedgeworth must know who murdered Brendan O'Sullivan. Please come forward to help us free these two victims of a conspiracy to pervert justice. Join our protest vigil outside Warwick Crown Court.'*

Just as he finished reading the leaflet, a burly police sergeant waddled across the road and slapped six-foot-tall George on the left shoulder.

'George Roscoe?' he asked.

'Yes, Sarge. I was looking for you.'

'Well, you've found me. Don't hang around watching the world go by, laddie. Come and join in the fun.'

The pair crossed the road. George smiled and nodded at his police colleagues, but he did not pay them much attention. He was intrigued by the claims made in the leaflet. He had noticed a woman in a wheelchair was among the protesters. She had stopped a passer-by, who was showing interest in the protest.

George listened as the grey-haired, wrinkled old lady, who was in her late seventies, claimed she was Winston Stevens' grandmother.

'We're pressing for an appeal,' she said loudly. 'I'm particularly aggrieved. My grandson was pushing me round Selfridges when he was meant to be shooting the artist. It's a travesty.'

One of his police colleagues appeared to be paying George a great deal of attention, continually leaning forward and peering at him. What's this officer's problem? George wondered. Then he realised that, beneath the helmet, was the smiling face of his close friend, Sean Munro.

'Sean!' he called. 'How are you doing? Have they roped you in as well?'

'Yes, George. I'm afraid so.'

'Quiet there!' called the sergeant. 'This ain't a mothers' meeting. Focus on the job and have your natter later.'

When the court closed at 5 p.m. the officers were picked up in a police carrier and driven to Leamington police station, where George and Sean enjoyed a coffee together.

'How's Shipston-on-Stour then?' asked George.

'Oh, it's too quiet. Nothing ever happens. I think everybody goes to bed at eight o'clock. There's more activity in a monastery garden.'

'Anyway,' said George, 'I wanted to ask you a favour. My grandad's having his retirement party at the tearooms. Bit boring, I know, but I've promised to be there. It's the second Monday in February. It's a little cheeky but I wondered if there's any chance you could give me and Amanda a lift over there and back because we're both on duty the next day?'

* * *

Sunita Roy was engrossed in reading the latest Preeti Shenoy romantic novel when there was a tap on her car window.

After overcoming her surprise, she smiled, put her book down on the passenger seat and stepped out. A slim, intelligent man in black-framed glasses was standing beside the car, grinning and holding a bouquet of mixed carnations.

'Sunita, how nice it is to be seeing you,' said the man, Samir Banerjee. 'Have you been waiting long?'

'Only ten minutes. I was reading a book,' she said. 'Oh, are these for me?'

'Yes,' he said, handing her the bouquet. 'I'm not late, am I?'

'Thank you so much for these flowers. No, we said eight o'clock. I got here early. Nice to see you, Sam.' She placed the flowers in the car next to her novel.

'Shall we go in?' she asked.

Samir, who first met Sunita after saving the life of her police colleague Tom Vickers when he was shot, led her across the car park on the northern outskirts of Coventry. He then followed her as she climbed the steps and made her way through the restaurant's double glass doors.

Within a few minutes, a waitress had found them a corner table amid the dimmed lighting in the plush hotel restaurant. Before departing, she lit a candle inside a red vase at the centre of the table. Sunita was shocked into silence as she gazed across the starched, white tablecloth at her companion.

'Sam, are you sure about this? I never expected to be invited to such an up-market place with stunning views over the golf course and lakes.'

'When you told me how much you like fish, this place sprang to mind at once.'

'I'm afraid I'm not used to this at all,' she explained. 'I'm more used to pub and cafe meals when I'm invited out.'

Sunita chose seabass from the à la carte menu, while Sam opted for a salmon dish. He suggested they had a bottle of white wine, but she insisted she would only drink orange juice as she was driving. In the end, they ordered an orange juice each.

'Sunita, I'm wondering how your colleague Tom's getting on,' Samir said after they had placed their order.

'Oh, Tom's fine,' she said. 'The doctors say it'll take some time for him to fully recover use of his arm, but he's getting better every day. He's back at work now.'

'Is he? That's wonderful, Sunita.'

'I'm sure he'll never forget your speedy response in stemming the blood with a towel.'

'I'm thinking anyone would be doing the same – finding a man in a situation like that,' he replied. 'Did police ever trace the black Volkswagen car the gunmen drove away in?'

She took a sip of juice before leaning back in her black, upholstered chair. 'We never found it. It had false plates in any case.'

'They are the most terrible men.'

'I know. We had one of them in custody in December, but, somehow, he gave the prison authorities the slip. We had a breakthrough at the end of last week. Their current car, a Mercedes, was seen outside a warehouse. But when we raided the premises, all we found were two Vietnamese men who'd been left in charge of a cannabis factory. The two guys we're after, Filipowski and Blake, have vanished.'

Chapter 6

A light rain was falling as Tadeusz Filipowski drove his silver Porsche Boxster into a side road in the Birmingham suburb of Handsworth.

He stopped his prized car on some double yellow lines before cutting the engine and stepping out.

'God, this place never gets any better,' he muttered to himself as he removed his umbrella from the rear boot, raised it over his head and locked the car.

It was nearly four o'clock in the afternoon as he walked to the main road in the inner-city suburb, where he was met by the smell of exhaust fumes and the constant drone of traffic. After taking a few paces along the bustling street, he reached a small supermarket, advertising wines and spirits, half-price pizzas and halal meat.

He stepped past the main window, found the grimy, black wooden door he was searching for – set back from the rain-soaked pavement – and pressed the buzzer.

Seconds later, a silky, persuasive voice he knew well purred from the intercom.

'Who is it?'

'It's the boss,' he replied.

'Come in, Tiff,' the voice replied before a buzzer sounded and he was admitted to the three-storey building.

Filipowski placed his rolled-up umbrella beside the bottom step. Then he climbed the steep stairway and was greeted at the top by a shapely young, dark-haired woman in a black Basque and stockings. He found himself on the dingy landing with several doors leading from it. Ahead of him lay a corridor with further rooms.

'Hi, Mr Tadeusz. How are you today?' the woman asked with a smile as he glimpsed a tantalising view of her cleavage.

'I'd be in a good mood if it weren't for the bloody weather, Anna,' he moaned. 'I must say you're looking gorgeous today, as always.'

'Thank you, Mr Tadeusz. Monika's in her office.'

He smiled. 'How did you know I came to see her? Maybe I've come to see you.'

She smiled back. 'You always come to see her.'

He reached across and clasped her hand. 'Maybe, one day,' he murmured before marching down the corridor and knocking on the door at the end.

Monika Kowalska, whose soft tones had greeted him over the intercom moments before, smiled broadly as she drew back the door. She had attractive blue eyes and a pale, milky innocence beneath her neatly coiffed blonde hair. She may have been in her early forties but was dressed in a stylish, navy-blue trouser suit and could have passed for a younger woman.

She kissed him on the cheek.

'Have you missed me, darling?' she asked.

'Of course,' he lied. 'I could've spent Christmas with you if it weren't for the bloody cops.'

She led him into her brightly lit office, which had a window overlooking the street and another looking over a cluttered supermarket yard. She swung her black, leather chair round and sat down, offering him a chair in the corner.

'So how was Spain, darling?' she asked.

'Hotter than here.'

'I don't doubt it. Why didn't you call me?'

'I kept my phone off. Didn't want to give my location away.'

'So you felt it safe to come back?'

'There was no choice. Lot of business to sort out. And my new house.'

Monika clasped her hands together and leaned forward. 'How's that going, darling?'

Filipowski shook his head. 'The builders are taking ages. May have to sack them and bring in new people from Poland.'

'The whole place is being gutted?'

'It's what the English call a makeover.'

'Not cheap at nearly a million pounds, darling.'

'I know but I want to get it right,' he said. 'I told you I'm having a swimming pool, tennis courts, garage space for six cars and an underground cinema, didn't I?'

'Yes, darling. I can't wait to see it when it's finished.'

'Me too,' he said. 'Listen, how's business here?'

'It's going very well, Tiff. It was boomtime over Christmas. Because you weren't around, I was here every day and the girls were kept very busy. But business has slackened off a little since the New Year.'

Filipowski took a small notebook from his pocket and began writing. 'Who've you got working here?'

'Anna, Sofia and Betina.'

'And in Hockley?'

'Lena, Maria and Angelika.'

'Give me the figures.'

After a brief discussion about finances, he shut his notebook and grinned at her.

'Do you fancy coming back with me to my new place?'

'You said on the phone it's in Balsall Common.'

'That's right. Is just a small place. Nothing special, but it suits me till the big house is ready.'

She nodded. 'Do you know what? I fancy a trip out. It would be really cool to get out of Brum and see your new place. I'll just go and have a word with Anna and then I'll get my things together.'

* * *

It was still drizzling when the pair left the building and set off in Filipowski's car. As they travelled, without asking, he placed his left hand on her knee. She caressed and fondled his fingers as he drove.

'Tiff, why did you leave your last place in Badminton Road so quickly?' she asked.

'No choice,' he muttered. 'We got a steer the cops were on their way over, so we got the hell out. Then I got arrested and held on remand.'

'And then they let you out again?'

'That's right. Everybody says I should've stayed in Spain but my business is in Birmingham. I had to come back. And I wanted to see you as well, of course.'

By the time they had passed through the Warwickshire countryside and arrived in the village of Balsall Common, seven miles west of Coventry, the rain had petered out.

After parking on the forecourt of his detached home in Whitstone Drive, he led her into his spacious living-room, which had patio doors leading to a medium-sized rear garden.

She threw herself onto the ivory-coloured three-seater settee.

'Your cousin's very kind to let you have this place while he's in Warsaw,' she said. 'Has it got a nice kitchen?'

She darted into the newly fitted kitchen, which had high-gloss white cupboards and a central island. Her eyes were wide – like those of a gourmet eyeing a hotel's cheese trolley.

'I could really see myself in here, Tiff,' she said with a broad smile. 'Hey, I could cook you a pierogi with beef. I know you miss your pierogi. I've found out where I can get all the ingredients.'

He stepped across the living room and stood watching her from the kitchen doorway as she opened some of the cupboards.

'What shall we do?' he asked, slipping off his jacket. 'Get a takeaway? There's a new Indian place that's opened along the road or there's Chinese.'

She gazed across the room, smiling. 'Food can wait,' she insisted.

'Do you want to do a line?' he asked.

'Maybe later,' she said, rising from the settee. She strolled across the beige carpet towards him.

'Come here, Tiger,' she cooed. 'Let me show you how much I've missed you.'

Chapter 7

The chief inspector found himself humming a tune as he negotiated the entrance steps at St James Street police headquarters the following morning.

His daughter was forever playing music around the house. He believed he may have subconsciously allowed it to infiltrate his brain. Perhaps it was the latest Ed Sheeran song.

He climbed the stairs to the first floor, turned right and, panting a little, found himself outside Tom Vickers' office. After knocking, he stepped inside the bright room with its floor-to-ceiling windows. He was shocked to find DC Wendy Hopkirk standing by the windows, listening to some music on a set of headphones and swaying in time to the beat.

She spun round as soon as she noticed the DCI and snatched the headphones off.

'Sorry, sir,' was her garbled response.

He decided to ignore her disregard for office rules and walked across to the far end of the office, where he waited for his colleague. A few moments later, the door opened and the inspector strode in, smiling.

'Sorry to keep you waiting,' Vickers exclaimed, hurrying to his desk. 'I just stepped outside for a cigarette. I'm glad to see you. We need to talk about Operation Temple.'

'Yes. Imagine you've been well briefed by the chief super?'

'Yes,' said Vickers, who looked dapper in a grey suit.

'So we're looking into the conduct of DI Seymour Trent from Summerstoke, and he looks to be in league with the pair who ambushed you last year, Filipowski and Blake.'

'Yes, guv. DS Roy's brought me up to date with that other incident near Meriden.'

The chief inspector nodded.

'It's a shame we've no idea where the pair are right now,' Vickers continued. 'It's pretty clear now that Trent helped Filipowski and his gang by framing the pair who went down for the "body in the bath" murder – just as that celebrity lawyer's been claiming.'

Roscoe shook his head. 'I think that might be going too far, Tom. The chief super says the evidence against the two convicted men was fairly clear-cut.'

'I'm not so sure, guv. Don't forget we found that witness, Nisa Shah in Albion Road whose evidence pointed the other way.'

The chief inspector leaned forward and clasped his hands together.

'I know,' he said, 'but she withdrew from testifying. Without her, there's little chance of a retrial.'

Vickers shrugged. 'Anyway, I've found out Filipowski's been inside a few times for drug offences. We believe Trent is aiding Filipowski's operations and tipping him off about police activity. As part of the deal, there's a suggestion Trent may be taking a percentage of the drugs profits. At the same time, Trent's been getting members of his team to target rival drugs gangs in Warwickshire and East Birmingham if they pose any threat to the 101 Crew's sphere of influence. The situation's got the potential to turn into a gang war on the streets of Brum.'

'Yes, the situation may be worse than we feared,' said Roscoe, shaking his head. 'You've been mugging up on Trent. What have you found out?'

'A colleague in the drug squad tells me he came over from Lincolnshire Police two years ago and, by all accounts, immediately set to work cosying up with people linked to the drugs trade. Somehow, he made a friend of

Filipowski. It's believed Trent's made a heck of a lot of money as a result.'

'We've got our work cut out here, Tom,' Roscoe muttered. 'I tell you what. I think we need to go back to Albion Road in Sedgeworth. Back to the scene of the artist's murder.'

'The house where Brendan O'Sullivan was killed?'

'Exactly. Trent was the officer in the case, and it looks as though he might not have been as thorough with that investigation as he should have.'

'I tried to hook up with the victim's nephew a few weeks ago but missed him. After that, I was in hospital because of the shooting and out of action.'

'Well, see if the nephew's around now and take DS Roy with you.'

'All right, guv.'

'I want you to keep me informed of everything, but I'll have to be a little careful about my personal involvement in any undercover work because I'm pretty certain Trent knows me by sight.'

Vickers nodded towards DC Hopkirk. 'Wendy here can run the office whenever I'm out and about.'

'Good,' said Roscoe. 'I tell you what, Tom, I'm going to call round and see one of my old informants. He always keeps his ear close to the ground. If you want up-to-date intel about inner-city gangs, he's probably the man to talk to.'

* * *

The chief inspector made a mental note to improve his fitness levels as, later that day, he walked across a car park close to Birmingham city centre. After clambering up two flights of stairs, he began panting.

Once he'd reached the top, he had to lean against a wall for a moment so he could regain his breath. He was in the heart of one of the largest council housing complexes in Birmingham, the Cumberland Estate. It comprised a mix of tower blocks, low-rise flats and maisonettes thrown up in the 1960s in an effort by town hall planners to cope with a post-war population boom.

Kenton House, where he was now standing, sweating profusely, was one of the newer tower blocks. The council had been promising for decades to replace the whole estate with up-to-date properties, but, for the moment, the long-suffering residents were forced to remain in these outmoded homes.

Roscoe made his way along the first-floor balcony until he reached a light brown, half-glazed door where he knocked. His jovial, silver-haired friend Pat Clancy appeared at the door moments later, smiling broadly.

'Gavin! What a great surprise! Won't you come in?' he asked.

'Thanks, Pat. It's really great to see you!' the detective replied.

As the genial Irishman led him along a narrow corridor to the living-room, he asked his visitor, 'How are you keeping? How are all the family?'

'We're all doing well, thank you, Pat,' said Roscoe. 'How about you and your family?'

'We're just fine. Just fine. And how's your lovely wife with her tearooms?'

'Well, a lot of our rivals are closing,' Roscoe admitted, 'but we're still coping well. Helen has worked hard to build up her clientele.'

'That's what I like to hear,' said Clancy, who was puffing on a home-made cigarette. 'Everyone likes a success story. Would you like a tea or coffee?'

'I won't just now, Pat. I'm in a bit of a rush. Got an important job on.'

'Nothing changes, Gavin.'

Roscoe sat down on the grey, three-seater settee in the bright living-room. His burly host slumped down into an armchair. He narrowly avoided knocking a silver ashtray to the floor as he did so.

'I wanted to raise a delicate subject with you,' Roscoe explained. 'I'm looking into a case of possible police corruption.'

'That's a terrible thing, to be sure.'

'This case is extremely serious, Pat, and I know, from working with you in the past, I can trust you implicitly.'

'Of course.'

'Do you remember a few weeks ago we were talking about the two men suspected of being framed over the "body in the bath" murder case? There was a suggestion of a bent copper being involved?'

'Of course I do, Gavin,' said the Irishman. 'I've been keeping my eyes and ears open. There's not much going on in the criminal underbelly of this city that old Pat doesn't get to know about. This is the corrupt DI involved with the 101 Crew who have been making moves on the big city?'

'That's right,' said Roscoe. 'We want to crack down on them before a gang war breaks out. Senior officers are concerned people are going to get killed and untold damage will be done to the reputation of the police unless we act quickly.'

'I see where you're coming from. Well, I'll help you in any way I can, of course. What've you got in mind?'

'Well, someone's got to go undercover and find out exactly what's happening on the inside. You know, to get the evidence. It's not a role I want to take on. More likely one of my team. I'm more office-bound these days and, in any case, I'm known to the detective concerned. What's more, I could never pass as a potential drug dealer and lesser still as a potential drug user.'

Clancy smiled. 'You'd stand out like a swan in a flock of sparrows.'

'I wondered if you knew of someone who's, say, in their twenties. Someone who's got a bit of free time at the moment and isn't frightened by the thought of befriending dangerous men. Someone who's got a bit of guile about them.'

Roscoe's friend, who was standing in the middle of the room, held both his hands out in amazement.

'Well, you could just be talking about my grandson, Liam,' he exclaimed. 'He's just the lad you need.'

Roscoe stroked his chin. 'Didn't I write a character reference for him a few years ago, which helped reduce his sentence for drug possession?'

'That's right. It was a turning point for him. Thanks to you, he served just a few weeks. It was the short, sharp shock that he needed, Gavin. The whole family will always be grateful.'

'I knew I did the right thing to visit you, Pat. Remind me about him.'

'Well, he's aged twenty-two and he's as sharp as a butcher's knife.'

'Same age as my son, George,' said Roscoe.

'And he's got good knowledge of the drugs trade, since he was dabbling with the stuff himself for a few years.'

Roscoe looked shocked. 'He's absolutely not involved with drugs now, I hope?'

'God have mercy, no. Not since he came out of jail and his father, Sean, and I gave him a good talking to, I can tell you.'

Roscoe smiled. 'Didn't know you'd a knack with anti-drug tutorials, Pat.'

'Our quiet, rational approach seemed to work with him. That along with the promise he'd get the hiding of his life if he upset his mother and grandmother anymore.'

'He sounds ideal. It would only be for a short time – just to get the lay of the land. I've got one of our own people in mind to go undercover, but your grandson's inquiries could prove a precursor to a fuller investigation by us. So can you set up a meeting?'

'D'you want to meet him now? He lives just three floors up. I've told him all about you over the years – the pranks we used to get up to. He'd love to meet you.'

'That would be splendid, Pat.'

'I'll give him a call.'

Clancy took out an ancient-looking mobile phone and pressed a few buttons. Within seconds, it sprang into life as the spirited sound of young Liam Clancy's voice filled the room.

'Grandad! How the devil are you?' he asked.

'Fine, Liam. Just fine. I've got someone here who's interested in meeting you. It's Mr Roscoe, the detective.'

'And he wants to see me? I'll be down in two ticks.' With that, Liam hung up.

'Oh, he's a grand boy. You won't be having any problem with him,' said Clancy.

Minutes later, ginger-haired Liam bounced into the room in a football shirt and jeans like an exuberant schoolboy on the first day of his holidays.

The chief inspector observed a close family resemblance to his grandfather – although Liam was more than forty-five years younger. The lad had the words 'Tada gan iarracht' – nothing without effort – tattooed on his right arm and, on his left arm, an Irish harp with a red rose.

'Liam, this is Mr Roscoe,' the old man explained. Roscoe held out his hand, which the lad shook warmly.

'I'm glad to meet you,' Liam declared. 'Grandad's told me about all the cases you've solved over the years. I remember there were some murders in a place called Oxford Lane. You solved that one.'

'To be fair, my sergeant played a major part in that,' said Roscoe, modestly. 'Look, have you got a few weeks free at the moment? We need someone to help us and you definitely look the part.'

'That's cool, Mr Roscoe,' Liam replied, sitting next to him at the far end of the settee. 'I've got a bit of time just now. How can I help?'

'We need someone to infiltrate a drugs gang for us.'

'A drugs gang? I'm not sure if I'm the boy for the job, Mr Roscoe.'

'Your grandad informs me you know about the drugs culture.'

Liam sat down on the settee next to Roscoe. He looked down at the carpet for a few seconds. Then he looked back at the visitor.

'I know a little about the Parish Killers, the Seven Days Gang, the West Side Gang, the Henhouse Boys, and the Handsworth Crew,' he said. 'Some of them guys have been caged. Who are we talking about here?'

'I'm talking about a gang called the 101 Crew.'

'Oh, I know them,' said Liam. 'We call them the kings of rock because they're always trying to sell crack to uni students.'

'Crack cocaine?'

'Yeah. Most of the 101 Crew dealers are cokeheads, trying to create a demand out on the streets. Yeah, I know the 101 Crew. I know where they operate. I know where they hang out.'

'What sort of age are the street dealers they use?'

'Guys like me, in their twenties.'

'So you'd stand a good chance of infiltrating their group?'

'Infiltrating, you say?'

'Yeah, befriending them to obtain information about their activities.'

'I guess so. What sort of information are you after?'

'Well, ideally we'd like to know how they operate; who their suppliers are; when the next big consignment is due and where; and, most important of all, who the people at the top are. D'you think you could tackle that? There'd be a handsome reward for you.'

'Sure, I reckon I could do that. What's the problem with your drug squad guys? Are they all tied up?'

Clancy winked at Liam. 'The DCI's on a special operation which is hush-hush,' he told his grandson in a low voice. 'There might be a crooked copper involved, so he's not wanting to involve his own people so much.'

The chief inspector looked embarrassed. 'That's roughly the size of it,' he admitted.

Liam sat thoughtfully at his grandfather's dining table and then stared across the room at the chief inspector.

'There'll be a reward for your trouble, of course,' said Roscoe. 'Oh and, on top of that, I might want you to help me on a couple of evenings with a little job I've got in mind. What's the matter? You seem a little hesitant.'

Liam was gawping at the table again.

'Is there something worrying you?' said Roscoe. 'Of course, if by any chance you get arrested while on the street, make sure you get a message to me promptly and I'll arrange for you to be released.'

'I wasn't concerned about that,' he said. 'I'm wondering how, if I'm wheedling my way into becoming a street dealer, how I get to know who the boss guys are? It might take a bit of work.'

'I think you'd be surprised how quickly you can discover that sort of information after you become a trusted member of their clique,' said Roscoe.

Liam remained pensive for a few seconds before a smile crept across his face.

'Well, there's only one way to find out, eh?' he said.

Chapter 8

Seymour Trent was beginning to lose his temper. He and his sergeant, Philip Bains, had arrived for their meeting ten minutes early at five minutes to eleven. They were sitting, as arranged, in the main bar of the Old Guildhall Tavern, a fourteenth-century building renowned for its oak-beamed ceilings and decorative stained-glass windows. Yet there was no sign of the man they'd come to meet. Trent took a sip from his glass of cool Amstel lager.

'You'd think he'd make a bit of an effort,' he muttered to his stocky friend. 'It isn't as if we have these meetings very often.'

Just then, Bains glanced through the window and spotted the tall, thin man they were expecting.

'There he is!' cried the sergeant. 'He's outside having a row with a traffic warden.'

Trent slipped his head into his hands.

'You'd better go and get him pretty smartish before he punches him and gets himself into all sorts of trouble,' he said. 'Tell him he can park round the corner in Nicholas Street. You can stay there for up to an hour. Should be long enough for us.'

Bains hurried out of the main door. He was just in time to prevent the argument on the pavement becoming more heated.

Filipowski followed Bains into the main bar, where he grinned and shook hands with Trent.

'What are you having, Tiff?' Trent asked politely.

'That's kind of you, Seymour. I always like the Hobgoblin when I drink here.'

'Phil, would you do the honours?' Trent asked, handing his sergeant a twenty-pound note. 'Another pint of Amstel for me, a Hobgoblin for Tiff and whatever you fancy.'

While his colleague strolled to the bar, he turned to Filipowski.

'Good holiday?' he asked.

'Bit last minute, Seymour,' he replied. 'Half the cops in the Midlands have been on my tail after that messy business with the nosy inspector in Sedgeworth.'

'But you felt it safe enough to come back now?' said Trent.

He shrugged. 'Things have cooled down and the cops have had their hands tied with other things. Did you read that report in the *Birmingham Post* about murders? There were more homicides in December than for the whole of last year.'

'Yeah. I helped compile the figures. It's true. We've been busy. Certainly we've had no time to interfere with the activities of genuine business people like your good self.'

'Thanks for that, Seymour.'

A few minutes later, Bains returned with a silver tray laden with drinks. As each man began to sip his beer, Trent was eager to start the proceedings.

'How are we getting on with this new batch of white?' he asked.

'I've found some good new suppliers,' said Filipowski. 'Everything's running very smoothly – maybe too smoothly.'

'What d'you mean by that?' demanded Trent.

Filipowski shrugged. 'Just that I'm surprised we haven't had any problems recently – either with the cops or from other gangs.'

'Well, don't forget we managed to get two of the West Side Gang's main dealers sent down,' said Bains with a smile.

Filipowski nodded and grinned back.

'Yes, I know,' he said. 'Their families aren't too happy about it, either. There was a picture in the paper last week of them protesting outside the court.'

'Yes, that was a bit of luck – getting those two lads put away,' Trent admitted. 'It means we've been able to up our sales substantially in North Warwickshire. But I'm eager to make more inroads into the market in Brum.'

Trent noticed Filipowski had, from time to time, been glaring at his pint of beer. He was clearly unhappy about something.

'Would you excuse me, gentlemen?' Filipowski asked.

Then he picked up his pint of bitter and marched up to the bar. Trent and Bains strained their ears to hear what was being said. It appeared Filipowski had found the drink cloudy and was demanding the barman pour him another.

'Phil,' he said. 'You'd better go and get him before he lands a blow on the barman. God, I don't know. That man's got major anger issues. This was meant to be a quiet business meeting.'

The sergeant dutifully proceeded to the bar as quickly as he could manage, nearly slipping on the highly polished oak floor as he did so. As he reached the counter, he realised his friend's request for a fresh pint was being declined. Filipowski was losing his temper.

'I regularly come in here and, nine times out of ten, the Hobgoblin's fine,' he boomed. 'It's just today it's cloudy and you ought to sort it out, for God's sake. What's the bloody matter with you, man?'

'Calm down,' said Bains.

'No, I'm bloody not going to calm down,' said Filipowski. 'This cheeky bastard knows me. He knows I come in here a lot. The beer's off and he just won't admit it.'

He reached across the bar, grabbed the young barman by the scruff of his shirt and lifted him off the floor.

'You'd better get me a fresh pint, mate!' he demanded.

'Put him down!' the sergeant said. 'Let me buy you another drink.'

'No. I won't let you,' Filipowski insisted. 'There's a principle at stake here.'

'If I have to call the manager, he'll throw you out of here!' the barman said. 'He doesn't take kindly to customers roughing up his staff.'

'Look, just pour him another pint and I'll settle up with you,' Bains said. 'All he wants is his Hobgoblin.'

'All right,' said the barman. 'But your mate will have to calm down. He was way over the top.'

Bains took his protesting colleague by the arm and led him back to his seat. Then he returned to the bar where the freshly poured pint of ale stood waiting. He paid for it, walked back to their table clutching the drink, and presented it to Filipowski.

'We're meant to be keeping a low profile,' Trent moaned. 'Come on. Let's have no more incidents. We've got important business to get through.'

Chapter 9

It was a cold, foggy Thursday morning as Tom Vickers and Sunita Roy set off from St James Street for the north Warwickshire market town of Sedgeworth.

'Well done on tracing that Mercedes, Sunita,' he said as they drove out of Solihull and followed a series of country lanes towards their destination, twenty miles away.

Within half an hour, they reached Sedgeworth, close to the Leicestershire border, and, without needing his satnav, he remembered his way to Albion Road, a quiet suburban street on the west of town.

'This is the first time I've been to this town since I was shot,' he said.

'They haven't put any flags out for you,' she replied.

Sunita had been quiet for much of the journey. She had been casting her mind back to the brutal murder of artist Brendan O'Sullivan two years earlier. It was while investigating that case more recently that Vickers had been gunned down.

O'Sullivan's body had been found in his bath, riddled with bullets that, according to forensic examination, had been fired from a Beretta pistol. Police from Summerstoke CID recovered a Beretta from a wardrobe in the home of father-of-two Winston Stevens. Following that, he and his friend Raj Kumar were arrested, charged, convicted and jailed. But Sunita was now aware that there were serious questions about whether the pair had been wrongly convicted.

'Not the easiest task we've got,' she muttered as she stepped onto the pavement and gazed across at the red-brick Victorian end-of-terrace house where the murder had taken place.

Vickers smiled at her as he got out from behind the wheel. 'Hey, we might be in luck,' he said. 'There are some half-decent curtains up in the windows now and the front garden is a lot neater. Looks like someone might be living here.'

She shrugged. 'Unless the family have sold it and some new people have moved in.'

The two detectives passed a grey Hyundai that was standing in the parking bay beside the house as they approached the front door.

'That's the victim's car,' Vickers murmured as she knocked.

After nearly half a minute, they heard the sound of footsteps. 'Who is it?' a deep male voice asked, sheepishly from behind the door.

'Police,' Sunita replied. 'We've got a few questions.'

'Hope you've got ID,' the man continued, peering through the misted glass in the door.

She held up her warrant card.

'All right,' said the occupant, releasing bolts and opening the door. 'You can't be too careful.'

'Too right,' Sunita agreed. 'Not in view of what happened to – your uncle, was it?'

'Yes,' he replied.

'I'm DI Vickers,' the inspector said. 'My colleague here is DS Roy. We're reviewing the evidence in the case.'

'Joseph O'Sullivan,' said the tall, slim man. He resembled a startled animal that had been cornered in his lair. 'You'd better both come in – although I can't see I'm going to be able to help you much. I'm just house-sitting.'

Sunita gazed into his tired eyes. 'You're trying to sell the house?'

'Been on the market since August but no one's buying round here at the moment.'

They followed Joseph through the hall into a light, spacious front room. It was sparsely furnished with a brown sofa and two matching armchairs, coffee table and bookshelves. Oil paintings of countryside scenes were displayed on either side of a marble fireplace.

'So what's all this about?' asked Joseph, as he sat on one of the armchairs.

'Well, I'm very sorry to bring up the death of your uncle again, but we're re-examining what happened,' she said, taking a seat on the sofa.

'It's all right. We weren't that close,' said Joseph. 'But why are you dredging it all up again?'

'A few questions have been raised about the court case,' Vickers said.

'I don't know about that. I just think that, whoever did it, must've been homophobic.'

'Your uncle was gay?'

'Yes. Didn't you know? He got beaten up outside a pub three years ago. I just think someone must've had it in for him.'

'It was suggested at the trial he'd been killed over a drugs debt.'

'This is what I get upset about. My uncle didn't do drugs, as far as I know. I saw drugs mentioned in the papers. It didn't sound anything like the Uncle Brendan I knew. Would you like some tea?'

Sunita and Vickers both nodded.

'That would be great,' Sunita said. 'By the way, has this room changed much since your uncle's death?'

'No, I've left it exactly as it was. I'll only be a moment.'

As Joseph went to the kitchen, the pair had a chance to examine the living-room. Some art magazines on the coffee table caught the inspector's attention. He picked one up and began thumbing through it.

While doing so, he happened to glance at the edge of the table and noticed a few tiny specks of white powder trapped between the edge of the glass top and the bamboo frame. Then he wandered round the room, studying the furniture before resuming his seat. Sunita was meanwhile peering about the room from her position on the sofa.

'So you didn't attend the trial then?' Sunita called out.

'No,' came the reply from the kitchen. 'There didn't seem much point. There were news reports online and in the local papers.'

As she leaned back on the sofa, Sunita gazed up at the ceiling. She tried to decide whether she liked the antique brass crystal chandelier which was hanging from the centre of the room. Does it suit the room or is it out of place? she wondered.

Then her eyes focused upon the large, ornate ceiling rose above the chandelier. The white plaster central rose was surrounded in a circle by eight white moulded leaves. Slits between the leaves appeared from beneath as small dark shapes. But something seemed out of place.

At last, she realised what it was. One of the dark clefts between the leaves was manifestly larger than the others.

'Oh, you like my uncle's chandelier, do you?' Joseph asked, as he returned, clutching two hot mugs of tea.

'I was looking at the ceiling rose,' said Sunita. 'There's something strange about it. Do you mind if I take a closer look?'

'Be my guest,' said Joseph, putting the mugs down on the coffee table.

'Do you have a set of steps, by any chance?'

'I'll fetch them from under the stairs.'

Vickers grinned at her. 'Would you like me to take a look?' he asked.

'Tom, I'm quite capable of doing this,' she insisted. 'Can I borrow your penknife?'

Moments later, clutching the inspector's knife in her left hand and the side of the steps with her right, she began to climb up. She took several hesitant steps until she was in reach of the ceiling rose. She released her grip and moved the chandelier out of her way with her left hand. Vickers held the side of the structure in case it swayed.

Joseph sat back bemused in his armchair, eyeing her. The inspector watched him and tried to read his mind. This woman – a total stranger – had only been in his house for ten minutes. Yet here she was, perched on top of his uncle's old metal steps, poking the ceiling about with a penknife.

What impression will he relate to his friends and family? Vickers wondered.

'This is just what I hoped to find,' said Sunita, as she prodded the plaster with the knife. A small piece of metal dropped into her hand.

'What is it? What have you found?' asked Joseph.

'It's a bullet,' said Sunita while climbing down. 'And, if I'm not mistaken, it probably comes from the same chamber as the ones that killed your uncle.'

Vickers was impressed by her discovery. 'Bloody hell, Sunita. That was a fine bit of detective work.'

She shrugged. 'Just following my instincts,' she said.

'Jesus, Joseph and Mary!' said their host. 'How do you work out the connection with the attack on my uncle?'

'We have it on good authority there were five shots – not four, as claimed at the trial,' Vickers explained. 'Only four were found by the police and forensic investigators. Therefore a fifth bullet had to be around somewhere. Seems it was hidden in the ceiling all the time.'

'Why would it be there then? You think the gunmen fired a loose shot first – maybe to test it was working?'

Sunita shook her head, as she placed the bullet on the platform at the top of the steps. 'It's too early to say,' she said.

Vickers turned to Joseph. 'The trajectory seems to have been straight upwards, showing the gunman was almost certainly in the centre of the room when he fired the bullet,' he told him. 'Maybe it was a warning shot – you know, to show your uncle the men meant business.'

Joseph tutted. 'If so, it's a bloody shame he didn't pay it any heed.'

Sunita handed the bullet to Vickers, who placed it in an envelope.

Then she cast her eyes around the room for the bullet casing that would have spun off after the shot was fired. It's unlikely to be found now, she thought. So much time had passed. Scenes of crime staff had been through the house and Joseph had lived there for a while.

'Joseph, you didn't find the bullet casing while you've been staying here?' she asked.

'What's it look like?'

'A small cylindrical piece of brass or copper,' said Vickers, helpfully.

Joseph looked askance. 'Don't think so.'

'Not to worry,' said Sunita.

She had read through all the trial notes. She knew that the Heart of England forensic team had explored the house with a fine-tooth comb. But somehow, despite all their best efforts, they had failed to spot the bullet lodged in the ceiling.

'I'm sorry about the ceiling rose,' Sunita said as she folded the steps and handed them back. 'I've damaged one of the leaves in my effort to dig out the bullet.'

'Don't worry about that,' Joseph replied. 'A little plaster filler will sort that out all right. Do you know, I noticed that small dark hollow in the ceiling rose myself a few weeks ago and thought nothing of it. I just thought the decorator's paintbrush had missed a bit.'

After the pair had said goodbye to Joseph and returned to their car, Sunita became engrossed in thought.

As she sat down in the front passenger seat, she turned towards the inspector.

'The prosecution made a big play of how four bullets were found at the house and four bullets were missing from Winston Stevens' pistol when it turned up at his house,' she said.

Vickers nodded. 'That's right,' he said. 'It was a key part of the evidence. I believe the gunman fired a warning shot into the ceiling first to show they meant business. But when O'Sullivan made it clear he wasn't willing to play ball, they shot him with the remaining four bullets and then dumped him in the bath. This ties in with Mrs Shah's evidence that she heard five shots and suggests it wasn't Stevens' Beretta that was used in the murder.'

Then he added, 'Sunita, we've blown a huge hole in the prosecution case.'

Chapter 10

The agile young prison officer's boots clanged on the iron steps as he sprang up the stairway that led to the first-floor landing in D Wing. He found the door marked 'D1, Cell 5' and banged hard. No one answered. Then a morose English-sounding voice from within inquired, 'What d'you want?'

Daryl Johnson was by now becoming accustomed to this inmate's bizarre ways.

'It's Mr Johnson,' he informed the prisoner as he unlocked the door. 'Got some news for you.'

'It isn't about my mortgage application, is it? It's about bloody time, if it is.'

Johnson gazed round the cell. The man who had brought terror to the Midlands just three years earlier by slaughtering two men and a woman was sitting quietly on his bed. Surely this unassuming fellow with wire-framed glasses, originally from Birmingham, could not have been responsible for the Oxford Lane atrocities? He was ruminating over *The Times* crossword. He looked as innocuous as a monk at prayer.

'What's this about a mortgage?' asked the young warder.

The prisoner frowned and looked up.

'Haven't you heard? I'm in the process of buying a country house with tennis courts, a fishing lake and stables. That's not to mention a set of garages for my vintage cars,' said the serial killer, a smile radiating across his pale, wrinkled face.

'Well, are you now?' said the warder, almost certain – though not completely – that the inmate was joking.

'Yes, and I've put your name on the form as one of my references,' the inmate continued. 'The bank should be in touch any day now.'

'I know you're having me on,' said Johnson.

'Of course,' came the reply. 'I got gazumped by one of the fraudsters on B Wing.'

'Look, forget your silly jokes for a moment. I've got some news from the governor.'

'Before you do that, give us a hand with this. Five across, "People turning up two hours before midnight to boogie." Ten letters. Something, *T*, something, something, *N*, and then a further five letters.'

'Well, two hours before midnight is ten o'clock, so *TEN* might be in there somewhere.'

'Got it!' said the prisoner as he continued to smile. '*Attendance.*' He began filling in the letters with his pencil.

'Now listen to me,' said Johnson.

'Oh yes. Your news.'

'There was a lot of debate, but your new name's been accepted under Home Office rules and we've all got to get used to it from now on.'

'The deed poll change has gone through?'

'Yes. With some reluctance on the governor's part, I can tell you. From today, we've been told to refer to you officially as Carl Innocent.'

'You're right. That's good news,' said the prisoner, sweeping his straggly greying hair towards the back of his head with a swipe of his right hand.

'You were supported in your application by the doctor, who cited psychological factors in allowing the name change.'

'You're making me sound like a headcase.'

'No, there was no suggestion of mental instability. It was simply decided you've been suffering from psychological pressure and the new name might help you adapt better to prison life. I'd love to hear your reasons for choosing that name.'

Innocent spat onto the stone floor in front of him.

'It's because I was sent down for crimes I never done. There was no evidence. If it weren't for one man…'

'What man?'

'I'd better not say. Don't want to get into any more trouble. But if it weren't for him and his Asian sidekick, I'd be a free man. You realise the killer of those people is still out there, don't you?'

'I don't know about that.'

'It's true, I'm telling you. The maniac who done those murders is free to strike again. My new name says it all. I'm innocent. Anyway, I'm not the only poor sod in here with the surname Innocent. There's at least two others.'

'Let's hope your mail doesn't get mixed up,' said the warder. 'You do realise all correspondence from now on will feature your new name but it must also include your prison number on the envelope as well.'

'I've been here long enough to realise that. I suppose you heard about the paedophile Timothy Vick?'

'Yes, the governor wasn't happy about that name change either.'

'It took him months to come up with that. He thought it might cheer him up to see his name listed everywhere as, "Vick, Tim". I thought it was a bit daft myself.'

'The governor's got limited powers in this area of inmates' names. He can only block a name change in rare cases – if the name's offensive or obscene.'

'I tell you what's offensive and obscene – people like me suffering for something they never done.'

'All right. That's enough of your moaning. I just thought I'd pass on the news. I've got to go – I've got a busy day.'

'You've got a busy day? What about me? I've got this crossword to finish. I've got to clean the toilet and then I'm off to the gym. It's all go in here.'

'Have you chosen a new course yet? You're coming to the end of the Maths course, aren't you?'

'I can't make my mind up. I'm spoilt for choice, aren't I? Barbering, industrial cleaning, speaking French. It's like a bloody university in here, ain't it?'

'You'll have to decide soon – or the governor will decide for you.'

'That's what I like about this place. You're all friendly on the outside, but deep down inside we're a nuisance, a hindrance. You'll push us into something we don't want, just to get us out of the way.'

'That's nonsense. It's not like that at all. We have to act under Home Office guidelines and all prisoners here at Ashwood Vale have to follow a course of education. Learning in prison's been shown to have a significant impact on reducing reoffending.'

'You're all full of crap. You've just been taught to say that and you repeat it, parrot-fashion. You're just part of the system.'

'It's a system that tends to work very well most of the time. Anyway I can't hang around here swapping banter with you. I've got to get on.'

Chapter 11

It was a bitterly cold morning as the chief inspector drove towards St James Street police headquarters. The temperature gauge on his car showed it was only just above freezing.

As he drew into the car park, he was recalling a phone conversation he had with his son, George, immediately after breakfast. George remained concerned that two men convicted of O'Sullivan's murder had been framed. He had been moved by some of the claims in the leaflets handed out during the demonstration at the Crown Court.

In response, Roscoe had warned his son against becoming emotionally involved in his police work. 'Always try and remain detached, and don't let sentiment come before duty,' he had told him.

But, deep down, he could not help sharing his son's concerns about the way police colleagues and the Crown Prosecution Service had handled the murder investigation.

After hanging up his coat and making himself a coffee, he summoned his sergeant, Sunita Roy, and they both walked to Tom Vickers' office. The room was deserted.

'Perhaps he's in the canteen?' she suggested.

'Who knows,' he replied wearily.

They both began studying the white evidence board which had been installed behind the door. Someone – presumably DI Vickers – had written 'Presumed innocent' in capital letters above a column on the left of the board. Beneath were photographs and descriptions of the jailed men, Winston Stevens and Raj Kumar. At the top of a column on the right were the words 'Key suspects'. Descriptions of the two men reported in a witness statement by the murdered man's neighbour, Nisa Shah, appeared directly below.

Her name jogged Roscoe's memory. He turned to look at his sergeant.

'Have you tried to reach Nisa Shah recently?' he asked her.

'Yes, sir,' she said. 'I've left messages for her everywhere, but it looks as though she's trying to avoid us. Don't think she'll have changed her mind about giving evidence.'

'Never mind,' said Roscoe. 'Keep trying. It's going to be much harder to breathe fresh life into this case without her – despite the advances we've made over the past few days.'

They had just finished browsing through the details on the board when the door opened and Vickers appeared in a smart charcoal-grey suit and red patterned tie – a far cry from the days when he gave the impression he had slept in his clothes. He was beaming like a student on graduation day.

'Good morning, guv,' he said. 'I was told you were here. Sorry, I was over in forensics, having a word with Dr Ling. As you can see, we've put the eye-witness descriptions up on the board. We've studied Trent's associates and other possible suspects. There are a few names in the frame, which I'll tell you about in a minute.

'Dr Ling's had a report back from our ballistics specialist on the bullet that DS Roy found. The bullet comes from a different Beretta from the one that featured in the trial. Dr Ling says it comes from a Beretta 9000S pistol. So that's obviously a vital new piece of evidence.'

'Great news, Tom,' said Roscoe, taking a seat at what was normally DS Hopkirk's desk by the door.

'I've also been checking the alibis of Stevens and Kumar,' Vickers continued. 'Two of our colleagues from West Midlands helped me earlier this week to go through CCTV camera footage obtained from the Bull Ring shopping centre at the time of the murder.'

'West Midlands have been helpful, have they?'

'Yes, guv, very helpful. After trawling through the footage, we found someone who looks like Stevens pushing a woman in a wheelchair past the River Island store. Luckily, it's well-lit there. The woman resembles Stevens' grandmother.'

'Oh yes – the woman in the wheelchair pictured in the press after the protest outside Warwick Crown Court?'

'Precisely. We've also checked into Raj Kumar's alibi. He claimed he'd got a dentist appointment in Summerstoke at the time of the murder. We've checked and the dentist's staff deny this.'

'So he doesn't have an alibi?' said Roscoe.

'Well, we've had a bit of luck. By chance, one of my old contacts from my Wolverhampton days called me. He spotted some CCTV showing Kumar with some other dealers peddling drugs on a street corner in Soho Road.'

'Bloody hell!' said Roscoe. 'That's a bit of luck.'

'The time on the frame is ten minutes past three. There's no way he could've been in Sedgeworth at around three. We've also tracked phone signals which show his mobile was in Soho Road.'

Roscoe smiled. He had some happy memories spent as a young constable patrolling the streets of that suburb while with the West Midlands force.

'I can see now why his defence team didn't want to delve into his alibi more closely,' Roscoe muttered, 'if he was out selling drugs. Not something you'd want to put before a jury.'

'Well, he refused to cooperate with them. He couldn't believe a murder charge would be pinned on him. He was reluctant to admit he was supplying drugs at the time O'Sullivan was shot over an alleged drugs debt.'

Vickers walked over to the whiteboard. He pinned two names under the heading 'Key suspects'. The names were Tyrone Blake and Tahir Khan. He turned to Roscoe.

'Thanks to the sterling work of our undercover lad Liam Clancy, we now know that Trent's main supplier is Filipowski,' he said. 'Liam's also provided us with information about these two other men – Blake and Khan. They're the two main street dealers who work for Filipowski. Liam believes Filipowski is importing cocaine from the Netherlands. The lad's only picking up bits and pieces, but it's thought to be coming into the UK through a port in the West Country – possibly Bristol.'

Vickers paused for a moment before remarking, 'I've got to say, guv, that our methods in this investigation have been rather unorthodox.'

The chief inspector glanced at his two colleagues and smiled.

'They have rather,' he admitted. 'But you sometimes have to take chances in our world. Anyway, we'll be replacing Liam at a later stage with one of our own undercover people.'

Sunita was unsure how to respond. She sometimes wondered if her boss took too many chances, but she smiled and said nothing.

Roscoe looked down at the floor. He was pleased at the progress they had already made in amassing evidence to clear the wrongly jailed men. His only concern now was that none of the evidence pointed to Trent's personal culpability.

They had to find a way to prove he was playing a major role in the OCG. It had to be incontrovertible evidence. It was much harder to pin guilt on a police officer than on an ordinary member of the public. Evidence had to be cast-iron. Judges might be tempted to give an officer of the law the benefit of the doubt if the prosecution case was weak.

He shared his thoughts with his colleagues. 'We've got to prove Trent is clearly linked to crime,' he said.

'Easier said than done,' said Vickers, walking to his desk at the far side of the room and sitting down in his usual chair.

'Yes, but I've got a plan,' said Roscoe.

Just then, DC Khalid knocked on the door and eased it open a fraction.

'Sir, there's a call come into CID for DS Roy,' he explained with a stern expression.

'Is it urgent?' Roscoe snapped.

'I think it's someone the sergeant was trying to reach yesterday.'

Sunita jumped up. 'I'd better go and take it,' she said. 'You never know. It might be Mrs Shah.'

'Unlikely,' said Roscoe. 'Very well. You'd better take it.'

After she left, the chief inspector revealed his latest plan.

'Young Liam seems to have been accepted into the gang, which is very helpful. But I've been thinking, Tom, he could be useful in another way as well.'

'How d'you mean, guv?'

'Well, I've been thinking the only way we can get direct evidence of Trent's involvement in crime is to bug his office.'

'Sounds sensible to me.'

'I've been to see Norris and she's applied to the chief constable for permission. We need to catch him giving instructions, passing on messages, discussing money – that kind of thing. We've got to get direct evidence of what Trent is up to, and the best way we can do that is to conceal a microphone over in Summerstoke. We can't run the risk of Trent being tipped off. So I'm going to suggest we involve Liam Clancy in this as well. I want to get him inside Trent's office to install a device.'

Vickers smiled. 'You've come to the right person, guv. I've got a selection of some of the latest recording gadgets. One of my favourites is a fake air freshener. I've also got a device which would be ideal for slipping behind a loose tile in a suspended ceiling. And I've got a bogus electrical double socket that records conversations as well as providing electricity. Name your weapon.'

'The double socket sounds interesting. Can I have a look?'

'Absolutely,' said the inspector, opening a drawer in one of the desks. 'Here you are.'

He showed Roscoe a gadget which resembled an ordinary white wall socket.

'It gives quite a high-quality recording once it's been fitted to the wall in the place of a standard double socket. The bug itself is battery-powered, so both mains sockets can still be used to power electrical gadgets. There are no outward signs of it being anything other than a normal socket because the on-off switch is underneath and not easily visible. The bug's voice-activated so there's no long gaps when the recording's played back.'

He added, 'Any recordings made can later be downloaded onto a laptop and saved. Trent's a sharp guy.

We could introduce an adaptor, air freshener or carbon monoxide alarm which have mikes inside, but they might stand out and make him suspicious.'

'The double socket sounds ideal,' said Roscoe. 'My plan is to get access to the CID office in North Warwickshire at night to fit the device. Then we'll have to return a week later to collect it.

'I realise there are several options, Tom. But I don't want anything over-complicated. I don't fancy taking a seat in a car outside Trent's office for a week listening into his phone calls. They'd be bound to spot me. No, I think our best option is to plant a device like this and return for it a week later.

'I know it's a nuisance having to go back, but even if we had recordings transmitted to us, we'd have to return to collect the bug. The last thing we want is for him to realise his office is bugged.'

Vickers held up the double socket. 'You're welcome to take this, guv. I'm off to Coventry this afternoon to meet Giles Farquhar.'

'Remind me who he is?'

'He's the solicitor working for the Stevens and Kumar families. I want to find out how the appeal is going.'

'That's good,' said Roscoe. 'With any luck and a bit more work, we can't be too far away from handing those men their freedom and getting the right villains behind bars.'

Chapter 12

The light drizzle that had been falling tailed off as the chief inspector drove into a supermarket car park in Chelmsley Wood, near Birmingham Airport, on Monday, 14 January in a small white van he had borrowed.

The palms of his hands were becoming slightly moist. The mission planned for that evening was full of risks. After stepping out of the vehicle, he paced up and down beside a clump of trees like an expectant father in a maternity ward.

He had decided to embark on this stage of Operation Temple himself, despite the risk that Seymour Trent might recognise him. He was taking a gamble by involving Liam, a civilian, in his cloak-and-dagger venture and he was determined to ensure it would pass off without a hitch.

Within a few minutes, Liam drove up to him in a ten-year-old red Honda Civic. Roscoe walked over to the ginger-haired youth. Liam stepped out of his car and the pair warmly shook hands.

'Sweet mother of God, Mr Roscoe,' he said. 'I'd never have expected to be seeing you in a poky little van like that.'

The detective glanced back at the Ford van. Emblazoned across the side were the words 'Avondene Electrical Services' along with a Queensbridge phone number.

'I've borrowed it from a friend,' said Roscoe. 'It drives very well. We'll take it to Summerstoke and, when we get just round the corner from the police station, I'll get out. Then you can drive it for the last few hundred metres and park outside. You'll have to leave it partly on the pavement because it's double yellow lines all along there. But it'll be after six thirty, so there shouldn't be any trouble with wardens.'

The pair set out for the seventeen-mile journey to the North Warwickshire town of Summerstoke.

Just before a quarter to seven, they stopped in a terraced street close to the police station.

Roscoe handed Liam a pair of blue overalls to slip on. By a quirk of fate, the youth was almost the same height and build as Roscoe's electrician friend so they were a near-perfect fit.

'Now here's the gadget you've got to install. It's called an audio surveillance device,' said Roscoe. 'Here's an old tool-bag containing a set of screwdrivers. I've shown you the basics of how to fit it, haven't I? And don't forget to bring back the old socket. We'll need to put that back in its place in a week's time.'

'Don't worry now, Mr Roscoe,' Liam insisted. 'I've done this kind of thing, replacing sockets, so many times with me dad and grandad. I'll just have to be extra careful with the wires.'

'How come?'

'I'm not going to be able to turn off the power, am I? In these big buildings, they've got a closet where all the distribution boards are kept. I probably wouldn't know where to look and, in any case, it may be locked. But don't worry. You just have to take care to keep the live wire well away from the others.'

'Well, if you're sure…'

'I'm sure. The only thing that concerns me is, and it's only a little thing…' He broke off.

'What is it, Liam?'

'Well, I've never been asked to break into a police station before. It seems a little strange, don't you think?'

'You'll be fine,' said Roscoe. 'This is the way to look at it, you're doing the force a favour. You're helping to root out a bent copper.'

'That's a nice way of putting it, to be sure. So you've dropped the idea of putting a tap on the guy's phone?'

'Yes, that's right. We thought it would be too tricky.'

'Well, I'm glad you decided against putting a tap on it, Mr Roscoe,' Liam continued with a twinkle in his eye. 'I'm sure the man would've noticed and he'd have called a plumber out in no time.'

'It's good to work with you, Liam,' said Roscoe, laughing. 'Now,' he continued, picking up an umbrella he had left just behind the passenger seat, 'I'm going to go into reception and have a word with the desk staff to keep them occupied. Give me a few minutes' head start and then you turn up with your toolkit. As I've explained, the CID office is on the second floor, unless they've moved. We'll meet back here afterwards.' Then he added, 'Don't forget your bobble hat and your grandad's old glasses. We don't want Trent or his cronies recognising you.'

'Don't worry now, Mr Roscoe. I know exactly how to play it.'

'And keep your mobile on,' said the detective. 'If a load of CID suddenly turn up, I'll give you a bell. All right. Let's rock 'n' roll.'

After Liam had driven away, Roscoe set off on foot. As he turned the corner, he saw the imposing justice building a hundred metres ahead on the left in Spring Street. The police, courts, prosecution service and probation staff were all housed in the thirteen-year-old red-brick building.

Roscoe mounted the steps and made his way in. To his relief, a constable he remembered from the past was manning the reception desk.

'Mr Roscoe,' the constable proclaimed. 'I've not seen you in what – six or seven years? How are you getting on?'

'I'm fine, Edwin,' Roscoe replied, removing a small map from his jacket pocket. 'We could do without this weather.'

'I've seen George several times. He's getting on fine,' said Edwin.

'Yes, he's loving it. Look, I'm a bit of a stranger here. Can you help me find St Margaret Street?'

He slapped his map down on the counter. As he did so, a young man with a blue bobble hat and glasses in smart blue overalls entered the foyer carrying a black bag. He boldly approached the desk and interrupted the constable to ask, 'CID? Is it second floor?'

'That's right. I wasn't told of any electrician coming this evening.'

'It's an emergency,' said Liam.

'All right. Take that lift over there. Turn right as soon as you come out on the second floor.'

Edwin turned to Roscoe as Liam stood a few metres away, waiting nervously for the lift to arrive.

'I should really get someone to escort him but we haven't got the staff,' said Edwin.

'He looks harmless enough,' said Roscoe.

'I wonder if I should leave reception just for a moment and go with him.'

'What if someone else comes in?' said Roscoe. 'I'm sure he'll be OK. There are a few people on the CID floor anyway, aren't there?'

'You think he'll be all right, do you, sir?'

'Yes, someone must've called him in. They'd have all his details.'

'I'm sure you're right, although I'd better put it in the log. What's it say on that van out there? Avondene Electrical Services?'

* * *

Liam took the lift to the second floor. It jerked upwards and arrived with a jolt and a 'ping' sound. He emerged gingerly to find he was in a huge, well-lit, open-plan office with a few small, private rooms at the side. The only staff present were two men and a woman in plain clothes sitting behind computers some distance away. They took no notice of him as, fearlessly, he turned right out of the lift and began to wander around, searching for Seymour Trent's desk.

Within seconds, he realised the word 'Detective' appeared on some of the side-room doors, confirming he was in the CID area. But none of the doors bore the name Trent.

He was starting to feel impatient and frustrated when, at the end of the room, he discovered a desk which was wider than the others. Unlike some cluttered desks nearby, the desktop was neatly arranged with a computer, an upright calendar, a silver paperweight, a bronze statuette of an officer in riot gear, and a wooden tray containing documents.

Rather audaciously, Liam put down the tool-bag and, for a few minutes, made himself comfortable in the high-backed executive chair in front of the desk. He examined the papers in the tray – most of which were marked 'Police – confidential'. The name of 'DI Seymour Trent' or 'Detective Inspector S. Trent' appeared on all of them. He picked up Trent's phone and put it to his ear.

'Right now, Malone,' he said quietly in a mock-American accent. 'Get down to the south side. There's a body been fished out of the docks. It looks like moyder. Tell O'Shaughnessy to get down to the Black Cat Club in the Bronx. There's bin a shootin' and a lootin'!'

Suddenly a female voice sprang forth from the phone.

'Switchboard. Which service?' the woman inquired.

He quickly slammed the handset down, realising it was time he focused on his task.

Rising from the chair, he quickly took some photographs of his surroundings on his mobile phone, as Roscoe had requested. Then he gazed round in search of the nearest electrical sockets. At first, there was none to be seen. Then, after shifting aside a pile of boxes containing printing paper beside the skirting board, he discovered a double one. It was just six feet from Trent's chair.

After making sure he was not being observed, he knelt down on the carpet and deftly set to work, unscrewing the front face of the socket. He disconnected the wires before taking the fake version out of his bag and carefully attaching all the wires to it. Finally, he screwed it to the base of the socket and placed the old plastic front in his bag. He turned the switch beneath the socket to activate recording and then used a socket-testing plug from his bag to ensure both sides were fully functional.

Just as he rose to his feet, he realised he was not alone. He noticed a pair of what seemed to be size ten or eleven shoes waiting, motionless, a few metres away. He peered up to see who was standing in this large pair of shoes.

It was a tall, stocky man in a light-brown suit with short brown hair. The man must have been watching him.

'All right, mate?' Liam asked.

'Yes. Just come to see what's happening,' said the newcomer. 'You're working a bit late, aren't you?'

'My van broke down,' said the bogus electrician. 'Should've been here a few hours ago. Anyway this is working now.'

'Didn't know there was anything wrong with it.'

'Yes,' said Liam. 'One of the cleaning ladies complained. Couldn't get any power from the socket.'

'Oh, OK,' said the man.

'Must be going,' muttered Liam. 'Promised to buy the girlfriend a meal.'

'Goodnight,' said the man.

Liam, carrying his tool-bag, took the lift back to the ground floor, where Roscoe was still chatting to the desk constable as if they were long-lost friends. Liam could faintly hear Roscoe saying, 'I'll have to shoot off now, Edwin. I think it must be the High Street I'm looking for.'

'Yes,' the constable was saying as Liam left the building.

* * *

'So you're quite clear now, sir,' Edwin told the chief inspector. 'It's round the ringway in a clockwise direction. Turn left into Queen's Road and it's the first turning on the right. You won't have any trouble finding it, sir.'

'Thanks for being so helpful,' Roscoe said as he headed for the doors. He was pleased to see it had stopped raining.

'Goodnight, sir!' Edwin called. 'Oh, don't forget your umbrella!'

But the detective had already emerged into the cold January air, confident in the belief that their task had gone as planned. The constable ran outside, still shouting about the umbrella. But his words went unheeded.

Chapter 13

Polly Cook watched the customers queuing to order food at the bar of the gastropub.

'Tell me, Seymour. Why d'you like this pub so much?' she asked as she watched him in adoration from across the table.

'Well,' her boyfriend said, 'it's got good beer and food. It's great in the summer because it's got a huge garden. The staff are friendly, and you can see the whole car park from the front windows.'

'That's important to you?'

'Too right.'

The inspector sipped from his cool pint of lager as she stared down into her margarita, twiddling the cocktail stick.

'Not only that – it's convenient. It's on the way home,' he added.

'You don't mind it being so busy?' she said, glancing through the window at the thirty or forty cars and vans parked in the large car park at the front.

'It's not usually like this. Maybe it's pay day.'

'Have you been here with Phil Bains?'

'A few times. He prefers his local in Hinckley. He's made a lot of friends there.'

'He's very loyal to you, isn't he?'

'Yeah, we're old mates. I've known him for about eight years. He worked in Lincolnshire with me for a short time and we kept in touch.'

'How come you both ended up in Summerstoke?'

'I had to pull a few levers to get him as my DS,' he admitted.

'What time's Tiff coming?' she asked.

'He should be here any minute,' he replied. He studied the small diary he pulled from his trouser pocket.

'Here it is,' he said. 'Monday, 14 January, 7 p.m.' He checked his Cartier watch, which gave the time as three minutes to seven. 'God, I hope he doesn't get lost. I told him it was the Three Gardeners at Vine Hill.'

'I like it here too,' she said. 'It's a pity I can't come home with you tonight.'

'I know,' he said. 'Polly, have you opened those new bank accounts yet?'

'I've left it till tomorrow because that's my day off.'

'And have you started looking for luxury cars to buy so we can process all this fresh money?'

'Don't worry. It's all in hand,' she said. 'I'm giving up the whole day to do it.'

'Good.'

Just then his iPhone rang.

'Here's our man now,' he said. 'Yes, Tiff?'

Polly heard only a few muffled words.

'What's wrong with your satnav?' Trent asked. 'Look, calm down. It sounds like you're on the right road. Have you passed a pub called the Five Bells? … OK. Just take the next road on the right and you should be here in a matter of a few minutes. See you then.'

Trent ended the call and then spent a few seconds looking down at his chrome handset.

'He's such a bloody idiot,' he said, putting the gadget away in the inner pocket of his grey casual jacket. 'I don't know how he got into this game and how he's stayed in it for so long.'

'He doesn't seem to have the right temperament at all,' said Polly, rising from her chair and moving round the table so she could sit next to him.

Trent continued, 'He's swearing away at ten to the dozen, complaining his satnav isn't working and he's going to sort out the car dealer. I don't know.'

Polly again cast her eyes round the dimly lit country inn with its exposed stone walling, brick fireplaces, heavily beamed ceilings and flagstone-style floor. She watched as customers continued to vie for the two barmen's attention in front of the rustic oak counter.

From time to time, just beyond the queuing drinkers, she caught glimpses of a few brave souls standing in the cold air on the terrace outside, smoking.

Her eyes returned to her boyfriend. How she idolised him. How she longed for him to leave his wife. How she wished he would set up home with her. She stroked his bristly hair and he smiled back at her.

'What did you do today?' she asked as she took his hand in hers. 'Anything you can tell me about?'

'You know I'd always tell you if anything fascinating happened.'

'So it didn't?'

'No. It didn't. I sent Clarkie to a terraced house in Summerstoke to look into a sudden death. At first it seemed suspicious, but it turned out to be natural causes. How about you?'

'Had to arrest a drunk last night. My colleague slipped up and called me "Polly". So then the drunk kept repeating, "Pretty Polly! Pretty Polly!" all the way back to the station.'

Trent shrugged his shoulders.

'You've got to expect a bit of banter from the punters, haven't you?' he said.

After a few minutes, as the couple glanced through the sash window next to their table, a silver Porsche Boxster arrived. The driver found a space at the far side of the car park. They watched as a tall, thin man stepped out.

'I'd better go out and do the business,' said Trent. 'Won't be long.'

* * *

Seymour Trent marched out through the main door of the pub and headed towards his associate. They shook hands warmly, but, as they did so, Filipowski noticed a scratch on his car's passenger door.

'Bloody hell! Look at that mark!' he shouted. 'That must've been someone at the Coventry car park, I'm thinking. Some bloody little kid, I expect.'

'Calm down, Tiff,' Trent implored him. 'They'll soon sort that out in the body shop.'

'No, I'm not calming down. It's going to cost money, for God's sake. These kids have just got no respect. I think I'm going to go back to the car park and see if there are any of those kids about.'

'Don't be so ridiculous,' said Trent. 'Whoever did it is probably miles away by now.'

'But there's a principle at stake here.'

'Look, let's just sort out the money and then I'll buy you a pint. How's that?'

'I'm not forgetting this in a hurry,' said Filipowski as he retrieved a carrier bag containing bundles of notes from his car boot.

As surreptitiously as he could, he handed it to Trent, who opened the driver's door of his black BMW, parked nearby. He slipped inside and counted the money for a few minutes. When he was finally satisfied with the amount, he returned the notes to the bag and placed it beneath the front passenger seat.

They both locked their cars and Filipowski followed Trent into the pub.

'You remember Tiff, don't you, Poll?' asked the inspector as they approached her at the table in the window bay.

'Yes, of course. How are you?' she asked.

The newcomer kissed her on both cheeks and offered to buy them drinks.

'No, you're all right, mate,' said Trent. 'We've only just got these. Let me get you one. I'm sure it's my turn.'

'I think this is an Everards pub,' he said. 'I'll have a pint of Tiger, please, if they've got it.'

Trent headed to the bar and joined a queue. A few minutes later he returned.

'All they've got is Marston's Pedigree,' said Trent, apologetically.

'God, I hate that stuff. Get me a lager, would you?'

Trent returned a few minutes later with a pint of cool lager. By then, Filipowski had made himself comfortable in the chair next to Polly. He had told her all about the scratch on his car door and how any pub that ran out of his favourite beer should be closed down by the government.

'There's no excuse,' he said. 'They advertise a certain beer outside or at the door or on a board inside, they've got to sell that beer. It's no good them saying, "We're sorry. We've run out." They've got to plan so they don't run out. It's all to do with management.'

'I bet a pub wouldn't run out if you were in charge,' said Trent.

'That's right. I'm something of a smooth operator, you know. Customers learn to trust me because I'm not the man who lets them down. If I run a pub, they come back because they know the beer will be here and will be cold.

Not like the disgusting dishwater they serve in some English pubs which is claimed to be beer.'

'If you want a guaranteed cold drink in an English pub, you have to have lager,' said Trent, sitting on a chair opposite Polly and Filipowski. 'Real ale isn't really meant to be chilled, you know.'

'No. All beer should be chilled. It's obvious,' said Filipowski. 'Who wants warm beer?'

'The English have a bit of a reputation for drinking warm beer,' said Trent.

'No, they don't. They've a reputation for poor standards. The English let foreigners mock them because they let pubs sell them the warm beer. It's different. It's time the English did something about it. But d'you know what? They won't do nothing. The English are too scared to complain.'

'I'm sorry, Tiff. The die-hard, traditional real ale drinkers enjoy their beer at room temperature or just slightly chilled.'

'No. This is absolute rubbish. No one can enjoy beer unless it's proper cold – especially in the hot summer.'

Trent felt Polly nudge his foot under the table as if to say, 'Time to change the subject.' He decided she was right.

'All right,' he said. 'Let's knock this on the head now. We've got other things to discuss.'

'No, we're not knocking this on its head,' Filipowski insisted, raising his voice. 'You're talking crap, man.'

'That's enough now,' said Polly. 'Let's just enjoy our drinks. What's your lager like?'

'It's OK. It's cold, but it's not the drink I wanted.'

'I'm fed up with this!' Trent declared. 'We're going. Come on, Polly, drink up!'

'No,' said Filipowski. 'Polly, he doesn't have to be leaving. I'm leaving. I'm going back to the car park where those little bastards scratched my car.'

With that, he swallowed the last remaining dregs of his glass and left. Trent went to the door and watched as Filipowski marched over to his car and roared off down the road at high speed. Trent returned to the table, red-faced and in a furious mood.

'I can't work with him anymore,' he told Polly. 'The man's totally impossible. He loses his temper every few seconds. He's like a walking volcano. Other people are also finding it difficult to get along with him. Not to mention he can be unreliable.'

'Have you tried telling him?'

'What's the point? He'd just kick off again.'

'So what are you going to do?'

'I'm going to have to go into business with someone else.'

He took his mobile phone from his jacket pocket. He dialled a number he had not used for more than a week. Then he walked outside into the car park so his girlfriend could not overhear the conversation.

'You remember our cosy little chat the other day about our mutual problem?' he said down the phone.

A man's voice replied, 'Of course, my friend.'

'Well, I've decided the moment's come,' he went on. 'I can't take his outbursts of rage anymore. On top of that his deliveries are becoming irregular and we're losing trade. D'you think you can manage the job? … Good.'

Chapter 14

Gas Street Basin in the centre of Birmingham was once a sad spectacle, cluttered with abandoned factory buildings. But, after a multi-million-pound regeneration, this former waterway cargo hub – which thrived in the Victorian age –

has been transformed. Now it has become a magnet for boat enthusiasts and tourists. It is a hive of entertainment with canal-side pubs, clubs and restaurants.

Tadeusz Filipowski clutched Monika Kowalska's hand as they strolled beside the canal like carefree holidaymakers and decided to call in at one of the bars. It had proved one of the mildest nights for some time, but they decided it would still be too cold to sit outside.

He bought two bottles of lager with two glasses and they sat quietly in a corner of the main bar by a window overlooking the canal. They watched a narrowboat glide past on the water as they sipped their drinks. Several couples were chatting and laughing at tables nearby.

The premises had a huge chrome bar counter in the centre with faux leather bar stools. A number of tables and chairs were positioned around it. Floor-to-ceiling windows offered breath-taking views across the canal basin.

'I'm glad you've calmed down,' she told him. 'You were in a terrible mood last night when I spoke to you on the phone.'

He nodded. 'Well, you've seen the scratch on my car door. I went back to the car park, but the little runts had vanished.'

'Don't work yourself up. I'm sure a garage can fix it.'

'That's not the point,' he said. 'Anyway, I thought I should mention I'm bringing some more girls over next month.' He placed his glass down on the table. 'So I've been making inquiries about getting a flat in Ladywood. Is possible I get Lena to run it.'

'She'd be good. She can be trusted.'

Monika touched his hand and smiled. She was gazing into his eyes.

'Tiff, are you happy with your life?' she asked.

'Of course,' he replied. 'I made more than half a million last year. I've got a team of men working on my mansion near Edgbaston. It's going to have a swimming pool, sauna, gymnasium, cinema, and tennis courts. I've got a Ferrari on order. Why wouldn't I be happy?'

She shook her head. 'No, I mean really happy. You need someone in your life, Tiff.'

'I think the world of you, Monika. I always have. I just don't know if I want to commit.'

She cupped her palms round his right hand.

'I worry about you, darling. You're a player in a very dangerous game.'

'Don't worry about me. I've always taken risks – since I was a young boy. It's what's made me the man I am today. The Facebook man, Mark Zuckerberg, said, "The biggest risk is not taking any risk."'

'Oh, Tiff. Why don't you let me come and move in with you? I'd like to look after you.'

'Keep your voice down a little,' he snapped. He was embarrassed by her flattery. 'Look, I'm considering it.'

His attention was captured for a moment by a canoodling couple who were strolling past the window. He watched them step along the towpath and disappear in the distance.

'Come on, let's head back to my place,' he said. 'I've got some really pure gear. It's not been cut with anything, and it'll blow your socks off.'

'I'm not wearing any!'

'Listen, there's no need to worry about me. Got Tyrone to watch my back and, in any case, very few people know where I'm living right now. So stop worrying, Monika.'

* * *

A group of five prison officers were reading newspapers or watching breakfast television in the main warders' office the next morning when the phone rang. It had been a quiet night at Ashwood Vale Prison in Worcestershire. But if they were hoping that it would prove a quiet, trouble-free day, they were about to be sorely disappointed.

His colleagues could not hear the conversation, but the warder who took the call said simply, 'We'll be right with you,' and hung up.

'It's Carl Innocent,' he announced. 'He's gone berserk.'

The five men – including Daryl Johnson, the officer who had been trying to enrol Innocent on an educational course – hurried through the main building until they reached D Wing. One by one, they dashed up the stairway to the first landing. Constant banging and shouting greeted them as they approached Innocent's cell. A solitary warder was outside the room, reluctant to enter on his own.

'I've been trying to get his attention, but he's been ignoring me,' the officer explained.

Other prisoners were shouting from nearby cells.

One voice called, 'Oi! Keep the noise down. I'm trying to sleep.'

Another yelled, 'Hey, Innocent! Pipe down, you noisy bastard.'

'You lot, be quiet!' Johnson demanded. Then, approaching the officer by the door, he asked, 'What's the matter with him?'

'He's had a letter from his wife,' came the reply.

The warders nodded. It was a situation they were all familiar with. A prisoner, shut off from the outside world for long periods, develops a personal view of how the world is and how it should be. Then a letter from their nearest and dearest in the real world arrives and, often, their view is shattered.

'How long's this been going on?' asked one of the group.

'About ten minutes,' said the warder by the door.

'Let me have a word with him,' said Johnson, producing his bunch of keys.

'Innocent!' he began, as he turned one of the keys in the lock. 'It's me, Mr Johnson.'

Through the doorway, he could see the prisoner had smashed his television and stereo. He had also wrecked his bookcase.

The floor was covered in broken glass, damaged wood and scattered bedding. As Johnson watched, Innocent was thrusting the legs of a chair against the bars on his window, creating a loud, metallic noise.

'Shove off, screws!' he yelled.

'What's happened? What's the problem?' Johnson asked from the landing as he held the door ajar.

'Mind your own business!' Innocent screamed.

Turning behind him to his worried colleagues, Johnson explained in a quiet voice, 'He's smashed up most of his cell.'

'Better take him to the hospital wing,' said a tall, muscular member of the group. 'The trick cyclist can have a look at him.'

Taking a single step inside, Johnson asked the inmate, 'Did you get a letter this morning, Innocent?'

'Yes. From the missus,' he fumed. 'She wants a bloody divorce. She ain't going to bloody get one.'

He stopped banging the window bars. Johnson could see tears were streaming down his red face.

'Come on, old fellow,' said Johnson. 'Let me come in and have a chat with you.' He might have thought this gentle approach would have a calming effect, but he was mistaken.

'Keep your distance!' Innocent demanded. 'I'm not in the best of moods.'

'I gathered that,' said Johnson.

His colleagues were losing patience. They felt Johnson's gentle technique was achieving nothing. The tall, muscular officer barged past Johnson and strode into the cell.

'Come on, Mr Innocent. Time for you to have a quiet chat with the doctor.'

'No flaming doctor's chatting to me!' he screamed.

The burly warder snatched the chair out of Innocent's hands and hurled it aside. The prisoner began pummelling the officer with his fists, but the warder reacted swiftly, seizing Innocent by the wrists and ramming the prisoner's body hard against the cell wall with all his might. The force seemed to leave the prisoner dazed for a few seconds.

Then two other warders advanced on the inmate. He raised his fists and punched one of the warders, knocking him back towards the door, but the second man grappled with him and, supported by the tall, muscular officer, they overpowered him. Within a few seconds, they were able to drag him, still struggling, out of the cell and onto the landing.

'You're off to see the doc before you cause any more damage to Her Majesty's property,' said one of his captors.

Johnson, disappointed at his workmates' decision to employ physical force, followed closely behind, shaking his head.

An hour later, Johnson was having his lunch in the warders' canteen when one of the senior prison officers spotted him and sat down beside him.

'I hear your friend Innocent caused a one-man riot this morning,' he began.

'Didn't he just,' said Johnson.

'What set him off, Daryl?'

'He received a letter from his wife in Norton Prior. She told him she wants nothing more to do with him and wants a divorce.'

'Must've been a hell of a surprise. Hasn't she been visiting him regularly?'

'That's right. But, apparently, she's found herself a new man and wants to sell the business.'

'They've had to put him in a padded cell in the psychiatric ward.'

'Have they?' said Johnson. 'Poor old Innocent.'

'Poor old Innocent, my foot,' said the senior officer. 'He's a vicious bastard. He threw his own glasses on the floor and stamped on them. Then, when the doctor tried to pick up the remains, Innocent nearly strangled him. It took two other doctors and two nurses to get him off him. That's why he's getting the padded cell treatment.'

'That letter must've really upset him,' said Johnson. 'He's generally a morose and surly man, but he normally shows a dry sense of humour.'

'No sign of the comedian today.'

'I know.'

'They'll have to keep him in the medical wing for some time until he's no longer considered a danger to himself and to others.'

He stood up and wandered out of the canteen, leaving Johnson alone with his thoughts.

Chapter 15

It was just after midnight four days later when a black Volkswagen Touareg gently drew up outside an unremarkable mid-terraced house in the village of Balsall Common. The tall man with close-cropped hair spent a moment loading his Glock 17 with several rounds of ammunition.

A full moon bathed the street in a dim light every so often as it emerged from behind the clouds. As he had expected, there was no sound from the red-brick house, although the presence of a silver Porsche Boxster on the forecourt signified the householder was at home.

The man, dressed in dark clothing and wearing gloves, took a can of petrol from his car boot and opened the garden gate. Blinds had been drawn in all the front windows and no light was visible.

'Good,' he muttered to himself.

He walked silently across the forecourt until he reached the front door. There, using a key he'd had cut a week before while the occupier was in a drug-induced stupor, he let himself in.

The house was as still as a nunnery at prayer. He knew where his quarry would be. Spark out – probably spread-eagled – in the middle of his bed. On his bedside table would be the remains of a line or several lines of cocaine. He may be snoring. The intruder would be careful in his every movement but, even if he made an accidental sound, it was likely the householder would remain comatose.

The uninvited guest passed through the sparsely decorated hallway and pushed the living-room door. It opened with a creaking sound. Newspapers were scattered over the settee. A laptop computer and some books lay on top of a low-level sideboard. Three packets of cigarettes had been placed in front of the widescreen television.

Assured no one was sleeping downstairs, he returned to the hall and mounted the stairs.

Nearly every step squeaked. Now and then, he paused to see if his presence had been noticed, but the house remained silent. He would have to have an excuse ready in the unlikely event that his associate was awake and lucid.

However, the only noise came from a ticking clock in the hallway. The intruder reached the top and placed the can in the middle of the landing floor.

Then he took his loaded pistol from his bag and stealthily pushed against the bedroom door. It creaked open, brushing against the dark-red patterned carpet.

He peered into the darkened master bedroom. Nothing stirred. He could not even hear the sound of breathing. But he could see the householder lying in his bed with the top of his head just visible on the pillow. Lying motionless. Oblivious to the peril that awaited.

A china plate, holding the remnants of a drugs binge and a narrow tube that had been used for snorting the powder, rested on a dressing table. He took three paces into the room and pointed the gun at the tufts of hair. He fired. The victim's head seemed to twitch and then lay still.

'Job done,' he muttered.

After searching around upstairs, he found three duvets in one of the other bedrooms and piled them up outside the door to the master bedroom. Then he sprinkled petrol over the heap and struck a match.

The mound of material caught alight at once and, within seconds, the whole landing was engulfed in flames.

The intruder retraced his steps to the hallway, where he found a black refuse sack in a cupboard. Then he hurried into the kitchen and filled the bag with packets of cocaine, which he knew were concealed inside the oven.

After picking up the laptop from the sideboard, he left, firmly locking the white double-glazed front door behind him.

He was glad to see the darkness closing in. The moon had dipped behind some clouds. Soon the house would become an inferno, destroying any evidence of his midnight mission.

Moments later, his car drew away and the cold-hearted assassin headed off into the night.

But without him knowing, his actions had been monitored. A figure with short, light-brown hair had, sometime earlier, parked his black BMW a hundred metres away along the street. On seeing the Volkswagen disappear into the distance, he turned on his lights and his engine. He too drove away.

Chapter 16

The white electrician's van rattled as it entered the supermarket car park and drew up beside the coppice of trees. The chief inspector kept the engine running while he stepped out.

Five days had passed since the surveillance device had been planted in Summerstoke police station. It was now time to retrieve it and find out whether any incriminating material had been recorded.

He gazed around the near-deserted expanse beneath the glowing lampposts in Chelmsley Wood, wondering whether Liam Clancy had remembered their arrangement.

But he was reassured moments later when, just before half past six in the evening, he heard the sound of a red Honda Civic with a noisy exhaust heading towards him. Liam parked, cut the engine and got out.

Roscoe smiled. 'Liam, d'you remember last week you took some photos of the CID office?' he asked. 'I was just wondering if you could email them to me? I need a clearer idea of the layout.'

'That's no problem. I'll send them over later tonight.'

'Tomorrow will be fine. I just need to familiarise myself with the place. Anyway, how are you getting on with the 101 Crew?'

'Oh, it's going just fine,' said Liam, who leaned against the van as they spoke. 'I didn't give them my real name, obviously. They just know me as Lee. That's easy for me because some of me pals already call me that – so I always respond straight away when someone speaks to me.'

Roscoe grinned.

'Tell me what sort of people you've got to know.'

'Well, I've got some of the dealers on side. I can give you a list of names if you give me some paper. We call them "trappers" or "trapper boys". Two are Polish brothers, Gabriel and Dominik. There's two locals, Harry, who's known as "Razor", and his girlfriend Mandy, who they call Milly. And there's a couple of West Indians, Donnie and Mikey. The last two aren't their real names, by the way.'

'Where are you mainly selling or supplying?'

'Balsall Heath and Aston.'

'Aren't they areas where other gangs are trying to sell?'

'Well, that's the point, Mr Roscoe. We operate in the known places – the designer outlets of the drugs world if you like. It's where junkies go to get their fix – so that's where we have to go. And, of course, we're competing with the other gangs. As you can imagine, sooner or later, someone gets hurt.'

'Have you seen anything of Seymour Trent and Tadeusz Filipowski?'

'I've never met the Trent fella. He's the big guy, isn't he? He keeps well out of the way. The other fella, that's the guy they call Tiff. I've met him once. Seems a decent fella, but I've heard rumblings.'

'Rumblings?' Roscoe asked.

'Yes. Just rumours that the folk at the top aren't altogether happy with him.'

'D'you know why?'

'No. I'm still new. They haven't explained. Maybe they don't fully trust me yet.'

'Have you been making good money for the gang?'

'I pulled a couple of grand this week. It all goes to a guy named Blake.'

'Blake?' said Roscoe.

'Yes. His first name's Tyrone. He's West Indian. I get on all right with him. He's a big fella, mind – more than six foot.'

'Interesting,' said Roscoe. 'And you're keeping a diary with all the details of what you buy and sell, the people you meet, the places you go?'

'That's right, Mr Roscoe. Just like you told me. You know, I've met some pretty unhappy people. People who've got no money, but still they crave the drugs, like. Some of them are pitiful. I hope I don't have to do this much longer. It's not a pleasure, you know.'

'I'm sure it isn't, but what you're doing is vital work,' said Roscoe.

'I know. I could never go back on the drugs meself, like. I knew it before, but this whole experience has made me more convinced than ever that it really is a fool's game.'

'We both know it is, Liam. It's just very sad that so many people haven't recognised that yet and maybe they never will.'

'That's true, Mr Roscoe.'

'Now, it's going to be the same procedure tonight as before. You put on the blue overalls. There's also the tool-bag, hat and glasses. I'll call in at reception and ask about the umbrella I left there last time while you park outside and enter the building. You go to the second floor and replace our gadget with the original socket. It's all pretty straightforward, isn't it?'

'Sounds it to me.'

'By the way, describe to me again the man you met in CID on Monday.'

'Well, I'd say tall, stocky, short brown hair, plump hands and clean-shaven. Oh and he had large feet – I'm thinking maybe size elevens.'

'OK,' said Roscoe. 'As I thought on Monday, that definitely sounds like DS Bains. All right. Well, if you lock your car and jump in, we'll set off.'

The van reached Summerstoke town centre at about the same time they had arrived there five days earlier – a quarter to seven. As before, Roscoe got out a short distance away and set off on foot for the court building. Liam climbed into the driver's seat, drove the van to the glass-fronted entrance and parked directly outside.

Roscoe was relieved to find his constable friend Edwin was manning the counter once more.

'You must be getting forgetful, Mr Roscoe!' Edwin joked as he spotted the detective walking across the foyer. 'You left your umbrella behind on Monday.'

'I thought I had,' said Roscoe. 'I've been searching a few places and this was my last port of call.'

'I called after you, but you didn't hear me,' said Edwin, as the bogus electrician approached the desk carrying his tool-bag.

'I've been called back to CID,' said the young visitor.

'You know where to go,' said Edwin. 'Second floor.' Then he turned his attention to his old friend. 'So what sort of a week have you been having, Mr Roscoe? Just a minute. The phone.'

The receptionist turned away for a moment to answer a call on his desk phone. Someone was inquiring about when the magistrates' court would open the following morning. Roscoe watched from the corner of his eye as Liam entered one of the lifts on his way to the CID office.

'So you found the place you were looking for the other day?' said Edwin, returning to the conversation.

'Bit of confusion. I'd been misdirected. It wasn't St Margaret Street I wanted after all. I've got to find someone who lives close to St Margaret's Church.'

'So my directions were helpful?'

'Your directions were spot on, Edwin. Thank you very much for your help once again.'

'You're most welcome. Now you've got your umbrella. Is there anything else I can help you with?'

Roscoe thought quickly. He wanted to be around in case Liam encountered any problem and he had to assist. He needed an excuse to remain in the reception area.

'Edwin, do you know a couple of officers called Trent and Bains?' he asked. 'Any idea what they're like?'

Edwin began telling Roscoe the few details he knew about the pair.

* * *

Talk about the luck of the Irish, Liam thought after the lift reached the second floor and he stepped out. As before, the CID department was empty apart from two people at the far end.

He quickly familiarised himself again with the double socket behind Trent's desk. He removed the gadget containing the recording device and had nearly finished replacing it with the original socket when he thought he heard a noise. It sounded as if someone was coming up in the lift.

In a rush, he quickly slotted the two screws in the front and did them up as quickly as he could. Then he grabbed the tool-bag and ducked down behind one of the desks to see if anyone was coming. After a few minutes, he became confident enough to raise his head above the desktops and was relieved to find that, whoever it was, had made their way to the far end of the office.

He hurried to the lift, made his way down and hightailed it out of the building like a hare pursued by a whippet.

* * *

Roscoe had usefully received from Edwin two thumbnail descriptions of the two detectives he was investigating. He could not let slip the reason for his curiosity. He simply explained he was intrigued by their apparent rapid promotion.

'Yes, they've done well for themselves,' said Edwin.

'Look, got to go,' said Roscoe, clutching his rolled-up umbrella.

'Lovely to see you. Drop in any time!' said Edwin.

Roscoe briskly left the building and walked up the road to his agreed meeting point with Liam.

'How did it go, Liam?' the detective asked.

'Fine, Mr Roscoe,' said the young man. 'Here's your gadget. I hope it's of help to you.'

'So do I,' said Roscoe, as the engine spluttered into life.

After the pair had travelled for just over a mile towards Chelmsley Wood, Roscoe noticed Liam was rather subdued and asked him why.

'I've got a confession to make, Mr Roscoe,' Liam explained. 'I got a bit spooked in the CID office. I'm not sure I fixed the last wire back properly. It's possible one of the sockets won't work.'

'Don't worry too much,' said Roscoe. 'The main thing is we've got the recording. Now some poor dogsbody will get the job of listening to it all and deciding if any of it's admissible as evidence in a court of law. In any case, it's a double socket, isn't it? The chances are one of the two will work.'

'You're right there, Mr Roscoe. I'm not certain, mind, but there's a good chance one or other of the sockets will be working all right.'

The detective steered with just his left hand for a moment while he placed the plastic socket front inside an envelope and put it in the inside pocket of his coat.

Later that same evening, after dropping Liam off at the supermarket car park, he drove to St James Street headquarters and left the envelope marked for Tom Vickers' urgent attention. He then met some colleagues for a pint in the CID's regular pub, The Golden Fleece, and joined them for a curry at a restaurant afterwards.

As he drove home, he was content to reflect that a member of the team from Operation Temple would be able to start listening to the recording as soon as the office opened in the morning. They would soon learn whether the surveillance mission had been a success.

He switched on the radio. After listening to a discussion on BBC Radio Birmingham about Brexit and the Midlands economy, the 1 a.m. news came on. The first report was about an horrific house fire in Balsall Common. A businessman had been found dead in his bed, believed to be suffering from the effects of smoke inhalation.

Chapter 17

Sunita Roy felt a shiver run down her neck as she climbed out of Samir Banerjee's black Volkswagen Golf and turned to face him in the cold January air.

'It's been a fantastic evening, Sam,' she said as she stood on the pavement outside her Warwick flat, fiddling with the buttons on her cardigan. 'I won't invite you in. I'm on duty in the morning and it's already late.'

He leaned across the passenger seat and glanced up at her.

'It's been so lovely to see you again, Sunita,' he said. 'It was so kind of you to pay for the meal.'

'I felt it was my turn to pay.'

She knew she had an important issue to discuss, but she felt as awkward as a clown at a funeral. She was unsure how to express herself without upsetting him.

'Look, there's something I ought to tell you,' she began.

'What is it, Sunita? Is it about your family?'

She shook her head and then her mobile phone rang. The chief inspector's face appeared on the screen.

'Hang on a minute, Sam.' Then, moving a short distance away, she answered the call. 'Yes, sir?'

'Sergeant, be ready to go straight out in the morning,' he told her. 'There's been a dreadful house fire in Balsall Common. That's not far from you, is it?'

'No, sir. Only about nine miles.'

'Looks like it's that Polish crime boss, Tadeusz Filipowski, although that's not confirmed. First reports suggest it was arson and he was trapped in his own house.'

'That sounds so much like the arson attack on Mrs Shah's home two months ago.'

'Yes. Maybe there's a connection. Anyway I've sent Omar Khalid there tonight, but I'd like you to meet me over there first thing in the morning.'

'No problem. Have you got the address, sir?'

'Yes. It's 47, Whitstone Drive. Shall we say half past eight?'

'Fine, sir,' she said as she jotted the details down in her pocket diary. 'I'll see you then.'

She returned to Sam, who was still sitting with the passenger door half-open.

'I'm sorry, Sam. Early start tomorrow, so I'll have to say goodnight.'

'You were wanting to tell me something before your phone rang,' he reminded her.

'Don't worry. It'll wait. Goodnight, Sam,' she said as she began closing the car door.

'Good night, Sunita. Sleep well.'

* * *

It was just before half past eight the following morning when DCI Roscoe's BMW came to a halt in Whitstone Drive, which lay on the edge of a private residential estate of sought-after detached houses.

It was a cold, foggy morning. He'd been reluctant to leave his warm bed – especially since he loathed working on a Sunday. He'd always considered it a family day. But it could not be helped. If the drug baron Filipowski had indeed met an untimely end, this constituted a major development.

He had no difficulty finding the fire-damaged house. One of the upstairs windows was void of glass and the wall around it blackened by soot. Two policewomen stood on the pavement outside while forensic staff in white suits were scurrying in and out of the open front door. An acrid smell of burning lingered in the air.

Roscoe was about to cross the police tape and enter the house when he noticed his sergeant's white car enter the street. She parked between two patrol cars and hurried towards him.

'Didn't keep you waiting, did I, sir?' she asked, zipping up her jacket as she approached.

'No, no,' he replied. 'Only just arrived myself. I'm hoping Omar's around somewhere and that he'll fill us in.'

They didn't have to wait long. After stepping behind the cordon, a man with unkempt, dark hair lumbered up the road towards them. DC Khalid looked as though a mantle of sleep and fatigue hung heavily upon him.

'Sir, I've been sitting in the car, waiting for you,' he explained. 'Dr Reynolds is with the body.'

'Good. Do we know the dead man's definitely Filipowski?'

'As sure as we can be at this stage,' said Khalid. 'The photographer who took images of the body recognised him from the wanted appeals. There's a couple of letters that turned up in a living-room drawer with his name on. And, of course, this silver Porsche here is registered to him.'

Roscoe nodded. 'All right. We'll have to wait for formal identification.'

'There's been some heroics in the middle of the night,' Khalid continued. 'One of the neighbours is an off-duty fireman who spotted flames. He kicked the front door open, raced upstairs and heaved the man's body off the bed and down the stairs, thinking there was a chance of saving his life. But when he got him into the hallway, he could see the guy was dead. He then made efforts to tackle the blaze singlehanded with his own fire extinguisher.'

Sunita's eyes lit up. 'We should be thankful for guys like that,' she said.

'Fire and Rescue arrived soon afterwards and put the fire out. Damage is mainly limited to the landing and front bedroom. A police doctor came over to examine Filipowski's body and pronounced him dead.'

Sunita drew a quick breath. 'Sounds as though the fire would've been a lot worse if that fireman hadn't been so prompt.'

Khalid nodded. 'Could've been a lot worse. I haven't been able to speak to the guy. He's called Ambrose Grant, apparently. But I've had words with a second neighbour, who also went into the house. He told me he could smell petrol and just now an investigator from Fire and Rescue has confirmed an accelerant was used.'

'Do we know if Filipowski owned the house?' Roscoe asked.

Khalid shook his head. 'No, the owner's a Polish shopkeeper who's thought to be Filipowski's cousin. Apparently, Filipowski only moved in three weeks ago. Not many people knew he was here.'

'Someone obviously knew,' Roscoe remarked. 'Someone with a grudge.'

'Yes, sir,' Khalid conceded.

Sunita had been watching forensic staff entering and leaving through the front door. She turned to her colleague.

'Omar,' she said, 'do we know what time the fire broke out?'

'It's thought to have started about a quarter past midnight. The fire crews were here around twenty minutes later.'

'What sort of things are the neighbours saying?' she asked.

'They all say they'd hardly had time to get to know Filipowski. That he lived here on his own, but he was away from the house a lot. Those that spoke to him said he had little to say. He mainly left home at dawn and returned late at night. Oh, I ought to mention one of the SOCOs got into the Porsche and there was nothing of much interest in there. Nothing to tell us who the woman might be.'

Roscoe raised an eyebrow. 'What woman?' he said.

'The woman found dead next to Filipowski,' Khalid replied. 'I'm sorry, sir. I thought you knew there were two bodies.'

Chapter 18

Portly, middle-aged pathologist Dr Silas Reynolds smiled as the chief inspector stepped into the hallway.

'Ah, talk of the devil. I wondered if you were going to grace us with your presence this morning, Gavin,' he remarked as he stood over a body on the fawn carpet which was covered with a white sheet.

Roscoe grinned back. 'Wild horses couldn't keep me away, Silas,' he said. 'I've been working on this case over the phone up till midnight.'

'Midnight?' the pathologist retorted. 'You've got such an easy life. I was called out to a stabbing in Gloucestershire and didn't get to bed until gone two o'clock this morning. Listen, old fruit, you'd better come and have a gawp at this.'

Reynolds, dressed in a white suit, drew back the cover to expose the tanned face of a man with bulging eyes which was streaked with soot. Blood had oozed over his dark hair. Bare-chested, he was wearing only faded blue pyjama bottoms.

The chief inspector cast his mind back to his interview with Tadeusz Filipowski at police headquarters a few weeks earlier. He could tell immediately it was the drug baron.

Sunita glanced over the chief inspector's shoulder and recoiled in horror at the grim sight.

'Mr Grant, the neighbour, carried him down here and began CPR, but he recognised it was no use,' said Reynolds, replacing the sheet over the dead man's head. 'You'd better come upstairs.'

Cautiously, the two detectives followed him up until they reached the charred remains of the first-floor landing. He then led them into the main bedroom.

'Is it safe?' Sunita asked.

The doctor turned and smiled. 'Yes but watch your footing. I can't vouch for the soundness of these floorboards.'

They followed him into a partly blackened room containing a king-size bed. Many features of the interior had been incinerated, but they could recognise a china plate containing a powder along with a narrow, grey tube on a grimy dressing table. Dark-stained clothes lay on a fire-damaged chair.

It felt bitterly cold since the glass in the window had shattered and the room was open to the elements. Yet there remained a stench of burnt wood and something faintly akin to rotting fruit, which Roscoe recognised as the smell of decomposing human flesh.

'We've been told there's a second body,' the sergeant said.

Reynolds glanced at the two detectives over his horn-rimmed glasses. 'It's on the floor the other side of the bed. There isn't room for all of us round there, so perhaps you'd like to take turns.'

'Sergeant, you go ahead,' said Roscoe, pointing across the room.

Gingerly, she stepped round the bed. She was confronted by the shocking sight of a naked woman's body by the skirting board. She crouched down to examine it more closely.

Strands of the woman's long, blonde hair clung to her slender, delicate face, which was smudged with grime but nonetheless attractive. The victim's eyes, fixed upon the blackened ceiling, were wide open and lifeless.

Sunita said nothing. What was there to say? A young woman's life had been cut short. And for what purpose? She stepped away and re-joined her colleagues.

A minute later, Roscoe took his opportunity to study the second corpse.

'Terrible tragedy,' he remarked after allowing himself a fleeting glimpse of the woman. 'By the way, Silas, there's a good chance the guy in the hall is the boss of a criminal gang.'

The doctor nodded. 'Looks that way, old fruit. I was chatting a few minutes ago to your DC Khalid. But there's no idea yet on the woman. Perhaps you might know who she is?'

Roscoe shook his head. 'Not a clue,' he replied. 'But she appears to be a good bit younger than our chum downstairs.'

'Anything to identify her?' asked Sunita. 'Anything in the pockets of her clothes? A handbag?'

'A leather clutch bag was on the floor beside the bed,' said Reynolds. 'But it only contained money, keys, lipstick, a hairbrush and some condoms. Her phone hasn't turned up.'

Roscoe stood back from the bed and folded his arms. 'So would you say they've both been murdered, Silas?' he asked.

'Everything points to the man having been murdered. He's been shot once in the head, but I'll have to reserve judgement on the lady. My gut instinct tells me she was almost certainly murdered as well. But gut instincts don't have a major role to play in the pathologist's world. We deal in facts and, at present, on a cursory examination of the female victim, no bullet holes are apparent.'

'I'm guessing the perpetrator started the blaze to try to cover their tracks,' said the chief inspector as he peered across the room.

'More than likely, old fruit,' said Reynolds. 'Listen, this may come as a shock to you but this couple didn't die in the fire. They've both been dead for several days.'

Sunita glanced at the pathologist. 'How do know that?' she asked.

'The process of decomposing is well under way with swelling and bloating around the eyes, faces and necks. That makes it harder to estimate a time of death, of course. That's why we sometimes have to look around the crime scene for other clues to help with the time of death.

'On this occasion, my assistant, David, came up trumps. He made an interesting discovery in the kitchen – a supermarket receipt for groceries bearing last Wednesday's date and a time of half past five in the evening.

'Whoever bought these items – and it's probably a safe assumption that it was either Mr Filipowski or his mystery lady – purchased a beef lasagne. Their dinner plates are lying beside the sink – still unwashed, and the packaging for this microwave meal is at the top of the kitchen bin, so that was probably their last meal and a clear sign Wednesday night was their last night alive.

'Ingesting food takes a matter of hours – usually a stomach would be empty of food within six hours – so I'd be totally astonished to find any trace of the lasagne in their stomachs when we get the bodies into the lab. We'll analyse the gastric contents and check their airways for soot.'

Sunita had been listening intently while gazing down at the blackened floor.

'Dr Reynolds,' she said, 'your findings present us with a bizarre problem. I'm sure you're right if you say the couple died on Wednesday night. But we know the fire broke out at around midnight last night. So are we to assume the killer came back after three nights to destroy the evidence? Because that's one implication of what you're saying. The only other theory that would make sense would be if the killer tried and failed to start the fire on Wednesday night after laying a trail of petrol and that someone or something else ignited it last night.'

Roscoe interrupted. 'No, Sergeant. I don't think that last idea is feasible at all. It's much more likely that the killer returned for some reason. Perhaps he or she'd left something behind.'

Sunita nodded. 'Perhaps there were some drugs in the house and he returned to collect them, sir,' she suggested.

'That's more plausible,' said Roscoe. 'He came back to collect something and used an accelerant to start the fire while he was in the house. It's still extremely unusual for a murderer to return to the scene though. He was taking a colossal chance, if that's how it happened. Perhaps he came back and shot them to make sure they were dead.'

'That's possible, old fruit,' Reynolds agreed.

Sunita glanced round the room. 'Dr Reynolds, do you know how many bullets there were in total?'

'The light is rather poor in here,' he replied. 'Accurate findings aren't possible until we've had a chance to make a thorough examination of both bodies back at the lab. However, it appears only one shot was fired. The man – whom I'm calling Filipowski, for the sake of argument – has been hit once in the cranium. There was blackening round the bullet wound, indicating the shot was fired at close range.'

'And the woman would've been in bed, naked beside him, when the gunman struck?' asked Sunita.

Reynolds paused for a moment before saying, 'I think we can assume they may well have been snuggled up together on the bed and that somehow the woman's body slipped onto the floor. I may be able to tell you more about that in a few days. Oh, while I think of it, we'll also be conducting toxicology tests – in view of the presence of cocaine in the room.'

'Definitely cocaine?' Roscoe asked.

'Yes. I've just carried out the standard test with some chemicals.'

The two detectives simultaneously gazed across at the plate of powder on the top of the dressing table.

'Do you think,' said Roscoe, 'that drugs played a part?'

'That's a definite possibility.'

'That leads onto another problem, sir,' said Sunita, gazing at the chief inspector. 'How did the gunman gain access to the house? Did he or she have a key?'

Reynolds interrupted as Roscoe was about to speak. 'I gather the have-a-go hero down the street – the off-duty fireman – booted in the front door before he dashed inside. It would be a good idea to have a word with him and other locals who joined in. Since the blaze broke out, I'm afraid the back door and some of the windows have been left open to let the smoke and smell out. There's probably no way of knowing exactly how secure the house was prior to the fire.'

Roscoe nodded. 'Sergeant, I'm going to place you in charge of the day-to-day running of this investigation. As you know, I'm up to my neck with Operation Temple. Get Khalid and Dawson on board. Look into Filipowski's private life. And we must find out who this lady was.'

Chapter 19

A mantle of fog shrouded the hills and fields of West Warwickshire as the chief inspector set off for work the following morning.

From time to time, trees or houses would loom out of the silvery haze and cars or lorries would emerge abruptly from the gloom as if from nowhere while he headed towards the M42 motorway.

His mind was retracing the events of the day before. The double deaths in Balsall Common were cloaked in as much obscurity as the countryside, he thought.

But this morning he had other priorities. He was eager to know whether the bugging device planted at Summerstoke CID had achieved any results.

No sooner had he parked at police headquarters and entered the building when a voice he recognised greeted him.

'Morning, guv!'

He glanced over his shoulder to find Tom Vickers was just a few steps behind.

'Good morning, Tom,' said Roscoe. 'Did you hear about Filipowski?'

'Yes. I saw it on the breakfast news. A man in his fifties named locally as Tadeusz Filipowski.'

'Yes. Nothing official yet. I gather his uncle's coming over from Poland to identify the body. You must be pleased in a way. He was one of the two guys behind the shooting that left you in hospital.'

The inspector nodded. 'Yes,' he admitted. 'I'm never comfortable speaking ill of the dead, but it's a relief he's not going to be around to cause harm to others.'

'I was coming to see you,' said Roscoe. 'Any luck with the recording?'

'Although it was Sunday, Wendy Hopkirk came in specially yesterday and spent a few hours going through it. I had a quick word with her on the phone last night. There's nothing much to tell you content-wise, but she did say the mike picked up the voices perfectly.'

Roscoe stopped still as he reached the top of the stairs. 'Well, I suppose that's something,' he muttered.

He followed Vickers along the corridor to the Operation Temple office.

'Wendy may be here already. I should imagine she'll have got through a lot of the recording by now,' Vickers added.

Roscoe pushed open the office door to find slim, dark-haired DC Hopkirk leaning back on her chair. She had her feet up on the neighbouring desk and was listening to male voices emanating from an audio file on her desk computer. As soon as she noticed Roscoe and Vickers, she put her feet down and scrambled to pause the recording.

'Oh, morning, Tom. Morning, sir,' she spluttered.

'Good morning, Wendy,' said Vickers. 'How's it going?'

'I'll be frank with you, Tom,' she began. 'It's very boring. There's talk of some kids fooling around on the allotments, a suspicious death, reports of a stabbing that wasn't a stabbing. You can guess the kind of thing.'

'Humdrum bread-and-butter police work, in other words,' said Vickers. 'But nothing incriminating?'

'No, Tom. I've gone through more than half of the recording so far.'

'That's very disappointing,' said Roscoe. 'Never mind. Keep at it. You never know.'

'Yes, sir. I'll keep at it.'

Roscoe smiled at the inspector. 'Have you had any breakfast, Tom? I think perhaps Wendy will get more done if she's left on her own. Shall we go and have a chat in the canteen?'

'Excellent idea,' said Vickers. Then, turning to her, he said, 'We'll bring you back a tea.'

Ten minutes later, they were tucking into their meal in a quiet corner of the canteen.

'Let's hope we get something good from this recording,' said the inspector, as he sliced into his egg.

'Yes, it's not looking too promising though,' said Roscoe as he slurped his coffee. 'Trent's clearly no fool. It was always touch and go whether he'd discuss his extracurricular activities while in the office. We were probably being over-ambitious to expect otherwise.'

'I guess you're right, guv,' said Vickers. 'Oh, by the way, I forgot to tell you about our little scouting mission. We've had Trent followed from his office every night after work last week. On the Monday, Wednesday, and Friday evenings, he stopped off at a country pub on his way home to Coleshill. Each time, he was accompanied by a woman and once Filipowski joined them for a short time.

'On the Tuesday evening, Trent went straight home and, on the Thursday evening, he travelled into the city centre. Unfortunately our man lost track of him on that occasion.'

'Interesting. What pub was it?'

'The Three Gardeners at Vine Hill. Each time Trent was there, he chose a table by the window.'

Roscoe stroked his chin. 'Any idea who the woman was?'

'She's since been identified as a policewoman, Polly Cook, who's based at North Warwick Traffic. Both times, our guy followed him from the pub car park, but he went straight home.'

'He lives in Coleshill with his wife, doesn't he?'

'Yes, he's got a house in one of those gated communities.'

Roscoe finished his breakfast and pushed the plate to the side. He said nothing as he stared down into his lukewarm coffee. Finally, he looked across the table at the inspector as if he had an important announcement.

'D'you know, Tom, we've got to have another go at getting Trent on tape,' said Roscoe. 'I don't know whether we should hide a bugging device in his BMW or if we should use some kind of surveillance at the pub you mentioned.'

'Or at his home?' Vickers suggested. 'People are usually very relaxed at home and talk freely.'

'No, not his home,' said Roscoe. 'Too much of a challenge because the place is behind gates. He doesn't seem to be at home much anyway. So it's got to be the car or the pub.'

'Neither of those is going to be easy, guv.'

'I know, but it's got to be done.'

After half an hour, the pair returned to Vickers' office, where a stern-faced DC Hopkirk was still listening to the voices of Seymour Trent and members of his CID team. She paused the recording.

'Tom, I've heard three-quarters now and skipped through parts of the last section, so I've now got a good impression of the whole recording. I can honestly say there's nothing about drugs, nothing about the O'Sullivan case and nothing to suggest anyone there's been associating with criminals.'

'Bloody nuisance,' said Vickers. 'Well done, anyway. I'd like you to go through the last section more thoroughly as soon as you can – so that we've got the full picture.'

'Of course,' she replied. 'I was going to do that anyway. I just wanted to give you an overall idea.'

'So nothing of any consequence for our investigation?' Roscoe asked.

'No, sir. Except one passage which caught my attention. About halfway through, Trent tells a telephone caller, "Can't talk right now. But congratulate Blake on his plan." I didn't understand what it meant, but I made a note of it anyway. It sounded as though it might not be connected with official police work.'

'That's probably Tyrone Blake,' said Roscoe. 'Could we listen to that part?'

After Hopkirk spent a few minutes rewinding the recording, she found the crucial passage. Trent's northern tones at once echoed round the office.

'It's good of you to call and let me know. Can't talk right now. But congratulate Blake on his plan. Anyway, I must get on. I'm having a busy day.'

'That northern voice is definitely Trent's, is it?' asked Roscoe.

'Definitely, sir,' Hopkirk confirmed. 'I know it pretty well now, it's the main voice I've been hearing for the past five hours of the tape.'

'Yes, he must be speaking about Tyrone Blake,' said Vickers, pointing to the photograph of the tattooed man pinned up on the whiteboard as a suspect in the O'Sullivan murder.

'Why would Trent be talking about congratulating an underworld character for something?' asked Roscoe. 'That's very suspicious. We'll bear those words in mind because Blake could be a suspect in the Filipowski shooting. Look, Tom, I've been thinking. I reckon we should bug Trent while he's in the pub.'

'How d'you propose to do it, guv?'

'Well, we know he chooses to sit by the window. Maybe we can conceal a device behind a curtain, on a shelf, in a wall-light – I don't know, anywhere. Then we can sit in the car park and listen in.'

'It might work,' said Vickers.

'He's much more likely to open up in a pub atmosphere and, if he's got his cronies with him, he'll hopefully talk about his involvement with them.'

'Could give us some key evidence,' the inspector agreed.

'We'll need to pick up the device afterwards,' Roscoe went on. 'If it's left behind, the pub staff would no doubt find it and, if they know Trent is in the force, they might tell him about it, and we don't want to compromise the investigation.'

'I take your point. We don't want him forewarned, if we can help it, do we? Overall, it sounds like a promising strategy, but it's a risky one.'

Chapter 20

Brett Dawson insisted he knew a quick way to reach Balsall Common by car as he and Sunita Roy left police headquarters early that same Monday morning.

'It means following winding lanes out in the sticks, but, by doing that, we dodge some of the traffic hold-ups,' he claimed as he unlocked his car and they both got in.

However, as they left Solihull behind and began passing along narrow country lanes with high hedges on either side, she began to doubt his knowledge of the terrain.

'You'll have to slow down, Brett,' she murmured nervously. 'We might meet another vehicle at any moment.'

He seemed to ignore her and continued at speeds of more than thirty miles an hour. But, seconds later, her fears were justified. A black van emerged from behind a bend. Dawson was forced to brake hard and was then obliged to reverse his red Ford Focus back fifty metres until he found a passing place.

Sunita was relieved when they finally arrived in the village after more than twenty minutes.

'I think we'll go back via the main roads, Brett,' she remarked as they drew up outside 41, Whitstone Drive, the yellow-bricked home of fireman Ambrose Grant.

'Remind us again why you want to speak to this guy,' said Dawson, locking the car with his remote.

'Well, Omar was down here in the early hours of Sunday. He took several statements, but Mr Grant had gone to bed by the time he knocked. He was the only witness he couldn't get to speak to.'

The detective constable, who was four years younger than his sergeant, swept his spiky blond hair back with his hand and then fastened his coat.

'Pretty important witness. First guy on the scene, wasn't he?'

'That's right,' said Sunita, stepping past a white Ford Transit van parked outside the house.

Shortly after she'd rung the bell, Grant, a tall, stocky, bearded man from a West Indian background, drew back the door with a smile. He had been expecting them.

'DS Roy?' he asked. 'Please come in. You'll have to excuse the mess – we've got two kids.'

'No worries.' Sunita replied. 'This is my colleague, DC Dawson.'

He shook both their hands before leading them into a bright, spacious living-room strewn with toys.

'Sorry I wasn't free to talk to your colleague yesterday,' he said as he cleared a space for them to sit down on a three-seater settee. 'I'd just gone to bed.'

'That's fine,' she said.

'So what would you like to know?'

Sunita removed a small black notebook from her jacket pocket. 'Well, if we start at the beginning,' she said. 'How did you come to notice the house was on fire?'

'It was pure chance,' he said. 'I was fetching something from the car when I heard some noise. I thought at first it was coming from next door because they were holding a fireworks party. But it must've been the bedroom window shattering at number forty-seven. I ran over to take a look and smoke was pouring from the house. So I came back in and shouted at my wife to dial 999. I grabbed the extinguisher from the hall and got a wet towel. Then I rushed round to see what I could do.'

'We hear you had to boot the door in?' said Dawson.

He nodded. 'Yes. I had little choice. There was a good chance someone was inside because there was a car outside – a Porsche – and the downstairs curtains were drawn. What surprised me was there was no shouting or screaming. Anyway I kicked in the door and ran up the stairs.

'The place was full of smoke by this time and the fire was going like a good 'un on the upstairs landing. I sprayed foam over the flames and then realised it had spread to the bedroom. So covering my face with the dripping towel, I kicked open the bedroom door.

'Fortunately, the fire had only just started to take hold in there and I ran over to the bed, where I could see a person lying. The fire and smoke was getting worse, so I knew I had to get him out of there for him to stand any chance. I hauled him out of bed and carried him downstairs, but it was no good. What's the phrase? Life was extinct.'

Sunita gazed at him sympathetically. 'It must've been a shock to find him like that.'

'It was. I thought about giving CPR but it would have been pointless. There was one strange thing about him.'

Dawson sat upright. 'What was that?'

'There was blood on part of his head.'

'So what happened next?' Sunita asked.

'After that, the crew turned up. They were bloody brilliant. The fire could have really taken hold if they hadn't been so prompt.'

Dawson laughed. 'Sounds to me you were the one who was bloody brilliant. Don't see how you can do your job.'

'At the end of the day, it's just a job you do, like everything else.'

'I can't see that, mate,' Dawson muttered.

'Listen, Mr Grant–' Sunita began.

'Ambrose,' he said.

'All right, Ambrose. Did you see any unusual vehicles in the street before the fire broke out?' she asked. 'You know, any car that seemed out of place?'

He shook his head. 'No. Well, I was watching TV before I went outside. I wasn't paying much attention to what was going on in the street. I'd been working earlier in the day, see. I was on days last week.'

'So you didn't hear a gunshot around the time of the fire?' Sunita asked.

'Some other neighbours were holding a fireworks party that Saturday night. Jerry and Ashley Richards, who live two doors along, had just got married. So there was lots of loud noise up until around midnight. If a gun went off, my first thought would've been that it was connected with the fireworks.'

She stared into his eyes. 'Ambrose, you know there was a second body in the bedroom, don't you?' she said. 'Was the fire raging so much that you couldn't go back in?'

'I read in the paper this morning about a woman's body being found by the fire crew, but I never noticed a woman, I have to tell you.'

He slumped down into an armchair and stared at the carpet. He glanced up when she started speaking again.

'Ambrose, we're considering a theory that the two victims might've been dead for several days before the fire actually occurred. Did you see anything unusual happen on Wednesday evening when you got back from work? Any strange cars appear in the street?'

Grant paused for a moment to think. 'We're talking about Wednesday just gone?'

'Yes.'

He looked as perplexed as a sheep trapped in a maze.

'Not that I can think of, but if anything occurs to me, I'll let you know.'

Sunita stood up and walked towards the hallway, followed by Dawson.

'I'm still thinking about that second body,' said the householder. 'I'm an experienced fire officer. I like to think that, if there'd been a second body in the room, I'd have noticed it.'

Chapter 21

As Sunita Roy and Brett Dawson travelled back to the CID office, they were debating about how the two victims might have died.

'Is it possible the gunman pulled the trigger without realising the man was already dead?' Dawson suggested.

'I'd already been considering that theory,' she replied. 'It makes as much sense as any of the other ideas floating around. I've also been thinking that the gunman might've known in advance about the fireworks and chosen that very night, knowing that people would associate any bangs with the fireworks.'

'Or he might have had a silencer fitted,' said Dawson.

Once the pair had returned to their desks, the sergeant asked Dawson to scan through the police files on Tadeusz Filipowski. He worked in comparative silence for fifteen minutes. The constable wasn't a fast reader.

While Sunita was racing through all the statements given by neighbours in Balsall Common, Dawson was struggling to find details of the dead man's antecedents. Then he broke into a grin.

'Here we are, Sarge,' he exclaimed. 'I tell you what. You've got to hand it to this Filipowski fellow. He kept himself well under the radar. He's done time for possession with intent to supply and assault on a shopkeeper eight years ago but nothing since.'

'Don't forget he was also on remand for conspiracy to damage Nisa Shah's house, cocaine possession and assault on police,' said Sunita.

'I know. He got released from Winson Green by mistake, according to the press.'

'That's right. Home Office blunder.'

She glanced up from her desk opposite him. 'He's rumoured to have been involved in people trafficking as well as drugs.'

'There's nothing about any of that here, Sarge,' he replied.

She was about to pass comment when her desk phone rang. She answered it and DC Hopkirk's mellow voice emerged from the handset.

'While you were out, a caller was put through to me,' Wendy explained. 'You know today's papers are full of reports about the 101 Crew?'

'Yes,' said Sunita. 'Tadeusz Filipowski's murder.'

'Uh-huh. This guy wouldn't give his name but said the dead man was running a string of brothels in Birmingham. He said one's in Soho Road and he thought we ought to know about it. It was time the force did something about massage parlours, he said. I then pointed out that we don't actually cover Soho Road and that he needed to get onto West Midlands regarding prostitution in that area.'

Sunita nodded. 'Thanks for that, Wendy. I don't suppose he gave a name or phone number for the venue, did he?'

'No.'

'No, that would've been too much to ask,' said the sergeant. 'Did he say anything else about Filipowski?'

'No, Sorry.'

'All right. Thanks for letting us know.'

The sergeant recognised this was an important lead and, for the next half hour, she and Dawson phoned several escort agencies and massage parlours in Handsworth which advertised online. At the same time, she notified West Midlands Police they intended making inquiries in their area.

After several attempts, Dawson came upon an agency offering the services of 'young, beautiful escorts' in the city. A woman with a smooth, seductive voice answered. When he mentioned the name Filipowski, she lowered her voice.

'You didn't get this from me, darling, but I heard he's been running the Gold Star Agency in Handsworth and the Dolls and Molls Agency in Hockley.'

The constable scribbled the names down on a piece of paper after ending the call. He stood up and waved the paper triumphantly in the air.

'Got details of two places which look like brothels run by our man, Sarge,' he told her with a smile.

Sunita stood up as well. 'Right,' she said. 'Let's get going and see what we can find out about our clever Mr Businessman.'

* * *

The fog had lifted by the time the pair reached Handsworth and parked in a side road off busy Soho Road. But the day remained cloudy and overcast. Temperatures were struggling to rise above three degrees Celsius.

After a short walk, they reached a supermarket in the main street named Global Mart and, next to it, found the escort venue's black, wooden door, set back from the street. A flashing neon sign above the entrance read, 'Gold Star Agency'.

Sunita pressed the intercom button on the door frame and they waited. After a few seconds, a young woman's voice asked, 'Who is it?'

'It's the police,' the sergeant replied. 'Need to speak to the manager.'

A buzzer sounded and she was relieved to find the door opened as she pushed against it.

When they reached the top of the steep stairs, a tall young woman with long, dark hair was waiting for them on the landing. Her only clothing appeared to be a lacy bra and black, satin shorts which could be discerned beneath a flimsy, white gown.

Dawson laughed. 'Are you sure you're warm enough, love?'

'That's enough of that,' Sunita warned before turning to the woman and showing her warrant card.

'You can imagine why we're here,' she said.

'Mr Filipowski?' the woman replied in a quiet, faltering voice. 'Yes, we're all dreadfully upset. His death's come as an awful shock, but that's not all. One of our girls is missing.'

Sunita looked blank. 'How do you mean?'

'Well, Mr Filipowski hasn't been seen since the middle of last week, and neither has one of our escorts, Anna Borowka.'

Sunita and Dawson exchanged glances. Could the woman's body in the house with Filipowski be Anna? they both wondered.

Before either could say another word, a door at the end of a corridor opened. An older woman appeared like an indignant ghost in the dim light.

'Sofia, what's going on?' she demanded.

'It's the police, Monika,' the young woman revealed. 'They've come about Mr Filipowski.'

'Have you checked their ID?'

'I'm DS Roy from Heart of England CID,' Sunita called out. 'This is DC Dawson.'

'I don't care. We need to check who you are. Especially at a time like this.'

The two visitors handed Sofia their police passes, which she inspected.

'They're both genuine,' Sofia concluded.

'Very well. If you'd both like to come into my office.'

The detectives followed the blonde-haired, older woman into her room at the end of the building, where she settled into a chair behind her desk.

'I'm sorry,' she told them. 'We've got to be so careful.'

'I understand,' said the sergeant. 'You're in charge here?'

'Yes. Monika Kowalska. You're here about Tiff?'

'That's right. We understand he was the owner?'

'Who told you that?'

'I can't divulge that, but your young lady, Sofia, knew immediately we were here in connection with his death.'

'All right,' she said. 'Yes, Tiff had a controlling interest in the agency. But I haven't really got time to talk about it. I've got a business to run.'

Dawson, who was standing by the open door, peered into her eyes. 'How well did you know him?'

'Fairly well. Everyone here is devastated, of course. He was a kind, considerate man who'd just turned a corner. Throughout his earlier life, he had a hell of a struggle. His father died in Poland when he was young and his mother was ill. So, as the eldest, he had to bring up five brothers and sisters. His life got better when he made the move to the UK and his various businesses have just started to take off.'

'Can you think of anyone who might've wished to kill him?' Sunita asked.

'No. Not really.'

Sunita raised an eyebrow. 'Look, you can stop the pretence. We know he was involved in organised crime. Drugs as well as prostitution. We know that must've made him a target in the world in which he operated.'

Monika shook her head. 'Sorry, don't know what you're talking about. And, if that's all, I think it's time you left.'

'Do you know where we can find his colleague, Tyrone Blake?' asked Dawson.

She stood up. 'Don't know anyone by that name. It's time to go.'

Sunita glared. 'Sofia mentioned one of your staff is missing.'

Monika shrugged as she stepped round the desk.

'I don't know if "missing" is the right word. Our girl Anna hasn't turned up for work for a few days. But that's not uncommon for her. She's got a lot of personal problems at the moment. I'm sorry. You're going to have to leave.'

Sunita was annoyed by the woman's brusque attitude. She was determined not to be ushered away until she had made a proper attempt at eliciting as much information as she could.

She walked towards the doorway but then stopped. 'We need Anna's address,' she said firmly.

'Well, you're not getting it from me,' said Monika. 'Look, I expect Anna will be back in a few days. If you give me your phone number, I'll call you when she reappears.'

'Now listen to me,' said the sergeant sternly. 'A woman's body was found in the bedroom where Mr Filipowski's body was found. You probably saw it in the press or on TV. It seems to me there's a good chance it might be your girl Anna.'

Monika gave a weak smile. 'I'm sorry. You've put me in a difficult position. I don't want you going over there, upsetting her flatmates and possibly her family. There's no way the woman found during the house fire could be Anna. And the last thing she needs, with all her problems, is someone from the police going round there upsetting people. Sofia! Can you see them out?'

As Monika returned to her office and closed the door, Sofia appeared on the landing, glancing anxiously as they made their way towards her.

'Don't mind her,' said Sofia. 'She's terribly upset. She and Mr Filipowski were two of a kind. They were very close and she's taken it very badly.'

'We understand,' said Sunita.

Sofia led them down the narrow stairway. As she opened the door, she handed the sergeant a piece of paper.

'That's Anna's address,' she said. 'But you didn't get it from me.'

Chapter 22

'DC Clarke!' Seymour Trent's deep northern voice rang out around the CID office in Summerstoke.

A smiling young detective in a light-brown suit who was peering through black, thick-rimmed glasses rose from his seat ten metres away and strode towards the inspector's desk.

'Yes, sir?' the fair-haired constable inquired.

'That sudden death in Attleborough you were dealing with – has it now been confirmed as natural causes?' Trent asked him.

'Yes, sir. I've emailed you a copy of the post-mortem report.'

'Good. Well, I've got another one for you, Clarkie. Death of a woman on the Dickens Estate. Body was discovered in a house there last night. Sergeant Bains can give you the details. He'll be back in a minute.'

'Right, sir,' said the constable as he returned to his chair.

'Is it just me or is it a bit cold in here?' Trent continued. 'Has someone turned the heating down?'

Heather Young, an information analyst on the support staff, was sitting a few feet away. She looked up.

'You're right, sir. It's exceptionally cold today,' she said. 'I think all the rads are on full. Shall I put the fan heater on if you're feeling chilly?'

'Good idea, Heather.'

She took a small fan heater from a metal cabinet at the side of the room and plugged it in one of the two sockets behind Trent's desk then turned on the switch. But the fan blades failed to whirr round.

'That's odd,' she said. She placed the plug in the neighbouring socket, but that one did not seem to be functioning either.

'Hope the heater hasn't given up the ghost,' Trent remarked as he gazed at his computer screen.

'I'll try it in another part of the room,' said Heather. 'Maybe it's the socket that's faulty.'

'Not much good to me in another part of the room,' Trent muttered, although Heather was several metres away by then and failed to hear him.

Moments later, she was back.

'It works all right over there, sir,' she told him. 'That's really strange because I used that socket last week to charge my phone and it was working fine then.'

'Better call out the electrician,' Trent muttered. 'Who is it we use now?'

'I'm not sure. Used to be LMT Electrics.'

'Maybe it's gone in-house now,' Trent suggested. 'D'you want to call reception? They'll know straight away.'

As she returned to her desk, DS Bains strolled into the room with two steaming hot drinks from a vending machine.

'Got you a fresh coffee, Seymour,' he announced, placing the paper cup next to his boss's computer.

'Thanks, Phil,' said Trent, without looking up.

After a few minutes, Heather returned.

'That's strange, sir,' she said, placing both her hands on his desk and leaning towards him. 'Reception say there was an electrician here last night working in CID and the same guy called in last week as well. They made a note of his firm, Avondene. The receptionist was a bit rude to me. He said CID shouldn't have called him out. We're still meant to use LMT.'

'I didn't hire a firm called Avondene,' said Trent. 'Someone else must've done. Whoever it was that came, they obviously didn't do a very good job.'

'What's this?' asked Bains, who was now sitting at the desk next to the inspector's. He had overheard the last part of the conversation.

'There's something wrong with the socket down there,' Heather explained, pointing to the defective electrical point.

'I told you about the guy I caught in here at the start of last week, didn't I, Seymour?' said Bains. 'He was working on that very socket.'

'Did you? I don't remember,' Trent replied.

'Yes. He was wearing blue overalls. He told me one of the cleaners had complained the socket was broken.'

'No one complained about it to me – and I sit next to the bloody thing,' said Trent. 'I tell you what, Phil. Since this has been flagged up as a bit of a riddle, why don't you make some inquiries, if you're not too busy? Maybe have a word with the superintendent and anyone else who might've called an electrician out. Maybe call Avondene as well, whoever they are. Keep you off the streets for an hour or so, won't it, mate? And at the end of it, if nothing else, maybe we'll get them to come back and repair it properly, free of charge. What d'you say about that?'

'Good idea, Seymour,' said Bains. 'I'll get onto it straight away.'

But after Bains had made inquiries for nearly an hour, he was no nearer solving the mystery of the defective socket and the mysterious night-time visitor.

Bains strolled over to Trent's desk. 'Have you got a moment, Seymour?' he asked.

'Of course,' the inspector told him. 'What have you found out?'

'Well, I've spoken to reception, the superintendent, and the cleaning manager. They all swear blind they didn't call an electrician out.'

'What do Avondene say?'

'They don't know anything about the job either. In any case, they're based near Queensbridge. Their boss said to me, "Who in their right mind would call out a sparky from thirty-five miles away?"'

'Something dodgy's been going on here,' said Trent, taking a small screwdriver from his desk drawer. He knelt down on the carpet, unscrewed the front of the socket and examined the wiring.

'It wasn't screwed up fully, Phil, and one of the wires isn't connected,' he revealed.

'Well, at least we know now why it wasn't working,' said Bains.

The inspector returned to his seat. He leaned his elbows on the desk and put his face in his hands. After a few seconds, he turned to look at the sergeant.

'Why does someone from thirty-five miles away come into CID late at night and tamper with the electrics, Phil? It doesn't make sense. Go and have a word with the people at reception. Try and get a description of this guy. Find out what he was carrying, how he got into the building, whether he'd got transport – everything you can.'

'Yes, Seymour,' said Bains.

He then walked off in the direction of the lifts.

'You're not going to be happy about this,' said Bains when he returned ten minutes later. 'The sparky turned up in a white van with Avondene on the side and parked it outside the building. On both occasions, DCI Roscoe from headquarters was in reception at around the same time.'

'Gavin Roscoe? This is a hell of a way from his patch.'

'I know. He lives in Queensbridge, which is where the van came from.'

'Bloody hell,' said Trent as he leaned back in his chair. 'It's starting to fit into place now. But it still doesn't explain why the lad was tinkering with the… Hold on! Hold on! Unless they were planting some device so they could spy on us.'

'We'd better get someone to check the socket thoroughly,' said Bains, suddenly lowering his voice to a whisper. 'Maybe they're listening to us now, even as we speak.'

Trent was not paying attention. He was engrossed in thought. What had been the intention of the young electrician? Why had a senior detective been present in the building at the same time? Perhaps they were working for the lawyers seeking a review of the O'Sullivan case. That might be it. Maybe they were collecting information.

If there had been an attempt to bug their office, had he or Bains spoken unguardedly over the past week and allowed incriminating remarks to be recorded? Negative. He made it a point never to discuss non-police business in the office.

Nonetheless, this was a serious matter. It was as though a red light had flicked on inside his brain. Perhaps, for now, it would be wise for them to curtail their activities… just until things quietened down, he thought.

Later that day, a bona fide electrician from the well-established firm of LMT Electrics called in.

'We think a listening bug may've been planted in the socket,' Bains told the man.

But although the electrician turned off the power and examined the electrical point thoroughly, he could find no trace of any electronic device.

He then searched for any tiny lights that might be visible – indicating the presence of a spy camera or recording device. He examined the walls for the presence of any fresh wires and removed several ceiling tiles above Trent's desk, searching for any unusual objects.

Finally, he recommended they buy a surveillance bug detector from an electronics shop and carry out a sweep of the entire office. He also advised Trent and Bains to listen for any strange sounds while using their phones.

'Can't understand it,' Trent muttered after the workman had left. 'The whole incident is completely baffling.' Then he whispered to Bains, 'We'll just forget about it for the moment,' as the pair resumed their normal work.

But Trent was concealing his true feelings. In front of his colleagues, he may have been displaying a cool, calm demeanour. Secretly, inwardly, he was seething with rage.

Chapter 23

Missing escort girl Anna Borowka lived four miles from her agency in the heavily built-up suburb of Bordesley, a short distance from Birmingham city centre. It was an area where industrial and commercial premises fought for space beside blocks of flats or rows of Victorian terraced houses.

After finding the building where she lived, Sunita Roy and Brett Dawson climbed the stairs to the third floor. The pair passed along a balcony where the only view consisted of a row of garages and a car park.

'We could be wasting our time,' the sergeant remarked as they approached the front door of the address they had been given – 36, Hanbury Grove. 'Sofia told us Anna shares this flat with two other escorts. There's a good chance they could both be at work.'

It was nearly two o'clock. She rang the doorbell and they waited. After nearly a minute, they heard footsteps and a shrill woman's voice demanded, 'What do you want?'

'It's the police,' Sunita replied. She held out her warrant card as a nervous woman in her late twenties drew back the half-glazed door.

'We're from Heart of England CID. I'm DS Roy. This is DC Dawson,' she explained.

'You'd better come in,' said the woman, who was smoking a cigarette. Her dark, shoulder-length hair was swept back and held in place with a band.

She led them through a dingy hallway into a cluttered living room where clothes were piled on a blue settee and armchair. A coffee table in the centre was stacked with empty wine bottles and cigarette packets; fashion magazines; coffee mugs; and plates of leftover food.

'Excuse the mess,' she remarked as she stepped round a drying rack laden with damp clothes to stub her cigarette out in an ashtray.

'I'm glad you're here,' she told them. 'We're worried about Anna.'

As she found places on the settee for them to sit by moving clothing, she explained she shared the flat with Anna and another girl.

'We haven't seen her since last Wednesday,' explained the woman, who had a curvaceous body and sparkling blue eyes.

'I'm sorry,' said Sunita. 'We don't know your name.'

'Lena,' she replied. 'Lena Adamska.'

'And what's the name of your other flatmate?'

'Maria. She's my cousin,' said Lena. 'Mr Filipowski's dead, isn't he?'

Sunita shrugged. 'It's not been officially announced, but it's highly likely the body at the Balsall Common house was his. There was a woman in the house as well and we're trying to work out who she was.'

'How terrible. We're hoping and praying the woman's not Anna.'

'Tell us about Wednesday,' the sergeant said. 'Where were you when you last saw Anna?'

'She got up before me, but we were both late. She was going to the agency in Handsworth and was worried because Monika, who's in charge, had been getting onto her about arriving for half past nine. She expects us to be ready for the punters at around ten o'clock. We had coffee together in the kitchen and then she left. It must've been nearly nine o'clock. I just said, "Bye. Have a nice day."'

Dawson glanced up at her with a smile. 'She arrived at work all right?'

'Yes. One of the girls that works with her, Betina, called me about something during the afternoon. In passing, she mentioned that Anna had left early, which had annoyed Monika.'

Sunita wondered whether the girls worked set hours. 'What time should Anna have finished work?'

'We work day shifts and night shifts,' Lena explained. 'It's a hard life. We're doing it for a short while to help our families back home. But we're aware that, if we don't keep the punters happy and keep Monika happy, bad things can happen. Look, I've probably said too much. I don't want to get into trouble.'

'We aren't looking into the ethics of the business, although if people have been mistreated, we might come to that at a later date,' the sergeant said. 'For the moment, all we're interested in is finding what's happened to your flatmate. Have you got a picture of her, by any chance? A photograph?'

'There's probably one in her room. Hold on.'

Lena hurried into the hallway and disappeared for a few minutes.

Sunita folded her arms and gazed at her colleague. 'It all hinges on the picture,' she told him.

'You've got a clear recollection of what she looks like, Sarge?'

'Yes, fairly good.'

Lena returned with a photograph showing a tall, smiling young woman flanked by an older man in a blue suit and an older woman in dark, casual clothes.

'This is Anna with her parents,' she announced. 'She was their only child.'

'When was it taken?' the sergeant asked, as she leaned forward and clutched the picture in her right hand.

'Well, she's now in her early thirties, so I'd say – five years ago?' said Lena. 'By the way, I called 101 for the police on Thursday or Friday, and I made a report, but they've not been in touch since.'

Sunita took the photograph and studied it for a moment without saying a word. She knew straight away that this was the woman whom she'd seen more than twenty-four hours earlier in the fire-damaged bedroom.

She had the same slender face and long, blonde hair. Her mind returned for a moment to the darkened room where she had gazed at the same appealing face. Here she was smiling innocently towards the camera. A woman without a care in the world whose life had now been snuffed out like a candle.

She was faced with a dilemma. Should she make this bombshell admission to Lena? A frank revelation at this moment would no doubt send Lena into a paroxysm of grief and despair. Their chances of obtaining vital information about Anna to aid their inquiries might be lost for the moment.

What's more, although she was convinced in her own mind that it was Anna's body that had been found beside Filipowski, additional identification checks had to be made.

What if she was wrong? What if it was eventually found to be another woman? Speaking out of turn and in error could have inconceivable consequences.

'I'm not sure,' the sergeant said. 'Can I borrow this picture? It might help to eliminate her from inquiries.'

'Oh my God,' Lena exclaimed. 'You think it might be her, don't you?'

'I can't say at this stage. I saw the woman lying dead in the Balsall Common house. I'm really not certain. Listen, I need to ask you some other questions. Did Anna take her phone with her?'

Lena pushed some lingerie aside on an armchair and perched on the seat. 'I've looked for it and it's not here. Maybe it's at the agency.'

'Does she have a boyfriend?' asked Sunita.

'I may as well tell you this. Anna's bisexual. She's just come out of a relationship with Sofia, who works at the agency. But she's single right now.'

'Who ended the relationship?' Sunita asked. 'Was it Anna or Sofia?'

'Anna ended it,' she replied. 'They'd been arguing a lot.'

'The woman found in the house was lying close to Tadeusz Filipowski. It appears they'd been sleeping together. Does that surprise you?'

Lena put her hand to her mouth.

'That's very surprising. I should tell you that, Monika told me he'd just moved to Balsall Common and she recognised the house from the photographs in the paper.'

Sunita drew a quick breath. 'She recognised the house because she'd been there?'

'Yes,' Lena replied. 'You have to remember Mr Filipowski owned the agency. Monika is the manager and she often had to visit him regarding the business. I know he could be a difficult man, but we all had a lot of time for him. So I was shocked when we realised it was him. But it certainly didn't occur to us he might've taken Anna there.'

Sunita nodded sympathetically. 'Another question. Does Anna ever take drugs?'

'Only occasionally,' said Lena. 'She's not hooked on anything, if that's what you're implying, like some of the girls are – particularly the street girls. No. She just dabbles from time to time. It helps make the world go by.'

Dawson glanced across at her. 'Does she have any knowledge of the gangs selling drugs?' he asked. 'We're wondering if Filipowski's death might have something to do with the rivalries between gangs in Birmingham?'

'Maybe Mr Filipowski's upset some people with his business dealings. But Anna wouldn't have been involved in anything like that. She's a straightforward young woman from Warsaw. She's no angel. She's been in trouble with the law over minor things in the past, like soliciting in the street. But nothing else. OK, she's not doing what she really wants to do. Like me, she's got into something that, if she'd had her wits about her, she wouldn't have got into. But for now she just wants to make some money and get back home to her family as fast as possible.'

As the pair said goodbye to Lena, and walked away along the balcony, Dawson was consumed with curiosity.

'It's her, isn't it, Sarge? I was watching as you studied the picture. I could tell by your reaction.'

'Yes, I'm pretty certain Anna's the murder victim, Brett. But what on earth was she doing in Tadeusz Filipowski's house and how did she come to die?'

Chapter 24

Seymour Trent sat smiling to himself after finishing work later that same day. He was tapping his fingers on his car's steering wheel as he listened to a music track from his youth, *Gangsta's Paradise*.

While sitting in his car in the multi-storey car park, he recalled the first time he ever heard the track. He was nineteen. It was one of the hottest Augusts that England had witnessed in recent times. He had achieved spectacular A level grades. He could have gone on to university.

Instead, he stunned his family and friends by opting for a police career. His father had been a railway worker and his mother toiled in a factory. The family was extremely poor. He had vowed never to spend his life scrimping and saving like his parents. He was going to make something of his time on earth. He was going to use the police as a means of turning his life around.

Weeks later, he had met police training officers for the first time. It was clear he was regarded as a promising young recruit. But even in those early days he had exhibited signs of a rebellious nature. He had annoyed his first sergeant by continually refusing to wear a tie.

After work, he had gone out drinking with his former mates from school – again risking his sergeant's wrath – and had met his first steady girlfriend, who, like him, was a Coolio fan.

How far had he travelled along the precarious highway of life since those halcyon days, he thought.

There was a knock on the passenger window. His new business partner had arrived. Trent wound down the window of his two-year-old BMW. 'Get in, Tyrone!'

Tyrone Blake opened the door and, lowering his head, sat down beside him.

'How are you doing, Seymour?' the newcomer asked as he adjusted the passenger seat to suit his lofty frame.

'I'm doing fine. You?'

'Never better, my friend. I've got some gear for you.'

'That's cool,' said Trent.

'It's the best,' said Blake, handing him a bundle wrapped in brown paper.

The inspector switched on an internal light in the car, which was parked on the top floor of the dimly lit stacker, and partly unwrapped the parcel. Then he announced, 'Yes. That's fine. Thanks, mate.'

'A pleasure, my friend.'

'So good to be dealing with someone reliable,' he told Blake. 'Unlike Tiff. And while we're speaking about him, congratulations on a job well done.'

'Thanks,' said Blake. 'I've also got some money.' He passed him a bundle of fifty-pound notes. 'There's £6,000 there.'

'But I've got to ask you something,' asked Trent. 'Why kill the woman as well? Because she was a witness?'

Blake shrugged. 'I didn't know about no woman till I read it in the paper. All I saw was Tiff on the bed. There was no one next to him.'

'Headquarters CID are investigating. I've tried to find out quietly what's going on. I keep getting told tests are being done to discover what happened to the woman.'

'Who was she?' asked Blake. 'She ain't been named in the press.'

'No idea. Anyway it doesn't matter. We'll find out soon enough. While we're on the subject of our dearly departed friend, I'm glad you took the petrol over there. Helps to destroy evidence.'

'Yeah. Good job, wasn't it?'

'Poor old Tiff! One bullet to the head and he's history. Listen, Tyrone, I'm very pleased with the way the business is going.'

'So am I. I haven't told you about Lee, have I? He's one of our newest recruits. He's a bright young guy who's red hot at street dealing.'

'Yeah? Where's he from – is he a Brummie?'

'Yeah. His family's Irish. What is it you English say? Gift of the gab?'

'That's right. Good. Glad everything's running smoothly. But there's something I've got to tell you, Tyrone. We'll have to be extra careful for a while.'

'How d'you mean?'

'Well, I haven't mentioned this before, but it looks like someone's been spying on me. I think it may be to do with the O'Sullivan case.'

Blake's face turned pale.

'Explain,' he said.

'It's well-known the families of the two men who got sent down have been causing trouble. They've been holding protests outside the court. They won't accept the trial verdicts. So they've pooled their cash and got a solicitor working on it. You know, it's called having a case review. They want to get as much evidence together as possible to launch an appeal and try and get the men off.'

'Will they succeed?'

'Who knows? But it looks like someone's been looking through paperwork on my desk and may've been trying to bug my office.'

'What? Someone broke into the police station?'

'Yes, crazy as it sounds, Phil found a young lad fiddling with an electric socket. An old cop I used to know was hanging around in reception at the time. We've done a sweep for bugs and nothing's been found. They're idiots anyway. I never discuss private business at work.'

'We must be extra careful, my friend,' said Blake.

'Yeah, you're right. We must.'

Chapter 25

Swinging a bunch of keys as he went, Daryl Johnson plodded up the metal staircase on Tuesday morning.

After reaching Landing 1, he walked a few more metres until he reached Cell 5, where, on the floor outside, he found a piece of crumpled white paper. He straightened it out. It was a sketch-map of Carl Innocent's home village of Norton Prior and the nearby town of Queensbridge. Johnson knocked on the metal hatch.

'Good morning, Mr Innocent,' he said.

'No callers today,' replied a muffled voice from inside.

'What d'you mean "no callers"?'

'I'm on a rest day,' the prisoner replied. 'I've decided I'm not taking any visitors. Can I have one of those "Do Not Disturb" notices that you get in hotels?'

Without answering, Johnson pushed one of the keys into the lock and turned it.

'What's the matter with you today?' the warder asked as he entered.

'Nothing. I'm OK,' said the prisoner, who was lying on his bed.

'You've recovered after your stay in the hospital wing?' Johnson asked.

'Yes, I'm more myself now. I got a little upset at the time.'

'A little upset? I wouldn't want to see you when you're really angry then.'

'No, you wouldn't want to see me then,' the inmate agreed.

Johnson unfolded the map.

'This yours? I found it on the floor outside.'

'Oh yeah,' said Innocent, taking it from the prison officer. 'Must've dropped it when I came back from the gym.'

'What's it for?'

'It's a map of my home area.'

'I can see that. What d'you need it for? You won't be going there for a while – if ever.'

'Oh, thanks for mentioning that. I only get a chance to reflect on that twenty-four hours a day, three hundred and sixty-five days a year. I don't know. I was just reminiscing about the good old days before I got banged up in here.'

'Wouldn't have thought you'd want to be reminded of the place. Anyway, have you got a new pair of specs yet?'

'No. They're on order. Should have them next week, all being well. I'm having to use an old pair. You're being all friendly and chatty this morning. Is there any particular reason for your visit?'

'Yes, I'll get to the point,' said Johnson, moving further into the room. 'The governor says we've got to find you another educational course. He doesn't think you'd have reacted so badly to your wife's letter if you'd got more to occupy yourself with.'

'And what if I don't fancy any of the courses?'

'Then the governor will choose one for you. You've got a week to make up your mind.'

'That's very nice, I must say.'

'So have you considered the options?'

'Not really.'

'You're good with words, aren't you? You're always doing crosswords. Have you thought about applying for a little part-time job on the prison newspaper, *Voice of the Vale*? They're looking for a science reporter and a showbusiness correspondent to write about the prison theatre shows. You should apply.'

'I don't much like the bloke who edits it.'

'What, Freddie Shelburne?'

'Yes, Freddie the Fence. I served time with him in Winson Green. Can't stand the man.'

'Oh, I thought he was such a nice chap.'

'He hates the screws.'

'Well, then, you could do bricklaying, barbering, printing, computer work – the options are endless. You could learn French or Spanish.'

'I can't see the purpose of me studying any of them. As you've so kindly pointed out, the chances are I'm never going to get out of the Vale – except maybe if they switch me to another prison. What's the good of being able to lay bricks or speak French if I'm stuck in here?'

'Don't be so defeatist. You don't know that. I'm thinking a long way ahead.'

'Don't be ridiculous, man,' said Innocent. 'I'm forty-seven, nearly forty-eight. The judge recommended a forty-year minimum stretch. What's the point of me being able to lay bricks, cut hair or speak French when I come out and I'm eighty-seven?'

Johnson tutted and looked at the ceiling.

'But, Innocent, the point about education isn't just to gain a skill you can use outside,' he said. 'It's also about improving the mind, about evolving as a person. One day there's a chance – a slim chance, I admit, but a chance nonetheless – that you might be rehabilitated back into society. You're more likely to achieve that if you've used your time here wisely and learnt a skill or several skills. If the governor can see–'

'Bloody hell. They'll never bloody let me out. I can see that, even if you can't. In their eyes, I'm a serial killer. It doesn't matter how much I deny it. In their eyes, I can never leave. There'd be a massive hue and cry at the very suggestion of letting me out of choky. It would be all over the press and they'd be forced to reverse the decision.'

'Innocent, you're too damned cynical. Aren't you ready to take a chance and spend your time here sensibly?'

'Look, it's my bloody time in here and I think I should be allowed to spend it as I please.'

'I'm sorry. You've got totally the wrong attitude,' said Johnson, despairingly. 'I've warned you what'll happen in a week's time. The governor will choose a course for you.' He pulled a leaflet from his pocket. 'Here. This is a list of all the courses. For God's sake, have a serious think about it or you could end up being enrolled on the needlework or pottery courses or something you really hate.'

'I doubt they'd let me anywhere near needles. Not with my reputation. All right. I've got the message. If I've got any time later on, I'll have a look at your leaflet.'

'I think you'll find it worthwhile. By the way, I've been told you're due for a trip out.'

'Oh, you mean my trip to Birmingham. Yes. That'll make a nice little outing for me, won't it?'

'You're giving evidence against your ex-cellmate, Frankie Dinwood.'

'Yes, that's the size of it. I don't know why I'm bothering really – except the Crown Court in Brum will be a bit of a change of scenery.'

'It's good of you to help the court, really.'

'I'm not doing it for that reason. I'm doing it to help myself. Altruism ain't one of my virtues, you might've heard that. Just fancy a day out. Anyway, can you help with this one, twenty-one down? "It has its attraction, the plea to a higher court." Six letters beginning with *A*.'

'No, you've got me there.'

'Hang on, I think I've got it,' said the inmate, squinting at his newspaper. 'Let's see if this fits. *APPEAL*. Yes, it fits.' Innocent filled in the word with his blunt pencil.

'That's a good one for you, isn't it?' said Johnson flippantly. 'Appeal. Seeing as you lost yours.'

'I know. My lawyer was only going through the motions, wasn't he? Anyway, I don't need you no more, so you can go now.'

'I was going anyway. I'll see you later, Mr Innocent.'

'See you later, Mr Johnson.'

The warder locked the door behind him, reattached the keys to his belt and walked away along the landing. Behind him, in Cell 5, Innocent put his pencil and copy of *The Times* newspaper down on the bed and picked up his map of Queensbridge.

His finger ran along the southern section of the town's high street. The town's red-brick police station was clearly marked. He remembered the row of black-and-white Tudor cottages that followed. And the next building was a quaint seventeen-century building which housed the Apollo Tearooms.

Chapter 26

The chief inspector strode across his room and opened the door.

'DS Roy,' he bellowed. 'Have you got a minute?'

Sunita jumped up from her desk and hurried across the CID office towards him, her notebook in hand.

'I'm putting in a call to Dr Reynolds and wanted you to be around to hear the conversation,' he told her as she approached.

'So he's made some progress on the deaths?' she said.

'He sent me a brief email, saying he's made some initial findings.'

After fetching a chair and closing the door, Sunita watched as he dialled the number for the pathologist's laboratory in King's Heath, Birmingham. Reynolds responded in strident tones that would have cowered a pack of wild animals.

'You'll have to make this quick. I'm off to a shooting in Stourbridge,' he said.

'Silas, I've got you on loudspeaker,' said the chief inspector. 'I want my sergeant to hear what you're saying. So you've got some updates for us?'

'Yes, that Filipowski fellow's been identified at the mortuary by his cousin.'

'So it is Tadeusz Filipowski, as we expected,' said Roscoe. 'Listen, we believe we've identified the woman found with him. According to our sergeant here, who's seen a family portrait, she's Anna Borowka from Hanbury Grove in Bordesley. She worked at the Gold Star escort agency in Handsworth and, like Filipowski, is from Poland.

We've been in contact with her parents and they're coming over to identify the body officially.'

'That's useful to know,' the pathologist replied. 'Look, Gavin, preliminary tests show both victims had high levels of fentanyl in their blood and that's what killed them.'

Roscoe shifted about in his executive chair. 'Fentanyl? The pain killer?'

'I'm afraid so, old fruit. Indications are they both ingested it with some cocaine on Wednesday evening or possibly Thursday morning. There was no soot in their airways, which also points to their being dead before the fire happened.'

'Wasn't it fentanyl that killed the pop star Prince, sir?' Sunita remarked.

Roscoe shrugged. He'd never been a fan of the late American music icon. 'No idea,' he muttered.

'Fentanyl,' Reynolds continued, 'is a synthetic opioid that can be fifty times more powerful than heroin. It's used by drug dealers to "bulk out" their wares. It used to be linked to heroin but more and more we're finding cocaine being laced with it. They'd been snorting the drugs through a tube. There was a trace of white residue around their noses. Filipowski had 26 micrograms per litre of fentanyl in his blood and was bleeding slightly out of one nostril. The woman had 24 micrograms. I expect the cause of death to be recorded as opioid toxicity.'

'What about his head wound?' Roscoe asked.

'Filipowski had a single gunshot wound to the head. There were no bullet wounds to the woman.'

Sunita had been sitting with her arms folded, listening intently.

'Dr Reynolds, if fentanyl was to blame for both deaths, how do you explain the bullet wound to the man's head?'

'Very interesting question, Sergeant. Everything points to the shot being discharged at around the time the fire broke out. The bullet entered the cranium through the right parietal bone and the exit wound occurred on the left portion of the frontal lobe. Analysis of the tiny fragments and tissue round the exit hole told us putrefaction had been well-advanced. In addition, if the man had been shot earlier in the week, the blood on the victim's head would've been much darker in colour – a reddish brown.'

Roscoe shook his head. 'All I can think is that the gunman didn't check the body and killed a man who was already dead.'

'Very likely, old fruit,' said Reynolds. 'I've been thinking along the same lines. He was in such a hurry to get the job done and get out of there that he didn't stop to check the man was breathing. He just shot him and set about starting the fire.'

Sunita drew a quick breath. It was becoming clear there might have been two separate incursions made against the couple's lives with murderous intentions.

'Maybe the gunman knew of Filipowski's drug habit,' she said. 'Maybe he noticed the white powder and just assumed his victim was in a drug-induced stupor when he shot him.'

'Again, that's a possibility,' said the pathologist. 'I should also mention a ballistics expert has examined the bullet and the casing that was dropped on the bedroom floor. That tells us the weapon used by this blundering assassin was a Glock 17 handgun.'

Sunita frowned. 'Dr Reynolds,' she said, 'do you think the two victims were aware their drug was laced with fentanyl? Could they simply have been taking it with the cocaine for a greater kick?'

A heavy silence hung in the air before the pathologist responded. 'I doubt it, Sergeant. If they'd both ingested a lower dose of the opioid, then they might've been taking it to enhance their intoxication. But at the levels we discovered, I'm sure they weren't aware of the high risk they were facing.'

'So someone must have added it without their knowing,' she surmised.

'Absolutely. I doubt whether this Filipowski fellow, knowing what we know of him and that he's no stranger to cocaine, would've deliberately chosen such a high concentration to increase a high.'

'Dr Reynolds,' she continued, 'wouldn't he have been able to tell that the drug was laced with extremely high levels of fentanyl?'

'No. Unfortunately, many forms of illicit fentanyl don't necessarily have a definite taste, colour or smell, which makes it very difficult to identify.'

'Well,' Sunita said quietly, 'if it was deliberately added to the powder on the dressing table, this is definitely a case of murder. And innocent Anna Borowka seems like an accidental victim who was unlucky enough to be there and share the powder with him.'

'Yes. I think we're looking for a killer who's been cool and calculated in their actions,' Reynolds continued. 'They've chosen a method of elimination that might be hard to prove as murder in a court of law.'

'Exactly what I was going to point out, Silas,' interrupted the chief inspector. 'This could turn into a tricky case. If a batch of cocaine mixed with extremely high levels of fentanyl is knowingly supplied – leading to death, that supplier could definitely be charged with murder. But if it was found that a dealer supplied them with a controlled substance unaware that it also contained fentanyl, we might be left with having to bring a lesser charge of constructive manslaughter.'

'That would be an exasperating result, old fruit,' Reynolds admitted.

'That leaves us with the gunman,' Roscoe went on. 'We'd need to charge him with attempted murder and, depending on the outcome of the fire investigator's report, arson.'

Sunita drew a quick breath. 'It looks as though Filipowski was being stalked by two murderers.'

'A man with enemies, Sergeant,' the pathologist remarked as the call ended.

Afterwards Roscoe leaned back in his chair, shaking his head.

'Looks like we've got our work cut out with this one, Sergeant,' he said, picking up a pen from his desk and twiddling with it.

'Sir, we know Ambrose Grant, the neighbour, had to kick in the door, which must have been locked before he tackled the fire. So I'm wondering how the gunman got into the house? Did he have a key? If so, he could be someone close to Filipowski – such as Tyrone Blake.'

'A right-hand man turning on his own boss?' said Roscoe. 'It's not unheard of. But you know that road rage incident? The gun used to fire bullets into the tyres was thought by forensics to be a Beretta APX Centurion. Different weapon altogether from the Glock mentioned by Silas.'

Sunita nodded. 'That's a good point, sir. But a crook can have more than one gun and Blake may've had a key to his boss's house.'

'We'll have to start interviewing close friends and colleagues of Filipowski,' Roscoe went on. 'As Silas said, he clearly had a lot of enemies and we've got to sift through them.'

Sunita grinned. 'Blake was a close associate who's almost certainly gained from his boss's death. He's now in line to take a larger role in the business.'

Roscoe folded his arms. 'Yes, I think we should start with him. He's almost certainly the guy who shot Tom Vickers in November and we need to speak to him about that in any case. Maybe he's got a Glock 17 stashed away in his wardrobe. Omar checked the CCTV for Balsall Common and spotted a Touareg which could be Blake's. Only problem was the reg number related to a car in Cornwall.'

'We definitely need to bring him in, sir. But don't you think the main focus of the investigation should be on finding out who provided the fentanyl?'

Roscoe nodded. 'You're right. Let's concentrate in the first instance on the events of last Wednesday. Who else is in the frame in your opinion?'

The sergeant gazed at the floor for a few seconds before responding.

'There's Mike Gainsby, the road rage victim. There's Sofia Kozak, who'd been having an affair with Anna. Filipowski might've been targeted by the bosses of a rival group of villains, such as Axel Makepeace, boss of the West Side Gang.'

'Don't forget our corrupt copper, Trent. Maybe he wanted the guy out of the way.'

'Anyone of those people could've had a hand in the deaths,' she said.

Chapter 27

Omar Khalid shivered in the chill morning air. He wished he'd brought a thicker coat for his journey to Sutton Coldfield as he stepped out of his blue Ford Focus and gazed around.

Hanover Drive was a highly sought after, tree-lined street where large, detached houses were shrouded by high walls, hedges and bushes. The home of Axel Makepeace and his family, number twenty-six, lay behind large, black gates with a block-paved driveway.

The front door of the imposing red-brick house was set under a canopy storm porch which stretched across the front of the house, providing cover on blustery days. As he peered through the gates, he suspected the main door at the front had been reinforced and the windows had bullet-proof glass.

Khalid pressed a button on an elaborate intercom. Immediately a light shone into his face and a gruff voice demanded, 'What do you want?'

'I'd like a quick word with Mr Makepeace,' Khalid explained.

'Who are you?' the man demanded as dogs began barking in the background.

'DC Khalid, Heart of England Police.'

'He's away at the moment,' said the man, raising his voice above the din.

Khalid sighed. 'Do you know when he'll be back?'

'No set time. They're north of the border. Can I ask what it's about?'

'No. It's something I need to speak to him about personally. Is any member of his family around?'

'No. They're all away.'

'Could you ask him to call me? As I say, the name's DC Khalid.' He recited his mobile phone number.

'If it's about the coaches, you need to speak to Sajid at the depot,' the man said.

'No. It's not about the coaches. Just ask him to call me, will you?'

Khalid stepped away from the entrance and watched as the light beside the intercom faded and died.

He decided he would try to speak to neighbours and walked along the pavement until he reached the front of the smaller detached house next door, which was fronted by a high hedge. He marched up the gravel drive, past a neatly cut lawn, and pressed the bell. Curtains in the front room quivered before, seconds later, the dark-brown front door opened a fraction and a woman's face appeared. He displayed his warrant card.

'Sorry to trouble you,' he began. 'Police. Do you know the Makepeace family?'

She shut the door at once. 'Don't know them,' she called from behind the door. 'Sorry!'

The exasperated detective decided to approach residents living on the other side of the Makepeaces' house. This was a smart, well-maintained detached house behind wooden fencing which had a 'For Sale' sign outside.

Khalid pushed open the small, white gate and followed a path to the front door. He pressed the bell at the entrance and, after more than a minute, a man appeared in the doorway.

'Sorry to bother you,' he said, showing his card. 'I'm from the police. Do you know the Makepeace family at all?'

'No.'

'They live next door to you.'

The man, who was short and stocky with a round face, frowned at his visitor.

'Don't know them.' Then, like the other neighbour, he promptly closed the door in the detective's face.

Khalid returned to his car, aware that, behind the trees and high hedges, lurked fear of a sinister and powerful neighbour.

He phoned Sunita Roy, who was sitting at her desk in CID. Her eyes had been fixed solidly upon her computer screen for a while as though in a trance. She blinked and stretched out her hand for her desk phone.

'Sarge, it's Omar,' he said before she had a chance to speak. 'I'm afraid it looks like Makepeace is away in Scotland. None of the locals are talking.'

She tutted. 'Bang on a few more doors,' she said. 'We've heard that Makepeace and Filipowski were deadly rivals. Makepeace is claimed to have spoken about wanting him out of the way.'

Khalid laughed down the phone. 'It's incredibly convenient, isn't it – him being more than three hundred miles away at the time of Filipowski's death?'

She nodded. 'It is, isn't it? Listen, if he's gone away, it would be good to know when he went, where exactly he is now and when he's due back. I've been reading through the files. He's been flagged up for various drug offences in the past, but he's only got minor convictions.'

'Maybe he's got a sharp lawyer,' Khalid observed.

'Maybe that's it,' she continued. 'What are you meant to be doing afterwards? Didn't the DCI ask you to make more inquiries about Tyrone Blake?'

'Yes, Sarge. I've found an address in Handsworth for Blake. We got a tip from someone. The boss has asked me to go over there with two constables and make an arrest.'

'That's good. Don't forget to give his place a thorough search.'

* * *

Half an hour later, Dawson glanced up from his computer screen.

'Sarge, the media team have released Anna Borowka's name to the press. I've just seen a piece on *Birmingham Live*.'

Sunita stood up and gazed towards him. 'What are *Birmingham Live* saying?'

'I'll read it.

> *The woman found murdered alongside Polish businessman Tadeusz Filipowski has been named as Anna Borowka, who worked as an escort in Handsworth, police have revealed. She was aged thirty-two and from Bordesley. Police are still refusing to outline how the pair died. A fire broke out at the house in Balsall Common where the bodies were found early on Sunday. But early reports claiming the pair may have died from smoke inhalation have been dismissed.'*

The sergeant tutted. 'Now we'll have all the lunatics on to us, making all kinds of weird claims,' she moaned.

'Here's the first now,' Dawson yelled as his desk phone rang.

After listening to a voice for a few seconds, the constable placed the call on hold.

'Sarge, it's a guy called Akhtar. He claims he's Mr Makepeace's solicitor and he's asking for Omar.'

'Put him on to me,' she replied.

'I was asking for your DC Khalid,' the man told her in an educated voice.

'He's out at the moment. Can I help? I'm DS Roy.'

'I represent Mr Makepeace, and your Mr Khalid's been round to my client's house without invitation, asking to see him. All requests like this should be channelled through me and made in writing.'

Sunita shook her head in exasperation. She had once considered a career as a solicitor herself after her three-year law degree. One reason she had not pursued a career in that field was the thought of having to work alongside some of the bumptious, arrogant individuals in the profession – like the current caller.

'DC Khalid was acting on my instructions, sir,' she said. 'We're making inquiries about a major incident last week and were wondering where your client was at the time. That's all.'

'What incident are you referring to?'

'I don't want to go into all the details immediately, sir. We're simply seeking assistance with inquiries. We need to find out if your client's been in this country recently.'

'Why should this be a matter to concern my client?'

'We can explain everything when we speak to Mr Makepeace. Where exactly is he right now?'

'If you must know, he's in Scotland on holiday with his family.'

'When did he travel there?'

'I'm not sure. I think it would've been on Saturday, last week.'

'And when are they due back?'

'I don't know. Look, can you tell me what this is all about?'

Sunita shrugged her shoulders. 'Mr Akhtar, we know your client is mixed up in the drugs world and it's an incident involving drugs that we're investigating.'

The solicitor raised his voice. 'It's true that my client's been named in the newspapers in connection with the hideous drugs trade in the Midlands and we're in the process of taking legal action against those newspapers. My client is a respectable businessman who's never been involved in that reprehensible business in any shape or form.'

'If that's true, that's reassuring,' said Sunita. 'If you could ask Mr Makepeace to call us, I'm certain we'll be able to sort everything out with a brief conversation. We simply want to eliminate him from our inquiries.'

Once the call ended, Sunita rose from her desk.

'Brett,' she said, 'I'm going off to Handsworth. I've got an appointment to see that woman Sofia Kozak, who was once in a relationship with Anna. I reckon there's a lot she can tell us. I'd like you to go and see Mike Gainsby, the road rage guy. See if he's got an alibi for last Wednesday or Saturday night.'

Chapter 28

Tyrone Blake sat in the interview room, nervously tapping his fingers on the table just after four o'clock on Tuesday afternoon. Omar Khalid had arrested him at his flat in connection with the November shooting in Sedgeworth in which DI Vickers had been injured.

But he had been warned that the police also wished to discuss other matters. He was concerned they were already associating him with Filipowski's death.

It was cold. The nearby radiator didn't seem to be working properly. The solicitor that had been assigned to him, a short, plump middle-aged man, had seemed pleasant enough and had accepted all his denials without question.

'Don't confirm anything for the moment,' Salman Siddiqui had insisted. 'Let's hear what they've got to say. Simply decline to give an answer. We can then decide how to approach things.'

Although he was on the ground floor, Blake was uncertain of the building's layout. He had been in a rather aggressive mood when he arrived at police headquarters and was placed in a basement cell. The arrest had taken him by surprise. He'd certainly not suspected he was already on the police radar in connection with the Sunday morning shooting.

He couldn't recall where the main exit doors were. There was no point him trying to make a run for it, in any case. The building was swarming with police – even if he could overcome the young officer who was standing guard at the back of this drab room. He spent a few minutes gazing through the barred window. It offered a view of vehicles arriving and leaving the car park.

Did they have evidence linking him with Whitstone Drive? He'd covered his tracks well, hadn't he? He'd worn gloves. He'd used false number plates. He'd disposed of the gun. Yet here he was – just three days later – in the frame for it. It wasn't like him to make mistakes. But perhaps, on this occasion, he had.

* * *

Ten minutes later, the door burst open and the chief inspector stepped in, followed by Mr Siddiqui.

'Right, I don't expect to keep you too long, Mr Blake,' said the detective. 'I'm DCI Roscoe and, of course, you know Mr Siddiqui.'

The chief inspector turned on the recording equipment before taking a seat opposite Blake.

'Just to remind you, you've been arrested in connection with an incident in Sedgeworth on Tuesday, 13 November last year when DI Tom Vickers was shot in the shoulder. We're also keen to speak to you about the deaths of two people in Balsall Common at the weekend. Now do you admit that you and Mr Filipowski were present at a house in Sedgeworth at 2 p.m. on that Tuesday in November?'

He referred to some notes in front of him.

'To refresh your memory, the house in Sedgeworth was 46, Sidney Road.'

Blake glanced at his solicitor before replying, 'No comment.'

'DI Vickers has identified you as the man who shot him in the shoulder and chest.'

Blake shrugged. 'No comment,' he said.

'Four days later a petrol bomb was hurled through the window of a house in Albion Road and the family inside were forced to flee for their lives. A car driven by you was caught on CCTV in Albion Road at the time of the incident.'

He shrugged. 'I was nowhere near there at the time. I was at my home in Handsworth.'

Roscoe stared into Blake's eyes. 'Can anyone verify that?'

'My next-door neighbour might remember. I was putting up a shelf and probably making a bit of noise.'

Roscoe interrupted. 'Afterwards you fled abroad and you returned to this country just after Christmas.'

'No comment.'

'I want to ask you about something two days ago. In the early hours of Sunday, a Volkswagen Touareg, which we believe was driven by you, was seen in Balsall

Common, close to the house where your friend Filipowski had been living. Shortly afterwards we believe you used a handgun to shoot Mr Filipowski in the head and then the house became engulfed in flames.'

'Not me.'

Roscoe frowned. 'Becoming a bit of an expert at starting fires, aren't we?'

'No.'

'This is your chance to explain what happened in Albion Road in November and in Balsall Common this weekend just gone.'

'You've got the wrong guy.'

'We know you drive a Touareg. Two neighbours near your flat have confirmed it.'

'Must be mistaken.'

'They're both absolutely certain of that,' said Roscoe. 'We believe you arrived at the house just after midnight on Sunday morning, let yourself in, shot your former boss in the head and started the fire in order to cover up the crime.'

'No comment.'

The chief inspector folded his arms. He stared into Blake's eyes. 'You let yourself in with a key that you'd cut at a locksmith's in Soho Road, Handsworth on 11 January.'

He leaned back in his chair and studied the suspect as the question flowed from his lips. He noticed Blake wince on hearing this revelation.

Blake quickly seemed to compose himself and mumbled, 'No comment.'

'You shot him in the head with a pistol,' Roscoe went on.

'No comment.'

'Then you made a pile of bedding and set fire to it on the landing.'

'No comment.'

'The officer who searched your flat, DC Khalid, found a laptop which belonged to the dead man.'

'We've spoken to Filipowski's cousin, who owns the house,' Vickers explained. 'He's confirmed the laptop is his cousin's and he last saw it at the Balsall Common house.'

Blake smiled. 'Oh, I wonder how that got into my flat? Maybe you bastards planted it there.'

Mr Siddiqui raised his hands in alarm and whispered furiously in Blake's ear.

'All right,' Blake said. 'I'll explain. He lent it to me.'

The chief inspector glanced across at the solicitor.

'Mr Siddiqui,' he said, 'your client is part of an ongoing investigation, but I'm prepared to release him for the moment on police bail. This will be for twenty-eight days initially. The conditions are that Mr Blake remains living at his Handsworth address, surrenders his passport and reports to a police station once a day. Could you ask Mr Blake whether he accepts those conditions?'

The solicitor held a brief whispered discussion with Blake.

'Yes. He accepts,' said Mr Siddiqui.

'Good,' said Roscoe, standing up. 'Interview terminated at 4.20 p.m.'

He turned round and switched off the recording equipment as Blake and Mr Siddiqui left the room. A constable outside led Blake back to his cell.

A few minutes later, as the chief inspector was walking along the corridor, Tom Vickers caught up with him and took him aside.

'I'm bloody annoyed that you've given him bail, sir,' the inspector grumbled. 'Why has that bastard Blake been released? He fled abroad after the shooting in Sedgeworth, and the chances are he'll make off again.'

'Calm down, Tom,' Roscoe insisted. 'He's made no admissions and this gives us a chance to gather more evidence. He's still under investigation. We've got his passport and we've confirmed his address.'

'He can get a forged passport. Why the hell are we letting him go? I'm still having physiotherapy after that attack on me,' Vickers continued.

'Sorry, Tom. It's out of my hands,' Roscoe replied. 'Norris and the assistant chief constable don't want anything interfering with Operation Temple, which is at a delicate stage. Once that investigation's over, we can throw the book at him.'

Chapter 29

The roar of heavy traffic greeted Sunita Roy as she walked towards the Gold Star Agency in Handsworth on Tuesday afternoon. She felt a biting wind on her back as she pressed the intercom and waited.

'Who is it?' asked a softly spoken voice.

'Police,' the sergeant replied as the buzzer sounded and the lock on the door was released.

Sunita climbed the staircase nimbly. The very woman she wished to see, Sofia Kozak, was standing at the top.

'I'm— I'm sorry,' the escort stuttered. 'I don't recall your name.'

Her long, dark hair was now tied back, and she was more modestly dressed than before in a pullover and slacks.

'It's DS Roy.'

'Well, look, DS Roy, I'm afraid the manager hasn't been here for a few days,' Sofia explained. 'You should've phoned. It would've saved you a journey.'

Sunita smiled. 'It's you I've come to see.'

'Why me?' The escort stared at the detective in shock as though someone had thrown a bucket of ice-cold water over her.

Sunita folded her arms. 'You've heard the news, I expect.'

Sofia's quiet voice became even quieter. 'Yes,' she whispered. 'Terribly sad.'

'Is there anywhere we can go?'

'I suppose we can sit in Monika's office. I'm sure she won't mind,' said Sofia.

Sunita followed her into the well-lit office at the rear of the first-floor premises. Then, instead of slipping into the manager's chair behind the desk, Sofia drew up a chair for the detective while she herself remained standing.

'Yes. It's terribly sad what happened to Anna,' said Sofia.

'How did you find out it was her that died?' asked the sergeant, removing a small black notebook from her pocket.

'Anna's father, Stanislaw, broke the news,' said Sofia. 'He was wanting information about what had happened and called me. He said he was coming to England to identify the body.'

'That's right,' said the sergeant.

'It was such a shock to me,' Sofia sobbed.

The phone on the desk began to ring. Sofia clearly decided to ignore the phone. After a few rings, the caller gave up. Sofia raised the handset from its cradle and placed it on the desk so they would not be troubled by it.

'They'll call back another time,' she insisted.

'You knew Anna was missing,' Sunita told her.

'Yes, but it's still a shock to hear dear Anna had… had…' She burst into tears before reaching for a tissue from a box on the desk. 'Anna was such a wonderful woman. I can't believe she's gone. Her family are devastated. She was meant to be going back home for good soon.'

Sunita, who was making a few notes with a pen, was concerned for Sofia.

'Are you all right?' she asked.

'I'll be fine in a minute,' Sofia insisted as she wiped her eyes.

'You were surprised, weren't you, when it was revealed she was found in Filipowski's bedroom?' said Sunita.

'Yes and no,' she replied. 'I know she liked him for some strange reason, but I wasn't aware they were dating or anything. That's why it was such a surprise when Stanislaw called and asked me for all the details of how she died. I couldn't really help him. I was as much in the dark as he was.'

Sunita nodded in sympathy. 'They'd been taking cocaine before they died. Does that shock you?'

She shook her head. 'Not really. She's used it before from time to time, and he didn't seem able to live without it.'

'It was laced with fentanyl.'

'Really? I suppose Filipowski must've come up with that. He was always trying different drugs.'

'Tell me again. When did you last see Anna?'

'Oh, my God. You'll set me off again. It was last Wednesday. She was working here.'

'Was it a normal working day for her?'

'Pretty much. She was working hard to build up a nest-egg so she could run a little business when she went home. A hair stylist's or nail bar or something.'

'Did she have any enemies?'

'No.'

'What about the men? Were there any regular clients who might've held a grudge against her?'

'No. There certainly wasn't anyone who would've wanted her dead.'

At that moment, a tall woman with short, blonde hair and boyish looks burst into the room.

'Have you seen my can of drink? Oh, sorry, Sofia,' she stammered. 'Didn't know you'd got a visitor.'

Sofia broke into a smile. 'It's all right, Betina. This is DS Roy from the police. She's looking into what happened to Anna.'

'Oh, God,' Betina snapped. 'The papers say she may have been murdered. You will catch the bastards who did this, won't you?'

'We're doing our best,' Sunita assured her. 'D'you know if she'd got any enemies?'

'No, no one.'

'Were you surprised she was found in the bedroom at Mr Filipowski's home?'

'Totally,' said Betina. 'I don't know what she was doing with a man like that. He's old enough to be her father. I know he'd invited her out for a meal. She couldn't decide whether to go or not. Now they're both gone. It's such a tragedy. Everyone who knows them is devastated. Particularly Monika. She's under the doctor. She's on anti-depressants.'

A male voice echoed down the corridor. 'Are you coming back or what?' the voice demanded.

'I'd better go,' Betina whispered before she called out, 'I'll be right there,' and hurried away.

Sunita was keen to find out from Sofia how Anna spent her last day alive.

'Sofia, you say you last saw Anna on Wednesday. Do you have any idea what she did on that afternoon?'

Sofia was silent as she stared down at the red patterned carpet. 'She was on the rota to be working the whole day. But she took the afternoon off without permission. She received a mystery phone call from someone at about two o'clock. When she ended the call, she told Monika she wasn't feeling well and left.'

'Do you know if it was Filipowski on the phone?'

She shrugged her shoulders. 'I don't know. He often tended to come over here on either a Tuesday or a Wednesday to speak to Monika and look at the accounts. But I don't know. A friend and I took two children to see

Peter Pan at the Hippodrome that afternoon, so I wasn't around.'

'We haven't been able to locate Anna's phone. Is it possible she left it behind when she went on Wednesday?'

'I don't know anything about her phone.'

Sunita slipped her notebook back into her pocket and stood up. 'Oh, there was one other thing,' she said. 'Lena told us you were in a relationship with Anna at one point. Is that right?'

Sofia nodded. 'Yes, we lived together for around two years in a flat just up the road from here. But then it all fell apart. We started arguing a lot.'

'Whose decision was it to end the relationship?'

'Mine. I felt our time together had run its course.'

'I'm sorry,' said Sunita as she prepared to leave. 'You've obviously been through an upsetting time.'

As Sunita walked back to her car, she contemplated what she'd just been told. Why did Sofia's account of the end of her relationship differ so greatly from Lena's? She was inclined to believe the flatmate's explanation that Anna had instigated the break-up. So was Sofia lying? If so, why?

She was about to unlock her car and drive away when Brett Dawson called her on her mobile phone.

'How did you get on with our Mr Gainsby, Brett?' she asked.

'His ground-floor flat's deserted, Sarge. His landlady says she hasn't seen him since Wednesday of last week.'

Chapter 30

Customers in the busy Three Gardeners public house hardly noticed the tall, slightly overweight stranger waiting patiently at the bar to be served. Dressed in a smart grey suit, Tom Vickers hoped he fitted in among the early evening drinkers at just after six o'clock that Wednesday evening.

He had tried partially to disguise himself – in case Trent or one of his cronies recognised him as a serving officer. He had a blue scarf round his neck, which he could raise over his chin if the situation required. He didn't feel out of place among the beer-swilling office workers on such a cold January night.

He also had a pair of reading glasses perched halfway down his nose, allowing him clear vision just above them. He had given his brown hair a darker tint by using a dye the night before and had shaved off the moustache he'd been growing for the past month.

After purchasing a pint of one of his favourite lagers, Blue Moon, he remained standing in the bar area, watching the other drinkers milling around in the roadside tavern.

He remembered reading a memo from a police colleague who had spent a week following Trent around after work. Their man always chose to sit at a table in an alcove in the front window – a position that afforded views across the car park.

Immediately next to this table, which had three chairs on either side, were the main doors and a small entrance hall. This meant that whoever claimed the table was in the privileged position of being partly divided off from the rest of the clientele.

The staff had added a touch of colour by placing a vase containing white and red freesias and yellow forsythia in the centre of the table.

When he had first walked in, after leaving his Audi close to the car park entrance, he had noticed two pairs of customers sitting in the alcove. One pair had left and now just two men remained in their seats, sitting opposite each other. Vickers decided it was time for him to move in and stake his claim to at least part of the table.

'Anyone sitting there?' he asked, sipping his drink and pointing to a chair by the window.

'No. Go ahead,' said one of the men.

Vickers squeezed past him and placed his pint on the table. Then, when he was sure the two drinkers were engrossed in conversation, he reached into an inner jacket pocket and pulled out a white plastic object. To other customers, it would have the appearance of an air freshener – the kind often placed in a room to remove any stale or unpleasant odours. But although it emitted a faint fragrance of lily of the valley, this deodoriser contained a secret compartment.

Unlike the camouflaged double-socket device Liam had planted in the CID office, this gadget contained a transmitter. Vickers intended to hide it somewhere on the window ledge. Then, when Trent and his associates unwittingly took their seats beside it, he would be able to listen to their conversation from his car – live – while making a recording at the same time. He covertly switched the gadget on and placed it just behind a striped linen curtain.

He smiled to himself and glanced at his watch. It was nearly seven o'clock. Seymour Trent was likely to arrive at any time. When he did, Vickers told himself, he would surely proceed to this very table.

The two men were still deep in conversation and he was now becoming concerned. What if they were still sitting there when Trent arrived? Would he opt for another table? If so, his entire evening operation would almost certainly have to be aborted. The minutes ticked by. The two men's glasses were nearly empty. Would one of them buy another round or would they depart? Trent's BMW was due to be gliding into the car park at any moment. Then, just as he was beginning to fear he may have had a wasted journey to Vine Hill, the two men stood up and left.

Vickers breathed a sigh of relief and quickly moved into one of the men's chairs. Now all he had to do was deter anyone else from taking the table until Trent arrived.

But, a few minutes later, a woman approached him.

'Are these seats taken?' she asked.

'Yes, I'm afraid so,' Vickers replied.

'I haven't seen anyone sitting there,' the woman haughtily continued.

'They're just at the bar. Won't be long,' Vickers insisted before the woman stalked off in a huff.

Moments later, he watched as a black BMW – which he recognised at once as belonging to Seymour Trent – roared into the car park. It was followed closely by a blue Ford Kuga. Both drivers parked a few metres from the pub entrance. He felt as tense as a cat in a dog pound.

Trent and Bains got out of their vehicles. Their eyes scanned around the car park.

'Bains as well!' Vickers said to himself as he watched from the window. 'That's a bonus.'

Trent wanted to wait for some reason. The two men were lingering by the BMW. They were pointing at each other's vehicles, perhaps discussing the respective merits.

Shortly afterwards, another car, a silver Mercedes C-Class, arrived with two men inside. Its driver parked next to the BMW. Trent waved towards the newcomers. Vickers believed them to be Tyrone Blake and Tahir Khan, who was behind the wheel.

Khan stepped out and remained beside the Mercedes, smoking a cigarette, while the other three men walked towards the pub. Vickers' fingers began twitching. He could feel the tension mounting. They came to a halt by the open doors.

'Oh God. Let's hope Blake doesn't recognise me,' Vickers muttered to himself.

Now he could faintly hear their voices. Blake was saying, 'It's a bit out in the sticks, my friend. I thought at any moment the satnav was going to ask me, "Are we there yet?"'

The two policemen beside him laughed. Vickers, who by now had raised his scarf to cover his mouth, could see Trent heading towards his favourite table. He noticed the dismay on his face as he realised there was a customer sitting there.

'It's all right. I'm just going,' Vickers mumbled, choosing to disguise his voice by adopting a deeper tone. He swigged back the last drops of his lager.

Then he stood up and brushed past the group, ensuring his head remained down as he did so. He was still concerned one of them might recognise him. But none of them took any notice. They were too busy settling themselves in around the table as the man in the grey suit stepped out into the night.

* * *

'Right, Phil, can you get the drinks in?' Trent asked with a smile. 'What would you like, Tyrone?'

'A pint of Coors would be great if they've got it,' said Blake.

'They've got Blue Moon here.'

'That'll be fine, my friend,' Blake assured him.

'Is Tahir coming in?' Trent inquired.

'Not at the moment,' Blake replied. 'I've got him keeping a watch outside for us.'

'So it's a pint of Pedigree for me,' said Trent, 'a pint of Coors and whatever you're having, Phil.' He handed his sergeant a twenty-pound note.

As Trent and Blake made themselves comfortable in their window seats, Vickers was inside his car, setting himself up to listen into their conversation. He turned on the battery-powered radio scanner with its short aerial.

'Trust our dear old force to be stuck with this outdated equipment,' he moaned to himself.

The speaker in the black handset produced a cacophony of radio noise. He pressed a button to reduce the jarring, discordant sounds. Then he spent a few minutes searching for the frequency of the transmitter hidden in the air freshener. He beamed with delight as Trent's voice boomed out clearly inside the car.

'They always do a nice pint here, Phil,' he was saying.

Vickers was jubilant. The voice was clear and the sound unaffected by the voices of other customers.

He switched on his police-issue voice recorder, ensured the red indicator light was on and sat back in his car seat, listening intently to every word.

Trent appeared to be speaking to Tyrone Blake, but for a moment the sound was indistinct. Vickers thought the inspector was goading his guest, saying police now believed, somehow, that Filipowski and his female companion were dead long before Blake reached the house.

Blake began to take offence, but Trent explained he found the circumstances amusing and was not being critical. Then the two voices became clearer. Vickers assumed the pair had moved closer to the microphone.

Trent was saying, 'I'm glad you could make it this evening, Tyrone. We might have a bit of a problem over in Sparkhill.'

One of the drinks thumped down on the table.

'How's that, my friend?'

'The West Siders are trying to muscle in on our trade. One of our lads, Danny Nelson, was trying to sell in the park with his mate Sam. While Sam was preoccupied, trying to arrange a deal, a scruffy black guy they didn't recognise came up to Danny. He said, "Tell your mates to keep off our patch." Then the boy got shanked.'

'Is he all right?' asked Blake.

'He'll live. He's in the Queen Elizabeth,' said Trent.

'God. We've got to hit back at those bastards.'

Twenty metres away, at the far end of the car park, Vickers was delighted to find the men were speaking so frankly.

'This is dynamite,' he said softly to himself.

However, he realised he was in a perilous position. If the gang members spotted him, his safety – possibly his life – was at risk. But he had to continue listening for as long as he could. Trent was conferring with Blake.

'You're right. We've got to hit them hard,' Trent was saying.

'Hang on,' Bains could be heard saying in the background. 'These little arguments have a habit of getting out of hand. We need to play it softly-softly.'

'I don't agree, Phil,' said Trent. 'We've got to hit them where it hurts. For sniff and smack, Sparkhill and Balsall Heath have been our best trading area for the past year. We've got more than a hundred junkies who are regulars. We'll have to find out who used the blade on Danny Nelson.'

'I'll get Tahir onto it, Seymour,' said Blake. 'He's good at getting answers to questions. Anyway, before we get onto the figures, have you heard any more about the O'Sullivan business?'

'That lawyer I told you about called Giles has been sniffing around,' said Trent. 'But I think I've given him enough false leads to put him off the trail. So don't worry, Tyrone. You can sleep snugly at night. No one will ever guess that you and Tahir were involved. Oh good. Here's Polly.'

Vickers was startled to hear the group at the table were being joined by a fourth person. He hadn't noticed anyone else entering the pub but assumed the new arrival to be Trent's girlfriend, Polly Cook.

'Polly, darling!' said Trent, greeting her. 'Let me get you a drink.'

'Seymour, there's a guy acting strangely in the car park,' said the newcomer.

'What?'

'He's a guy in his thirties sitting in a white Audi A3 at the far end of the car park,' she went on. 'He's got some kind of scanner with him.'

Trent peered out of the window in concern and saw the white car she was speaking about.

* * *

On hearing Polly Cook's warning words over his surveillance device, Vickers knew it was time to leave. He dropped his handset on the passenger seat, beside the voice recorder, and started the engine.

'You didn't take a note of the reg, did you?' he heard Trent ask.

'I've checked the number. It's come back as "Not on file."'

'That could mean anything,' muttered Trent before raising his voice and shouting, 'Tyrone, quick! Let's go and sort this out!'

'Who do you think it is?' demanded Polly, who had swapped her traffic uniform for a suede jacket and jeans.

'No idea,' yelled Trent. 'Do you remember what I told you the other day about Gavin Roscoe? This could be one of his colleagues. Or it could be someone working for that solicitor – Giles. Hold on here! I'll be back!'

Trent dashed out of the Three Gardeners with Blake close on his heels. They at once saw the white Audi had gone.

'We need to sort that guy out,' said Trent.

'You go with Tahir,' Blake said. Then he opened the Mercedes' passenger door. 'Tahir,' he ordered. 'Get after that white Audi and take Seymour.'

The Summerstoke inspector climbed into Khan's Mercedes and the pair sped off up the road in pursuit of Vickers.

'Put your foot down. He must have a clear two minutes on us,' said Trent. 'The bastard's got some kind of recording equipment which he's used to spy on us. It's vital we get hold of it.'

'Don't worry, Seymour,' came the reply. 'He'll probably be held up at the roundabout a mile ahead. We should soon catch him.'

Vickers was meanwhile driving as fast as he could in the Birmingham direction. He already feared Trent might try to pursue him and he had to avoid being caught at all costs.

He was soon touching sixty miles an hour – a precarious speed along country roads. He intended to make for the M42 motorway, which would take him back to St James Street.

But he was concerned about being unfamiliar with the area. He also knew that, if the rogue inspector caught up with him, he might try to seize his receiver and voice recorder. That would be disastrous for Operation Temple. He made a hands-free call to Roscoe.

'Tom, are you OK?' his colleague responded.

'I'm on the main road between Vine Hill and Coleshill,' Vickers shouted. 'I'm heading for the M42. Trent, Bains and Blake are all on tape. They've just been joined a few minutes ago by Polly Cook, Trent's girlfriend. I've got a brilliant recording.'

The chief inspector was delighted.

'You've done well, Tom. As we agreed, I've been parked close to the pub. I saw you drive off, but Trent and a guy who looks like Tahir Khan are just behind you. Look out for a black C-Class Mercedes. What do they actually say on the tape?'

'Trent's talking about cocaine and heroin. They're saying one of their dealers got stabbed and how they're going to get revenge on a rival outfit, the West Side Gang. Guv, we've got Trent bang to rights. He's even admitting setting Giles Farquhar a false trail.'

'You've hit the jackpot there, Tom. That's excellent! I've got timed photos of the whole gang arriving at the pub.'

'The problem is I've still got to get the recording somewhere safe,' said Vickers.

'Don't worry. You'll be all right, Tom,' said Roscoe. 'I've called my old pal, Pete Northfield, who's an inspector with North Warwick Traffic. I've explained, without giving too much away, that you're working for me and that you're in a spot of bother and you're being pursued.'

'Confusing or what, guv?'

'Don't worry. He'll sort things out. Meanwhile I've just pulled into the pub car park. I'll nip in and pick up the transmitter from the window. Then I'll follow you back to the office. I'm sure you'll be OK.'

'I hope you're right,' said the inspector, as he ended the call.

Vickers drove on, passing countless fields and woods. He was in farming country and, twice, the winding road led him along quiet village high streets. Within seconds, he would emerge at the far end of the village to be met by further fields and woods.

Eventually, he reached the outskirts of the small town of Coleshill, close to the M6 and M42 motorways. He noticed in his rear-view mirror a black Mercedes racing towards him, becoming closer with every second.

'Oh God,' he muttered. 'Now I'm in trouble.'

Chapter 31

'Have you got a gun?' Seymour Trent asked as Tahir Khan drove them at breakneck speed through the Warwickshire countryside.

'Yes, it's in the glove compartment,' Khan replied. 'But I'm not sure we're going to get a chance to use it.'

They were interrupted by a call on Trent's phone. The inspector glanced at the driver. 'It's Polly,' he revealed as he answered.

'Yes, Poll?'

'What's happening?' she asked.

'I'm sorry, darling. It looks like we're going to be some time. This guy's got a good head start on us,' he told her.

Polly sighed. 'Don't worry, Seymour.'

'I'm so sorry not to be spending time with you,' he went on. 'I'll make it up to you later in the week.'

'OK. I'm free tomorrow night if you like.'

'That'll be fine. But I've got to catch this guy. He could cause us a lot of grief if he's picked up our little chat in the pub. Listen, can I ask you a favour? I want you to look around where we were sitting for anything strange. This guy obviously tried to bug our conversation.'

'What am I looking for exactly?'

'Just a small electronic device – you know, a tiny radio transmitter. Check the flower vase. That's the most likely place. Oh, and is Tyrone still there?'

'Yes.'

'Would you be a darling and stay and chat with him for a while? He's had a long journey. Could you buy him a drink? He's playing a major role in our organisation now.'

'All right, since it's you,' said Polly.

'Thanks, love. I'll make it up to you.'

'You will,' said Polly with a twinkle in her eye.

'Could I have a quick word with Phil?'

Polly handed her phone to Bains. As Trent chatted to him, she took the flowers out of the vase and checked them. She also examined salt and pepper pots, the menu rack and an empty plant pot in the middle of the window ledge. But there was no sign of any tiny electronic device. Meanwhile her phone had been passed to Blake.

'Our little chat will have to wait,' Trent was telling Blake.

'That's all right, my friend,' said Blake. 'I've got to get back to Handsworth. In any case, you've left me with this most charming lady. We've been getting on fine.'

'That's good,' said Trent, who was far too concerned about their mysterious spy to allow the slightest hint of jealousy to cross his mind.

'Catch up with you later in the week. Bye,' said Trent, as he ended the call.

* * *

Throughout this conversation, a tall, amiable grey-haired stranger with ruddy cheeks and a broken nose had been watching the group at the window table from the far side of the bar.

Gavin Roscoe knew Bains well. He also recognised Tyrone Blake, whom he'd questioned at St James Street the day before. He realised the woman must be Trent's girlfriend. She was trying to discuss a matter with Blake, but she was doing all the talking. Perhaps he wasn't much of a conversationalist.

After a few minutes, she gave up. All three finished the remains of their drinks and strolled out.

The moment they left, Roscoe grabbed his pint of Pedigree and headed towards the alcove. But sadly, three women on an evening out snatched the table just before him.

'Good evening, ladies,' he said loudly. 'I'm sorry to intrude. I think I've left something on the window ledge.'

Two of the women stood up obligingly as he squeezed past them. He reached behind the curtain and retrieved the air freshener.

'A friend left it here earlier,' he murmured as he placed it in the pocket of his navy-blue coat and made for the doors.

The women looked at one another in embarrassment. One remarked, 'God, did you see that? That bloke nicked the pub's air freshener. What are people like?'

Roscoe overheard the remark and smiled to himself. He stopped by the exit doors. He overheard a second woman saying, 'He's so smartly dressed too.'

While rushing out to his car, the chief inspector gauged that Vickers would be more than ten miles away by now and, no doubt, still the target of pursuit.

* * *

As it approached half past seven, Tom Vickers was driving as fast as he could away from Vine Hill. He had been involved in high-speed chases several times during his career in the force, but he had always been the pursuer – never the pursued. It felt very strange. There was a slight adrenaline rush. He did not want to be caught. He did not want to hand over his surveillance equipment. Moreover, he did not want to crash his car – particularly when it was still on finance.

On he raced, taking every care he could with the road, until he reached the bottom of the hill that led to the centre of Coleshill. He roared up the road leading to the high street as Tahir Khan's Mercedes began to gain on him.

The Audi swept past a parade of shops before Vickers realised he was approaching a pedestrian crossing controlled by traffic lights. A woman and two children were walking towards it but were still a few metres away.

Just as the lights changed to amber, Vickers managed to speed past. He punched the air as he realised the crossing might delay his pursuers.

Khan was forced to brake hard as the lights turned red. The family stepped into the road. The woman waved in thanks.

Vickers accelerated up the hill. He had gained some precious seconds, but he knew his adversaries would soon be close behind him again. He had to get his vital evidence to a place of safety.

He called Roscoe again and learned his colleague had left the pub. He was now travelling in his direction. Vickers could hear the drone of his colleague's BMW engine in the background.

'Where are you now?' asked the chief inspector.

'I'm in the middle of Coleshill, guv,' said Vickers. 'But I've got a bit of a problem. I've got two guys in a black car sitting on my back bumper.'

'Listen, the only place I know in Coleshill is the Fox and Hounds in Birmingham Road,' said Roscoe. 'I could meet you there.'

'Guvnor, that closed years ago.'

'I know, but it's the only landmark I can think of.'

'OK, I'll see if I can give them the slip and I'll try to meet you there.'

The inspector reached the crossroads where the main road leading to Birmingham was intersected by the town's high street. He glanced in his mirror. There was a lorry approaching. He couldn't tell whether the Mercedes was behind it. After pausing for a passing car, he drove straight across into Birmingham Road and found two vehicles driving slowly in front of him.

'Not much further,' he told himself, remembering the Grade II-listed Victorian free house, now shut, was a few hundred metres ahead on the left-hand side.

But then calamity struck. The car and van in front of him slowed to a snail's pace and then drew to a halt altogether by the entrance to a supermarket. Vickers applied the handbrake, leaped out, raised his hand to his eyes and scanned the road ahead. Temporary traffic lights were holding vehicles up next to some roadworks.

As he stood cursing his luck, he heard a shout, turned round and found the Mercedes had drawn up behind him.

Trent jumped out and ran towards him, shouting abuse and gesturing wildly. His eyes were crazed like those of a rabid dog. He charged towards Vickers and punched him hard on the jaw, knocking him off his feet.

While sprawled on the ground, he noticed Khan standing behind his assailant with a broad grin on his face.

'What were you up to, you sneaky bastard?' Trent snarled as Vickers struggled to his feet and glanced around. A small group of shoppers were watching from a distance.

'I don't know what your problem is, mate,' Vickers muttered. 'Why've you been following me? I've no idea who you are. Looks like mistaken identity.'

'Oh, no. You're not getting away with that excuse,' Trent insisted. 'You were spying on us. Who are you working for? Giles?'

Vickers failed to notice Khan approaching the nearside of his car and opening the passenger door. He was too busy squaring up for a fight with Trent.

Despite being slightly overweight, Vickers had played rugby in his twenties and nowadays frequently trained at the gym. He was ready to give the older man the hiding of his life.

But then a siren could be heard in the distance and Vickers peered back down the road. Fellow officers might be on their way.

Beads of perspiration were trickling down Trent's face after the physical exertion of assaulting Vickers.

'What's your name, pal?' demanded Trent.

Vickers recalled agreeing with Roscoe in advance that, if he was forced to, he would give a false name and address.

'Michael Edwards,' he replied.

'So, Mr Edwards, Gadget Man,' Trent sneered, 'what's your address?'

'Number three, Trident Court, Nunnery Way, Coventry.'

'Sounds like a solicitor's. Who you working for?'

Vickers stared at the ground and declined to answer.

Then the siren blared out again. This time it was louder. A vehicle with a flashing blue light was approaching. Trent's facial expression changed from one of anger with Vickers to concern for himself.

'Come on, mate,' he yelled to Khan as the light ahead turned green and traffic began to move off. 'If you've got what we wanted, it's time to go.'

The inspector felt a surge of relief as the two men leaped back into their Mercedes and sped away. But what had Trent meant by the words, 'if you've got what we wanted'?

No sooner had the pair left than a BMW police car in Heart of England's blue and yellow livery roared up behind the Audi and two traffic officers stepped out.

'I'm PC Michael Taylor from North Warwick Traffic,' said the slim, blond-haired driver. 'This is PC Ali. We received a call from our control room to say that an undercover officer was in trouble. I take it that's you?'

'Yes,' said Vickers with a sigh of relief. 'Really grateful to you both for coming out, but it's all over, guys. I was being pursued by two blokes in a Mercedes. They got out and attacked me but the sound of your arrival scared them off.'

'Oh, God. Are you all right, mate?' asked PC Taylor.

'Yes, bit of a bruised chin, but I'll be OK.'

'What was it all about then?'

Vickers was about to try explaining when the chief inspector's car drew up.

'Tom, are you all right?' Roscoe asked as he jumped out and ran towards the group.

'Yes, I'm fine, guv. These two guys arrived in the nick of time.'

'You look all right, although something seems to have happened to your hair,' said Roscoe. 'It's gone quite dark overnight. And there's a pink mark on your chin.'

Vickers shrugged. 'I'm all in one piece after meeting up with Trent. That's the main thing.'

'You always come up smelling of roses,' said Roscoe.

'I know. I amaze myself sometimes.'

The chief inspector shook hands with the traffic policemen. 'DCI Roscoe,' he said. 'Thank you so much for your assistance.'

After Taylor and Ali left, Vickers inspected his car and made the shocking discovery that the scanner and voice recorder were missing. At first, he said nothing to his boss, who was in a buoyant mood.

'When I first realised you were outside Morrisons, I thought to myself, surely he hasn't stopped to do his shopping!' said Roscoe.

The two men laughed. Vickers leaned against the side of his car and lit himself a cigarette. The chase through North Warwickshire had been dramatic. He was glad his encounter with Trent was over – at least, for the time being.

'Those two men are dangerous,' he said. He pulled deeply on his cigarette and inhaled the smoke. 'I overheard them talking about a gun. It wouldn't have looked too good on my epitaph, "Gunned down at Morrisons!"'

'Well, it's all over now. So where's the equipment, Tom?' asked Roscoe, peering inside the car. 'What have you done with the two gizmos you used – are they in the boot?'

'No, guv. I've got some bad news. While Trent was quizzing me, Tahir Khan sneaked in through the passenger door and took the equipment.'

'Oh, God!' said Roscoe, looking shocked. 'So we've lost our key piece of evidence and all our hard work's come to nothing?'

'It does rather look like it, doesn't it?' said Vickers.

Chapter 32

The deaths of Tadeusz Filipowski and Anna Borowka constantly preyed on Sunita Roy's mind as she drove towards Balsall Common that same afternoon. She couldn't erase from her brain the image of poor Anna, sitting proudly beside her parents in Warsaw, unaware that, five years later, she would be dead.

Other memories of her visit to Soho Road passed through her thoughts – Sofia's tears and her account of Monika's dark depression. Betina's muted anger. All their lives had been so badly affected by this double tragedy.

Her car was passing through the gentle, undulating farming country to the north of Balsall Common. The last time she'd travelled along this road, she recalled, she'd believed she would be tackling an arson attack. Now they knew the two victims had died from ingesting high quantities of fentanyl.

She also remembered the chief inspector's words immediately after the pathologist had explained the cause of death had been fentanyl poisoning.

'If a batch of cocaine mixed with high levels of fentanyl is knowingly supplied – leading to death, that supplier could definitely be charged with murder,' Roscoe had said.

So, she told herself, if evidence of murder was available to be found, it was vital that they found it.

She reached the village just before four on that cold, cloudy afternoon. A police tape remained in place at 47,

Whitstone Drive and a constable stood on the pavement outside. The blackened first-floor window had now been boarded up.

Brett Dawson had arrived a short time before her. He stepped out of his car and strolled towards her, smiling, as she drew up close by. She took a pair of gloves from the back seat and put them on before clambering out and locking the car.

'All right, Sarge?' he asked.

She nodded. 'Yes. Let's have a good look round, Brett,' she remarked as she showed the waiting constable her warrant card.

He unlocked the front door and let the pair inside.

'Don't you think the forensic team will have done a thorough job already, Sarge?' Dawson asked while standing behind her in the hall.

'Yes, but I want to go through the place again – just in case something's been missed. Then I want to do some house-to-house.'

'I thought all that had been done,' mumbled Dawson, who was clutching a pair of plastic gloves.

'Yes, Brett, but previously the team would've been asking about Saturday night and Sunday morning. We now know the crucial time was last Wednesday evening. By the way, any more news about the road rage man?'

'Oh, I haven't had a chance to tell you. I went back to see Mike Gainsby. He's a locksmith with shops in Solihull and Handsworth, and he's been away on a course.'

'So he's got an alibi for Wednesday?'

'Yes, Sarge. Afraid he has.'

He followed her as she glanced into the living-room and the kitchen. Wherever they went, the stench of smoke and charred wood pursued them.

'You check the kitchen,' the sergeant urged him. 'I'll take a peek upstairs.'

'What exactly are we looking for?' he asked.

'It sounds stupid, but I'm not sure,' she replied. 'Anything that may tell us more about what happened here on Wednesday. Don't worry. We'll know when we find it.'

'If we find it,' he muttered to himself as she mounted the stairs and disappeared from view.

Apart from the window being boarded up and the front door repaired, no remedial work had been carried out to the house. The carpet lay partly burned on the landing. The door frame, floor, walls and ceiling in the bedroom remained charred or streaked with soot.

She ventured inside gingerly with a torch, testing each floorboard as she passed. Eventually, near the window, she gazed at the top of the dressing table where the plate of cocaine had once stood. It was missing – no doubt it had been bagged up and despatched to the forensic labs at headquarters.

The clothing on the chair had also been removed. She drew back a door in the double wardrobe. It simply contained some men's clothing which reeked of smoke.

'Sarge, do you want me to go through the kitchen cupboards?' Dawson called out from the foot of the stairs.

'Hold on!' she replied. 'I'm just coming down.'

The stylish kitchen at the back of the house contained a picture window offering views across a secluded rear garden, mainly laid to lawn.

'Old Filipowski didn't have a brilliant diet,' Dawson bragged as he leaned on the black granite worktop. 'All he's got in his food cupboards is some soup, some corned beef, sausages, pickled gherkins and beer.'

'Maybe he ate out a lot,' Sunita remarked. 'What's in this cupboard?'

She bent down and opened a base unit near the sink. An empty chrome waste bin was screwed to the back of the door.

'The contents of the bin must've been removed by Dr Ling's staff,' she muttered.

'I've had a look out the back,' he said. 'There's a black wheelie bin for household waste, a brown one for recycled stuff and a small black box for glass.'

'We'll have to check the two wheelie bins.'

Dawson turned up his nose at the suggestion, like a two-year-old being offered cabbage for lunch.

'Sarge, don't you think they'd have been searched already?' he said.

'This is your chance to shine, Brett,' she replied. 'Think how proud your mother will be if you find a major clue hidden among that rubbish.'

'Nothing like that would impress my mother. She thinks I'm a clown for ever leaving the wooden tops.'

He turned on an outside light, opened the half-glazed back door and led his sergeant round to the left of the house. The three bins stood on a concrete path near a side gate.

He tipped the black bin on its side and allowed its contents to spill onto the narrow strip of grass beside the path. A smell of rotting food pervaded the air as old cans, plastic bottles, yoghurt pots, light bulbs and discarded groceries tumbled out.

'Some of the dead fellow's last meals here, Sarge,' he remarked as he donned his gloves and began searching through the waste.

'Come on. I'll give you a hand,' she insisted, kneeling down and inspecting the rubbish.

She glanced at some of the labels on food packaging.

'Looks like he was a fan of Sainsbury's,' she observed. 'Might be an idea for one of us to take a spin over there. There's one in the main street. Maybe some of the staff will remember him.'

She turned round to find Dawson had now tipped the brown wheelie bin over. He was kneeling on the path, examining some screwed up letters, cardboard packaging and Polish newspapers along with a mail order catalogue and sheets of cardboard.

'Hang on, Sarge,' he said. He was holding up a cereal packet and shaking it. He peered inside the cardboard box and pulled out some brown paper. 'What have we got here?'

The constable tossed the empty cardboard box onto the grass while he examined the wrapping.

'What is it, Brett?' the sergeant asked.

'It's a small bundle of torn packaging held together with sticky tape. There's a typed address on white paper which has been taped on the front. There's no name. It just says, "Deliver to 47, Whitstone Drive, Balsall Common." Hold on.'

He peeled back part of the paper and peered inside.

'Looks like a few grains of powder,' he said. He raised the empty packet to his nose and inhaled. 'There's a sweet floral smell, I bet it's cocaine.'

She stood up and stepped towards him, smiling.

'Brett, I told you this was your chance to shine. You bloody hero. This could be the packaging their cocaine came in.' She took the packet from him and sniffed it. 'Yes, smells vaguely like cocaine.'

As she handled the brown paper, a note scribbled on white paper fell to the ground. She picked it up and read it. The handwritten message said, 'Try this. It's brilliant. Tyrone'.

She took a paper evidence bag from her jacket pocket and placed the wrapping and note inside.

'I'm going to take this to the car and, this afternoon, I'll hand it over to Dr Ling. Well done, Brett.'

By six o'clock the pair had completed their search of the bins and Sunita suggested they begin house-to-house inquiries but they soon found many of the neighbours had not yet returned from work.

Among those householders they managed to speak to, none could remember seeing a couple arrive at number forty-seven in a silver Porsche Boxster on the Wednesday.

Neither could they recall any unusual incident in the street during the whole of that evening.

Sunita quickly became disheartened.

'Look, Brett. This is getting us nowhere. I think it would be a better idea if you took the bag with the packaging over to Dr Ling. The sooner we get that examined, the better.'

'Yeah, sure,' he replied. 'I'll drop it in to her.'

'I'll carry on here for another hour or so and catch some of the residents returning from work,' she said.

After he drove off, she began knocking on doors in Frobisher Way, a turning off Whitstone Drive which began almost opposite Filipowski's house.

No one answered the door at the first two properties, and she felt even more disillusioned. But she was determined to carry on – partly because the image of Anna Borowka with her parents kept flashing into her mind. She felt great sympathy for Stanislaw and his wife, who had lost their only child.

Number five, Frobisher Way was a modern, yellow-brick, detached house. It was similar in style to Filipowski's, but slightly smaller. A small white car was parked on the forecourt.

She marched up to the entrance and pressed the bell. After a few seconds, a short, young man drew back the red door. He was about her age and had a round, slightly podgy face with alert brown eyes.

'Sorry to trouble you,' she began.

'No trouble at all,' he said with a smile. 'Are you our new neighbour?'

'No, DS Roy from Heart of England CID. Just making calls about the murder, I'm afraid.'

The householder emerged from the doorway and glanced towards Whitstone Drive. He had an unimpeded view of the fire-ravaged house.

'Yes, we've all heard about that, of course. Such a tragedy.'

'I just wondered if you saw anything out of the ordinary on Wednesday evening last week'

The man returned to his doorway. He put his hands on his hips and peered down at the block paving.

'Yes, Wednesday is the night my wife and I always have a Chinese meal,' he said. 'We've only just finished this week's takeaway, actually. I did see something last week, now you mention it.'

Sunita's eyes lit up. This was an unexpected response after such a draining, uneventful hour of door-knocking.

'May I take your name?'

'Graham Langley.'

'What did you see, Mr Langley?'

'Well, we ordered a meal from the takeaway in the high street just before six o'clock. It usually only takes the delivery driver about half an hour. But on Wednesday of last week, our food still hadn't arrived by a quarter to seven. I was pretty hungry. I heard a motorbike roar onto the estate and told my wife, "This sounds like our food now." I opened the front door and looked out, but it wasn't our driver. It was a courier with a parcel. He stopped right outside the house where the two people died.'

Chapter 33

The chief inspector found DC Wendy Hopkirk on her own on Thursday morning when he visited Tom Vickers' office.

She was leaning back on her chair, running a brush through her long hair.

'Morning, Wendy!' said Roscoe.

The startled constable only just managed to stop herself from toppling onto the carpet. She turned to see him standing in the doorway.

'Good morning, sir! DI Vickers has gone to the canteen to get some teas.'

'Did you hear about the fiasco yesterday, Wendy?'

'How the inspector got chased through North Warwickshire and punched on the chin? Yes, I've heard the story. He certainly goes through the wars, sir, doesn't he?'

'He always comes up smiling though, doesn't he?' said Roscoe, grabbing a chair by the window and sitting himself down.

Moments later, the inspector arrived, pushing the door open with his foot and shuffling in with two cups of steaming hot liquid.

'Oh sorry, sir,' he said. 'You've missed out on the teas. Here you are, Wendy.' He put her cup down on her desk.

'Have you recovered from your exploits yesterday, Tom?' Roscoe asked.

'Yes. I'm fine now,' Vickers replied as he made his way to his desk.

'It's such a shame that you lost your recording after all the effort we put in. You must be gutted.'

Vickers sat down, took a sip of tea and then glanced up at them both with a smile on his face.

'Yes, if I had lost the recording, I'd probably feel like that. But the fact is I didn't.'

Roscoe frowned. 'You didn't what?'

'I didn't lose the recording,' Vickers replied. 'Guv, you didn't think I'd only have one copy, did you? Throughout my time working for you, you always impressed on us we should aim to have a back-up plan in case of emergency. Especially in a situation like this, when we're trying to bring a bent copper to justice. I had the recording function on my smartphone on constantly in my jacket pocket since the moment Trent and his cronies arrived at the pub. It's registered everything.'

A broad smile crept across Roscoe's face, while Hopkirk, who often took a while to grasp essential facts, looked bemused.

'What's more, all the incriminating talk from Trent has come out beautifully.' Vickers looked as pleased as a dog with a fillet steak.

Roscoe stood up and stepped towards the inspector's desk.

'Tom, you old goat, that's brilliant. That's the best news since the Blues signed Emile Heskey. Why didn't you tell me before?'

'I needed to listen to the recording and check it had picked up the key evidence before telling you. I've now had a proper audio copy made.'

Roscoe bent down and slapped him on the back.

'That's really terrific.'

'Every word's come out clear as a bell, guv,' the inspector added.

'It's still a shame we lost the equipment to Trent,' said Roscoe. 'He knows for certain now we're on to him.'

Vickers nodded. 'Would you like to hear the recording?'

'Definitely.'

'I was here for much of the night, producing a full transcript of the conversation at the Vine Hill pub. Here you are.' He stretched across his desk and picked up some documents. 'There's one for you and I've got one for the chief super.'

Roscoe studied his printed copy for a moment. 'This is excellent,' he murmured. 'Have you got an audio copy I can take away, Tom?'

'Yes, sir.'

'Good. I'll need that to play to Norris. Perhaps you could play the key part of the conversation to us right now and I'll try to follow it in the transcript.'

'Yes, sir,' said Vickers, who was groping round in his inside pocket for his small black audio recorder.

'I'll just rewind it a bit. It's on page seven.'

After a few seconds, he pressed the play button. Seymour Trent's voice boomed out around the office, revealing how he wanted revenge since Danny Nelson, from the 101 Crew, had been stabbed. He bragged that drug sales had been soaring and, regarding the O'Sullivan murder, that he had given the lawyer Giles some 'false leads'. Trent also claimed no one would ever guess that Tyrone Blake and Tahir Khan had been involved in O'Sullivan's death.

Vickers pressed the stop button on the audio recorder and placed it back in his pocket. When he looked up, both Roscoe and Hopkirk were gazing at him.

The chief inspector leaned back on his chair.

'No jury could listen to that and be in any doubt that Seymour Trent was heavily involved in drugs,' said Roscoe. 'He's got at least a hundred drug addicts regularly buying from his dealers and one of their areas of operations is Balsall Heath. It's class A stuff as well.'

Vickers pointed out that the hundred people mentioned were only the regular clients.

'He's obviously got far more casual buyers, guv,' he said.

Roscoe seemed deep in thought. He stared at the floor. Then he looked up.

'Yeah,' he said. 'Look, we've got more than enough evidence to bring Trent and his cronies in for questioning. In a minute, I'm going to go and speak to Norris. We must get all their addresses so we can get search warrants. Then we can hold simultaneous early morning raids across Warwickshire. I want to minimise any possible collusion. You'd better start preparing for these raids, Tom. Could be just a few days away.'

'It's good to hear Trent talking about the O'Sullivan murder,' said Vickers. 'It shows clearly that he knows the truth of what happened.'

'Absolutely,' said Roscoe. 'That phrase, "No one will ever guess that you and Tahir were involved," will be such a crucial statement in court proceedings and should, of course, help the two jailed men get justice.'

'Although you can never totally count on juries,' said Vickers, who sounded as if he was speaking from bitter past experience.

* * *

The chief inspector looked apprehensively at his watch when he returned to his room in CID. He had an appointment with Nicola Norris at 11 a.m. and he dreaded the thought of being late.

He re-read the transcript of Tom Vickers' recorded conversations and then, after checking the time again, climbed the stairs to her office on the second floor.

The chief superintendent greeted him with a frown after he knocked and walked in.

'Gavin, I'm very concerned about this incident in Coleshill yesterday,' she said. 'I gather Inspector Trent found out his conversation was being bugged.'

'Yes, ma'am,' he replied, taking a seat near her desk. 'It was all rather unfortunate. His girlfriend, who works in North Warwick Traffic, spotted Tom sitting in his car and holding a receiver.'

'Is that the device that looks like an old-style mobile phone?'

'Exactly, ma'am. When the inspector drove off, Trent pursued him.'

She shook her head. 'I understand there was a showdown in the middle of Coleshill. Three members of the public have phoned in about it.'

'Yes, ma'am. Trent assaulted Tom Vickers before driving off with Tom's surveillance equipment.'

'We mustn't take any action about either of those matters for the moment, Gavin. We mustn't allow what happened in Coleshill to impede our main investigation.'

Roscoe rose to his feet and placed a copy of the Vine Hill transcript on her desk.

'Ma'am, this is the transcript of the conversation involving Trent at the Three Gardeners pub,' he said. 'I think you'll be pleased we opted to carry out this surveillance. There are some very incriminating statements.'

'Thank you,' she said with a smile. 'I'll look at this later. Listen, do you feel that Operation Temple has been compromised by yesterday's events?'

He shook his head. 'We're not sure if Inspector Trent is fully aware that Tom works here in CID. He gave the impression yesterday that he suspects him of working for the solicitor, Giles Farquhar.'

'What, as a private detective or something?'

He nodded as a text came through on his mobile phone, which he chose to ignore.

'Possibly, ma'am. But Trent may well have made inquiries by now and realised Tom's true identity.'

As the chief superintendent picked up the transcript and began reading through it, Roscoe glanced down at his handset. It was a message from Pat Clancy which shocked him. It said, 'Liam's been stabbed.'

Chapter 34

Sunita Roy had just parked her car outside police headquarters on Thursday morning when her phone rang. She recognised her friend Samir's phone number.

'Hi, Sam. How are you?' she asked as she switched off the engine.

'I'm absolutely fine, Sunita,' he replied. 'How's work?'

'There's a lot going on at the moment. You busy?'

'I'm always busy. People are always breaking their computers. Look, I've heard about a really cool fish restaurant in Ladywood. I wondered if you fancied coming along with me?'

Sunita sighed. 'I'm sorry, Sam. Just now I'm involved in a really big case and it's reached a critical point. This week's totally out and probably next week as well. How about the first week of February? Are you free then?'

'Yes, I think so. Shall I call you again nearer the time?'

'No. Let me call you at the end of the month and we can sort something out then. How does that sound?'

'Sounds good to me. I'll look forward to hearing from you.'

After climbing the stairs to CID and turning her computer on, she heard a panting sound and turned round. Brett Dawson was hurrying towards her with his coat half undone, clutching a carrier bag.

'I've got the disks from the two CCTV cameras on Kenilworth Road in Balsall Common,' he announced as he hung his coat up on a hook.

'Good. Let's have a look.'

'Sarge, I went back to the village last night, like you told me. Filipowski's neighbours confirmed none of them received a delivery of any kind on Wednesday evening last week. So there's a good chance the package was drugs arriving at number forty-seven.'

'Excellent,' she replied.

After he had handed both disks to her, she could see one was labelled 'Sainsbury's Local' and the other 'Balsall Common shops'. She took the supermarket one and gave him the other.

'Right. Let's see if we can find this motorcycle guy,' she said.

They both settled themselves down in front of nearby monitors and, for nearly an hour, stared at their screens like TV soap fans hooked on a dramatic episode. They studied traffic coming from both directions into the village on the evening of 16 January.

'What about this, Brett?' she asked her colleague after finding a hazy figure on two wheels travelling towards the village from the Birmingham direction.

He got up and gazed over her shoulder at the poor-quality image of a dark figure on a motorbike or scooter, travelling past Whitstone Drive in the direction of Kenilworth.

'That image is so poor, I doubt we'd ever get the registration from it,' he said, squatting down on the carpet beside her. 'In any case, he's not turning into Whitstone – he's going past – and the time given is just before 6.10 p.m. Isn't that too early? Your witness, Langley, said it was around 6.45 p.m. when he saw the courier.'

She glared down at him. 'Brett, I'm not a complete muppet. I'd thought of all that. But it's the only motorcyclist I've found going past the supermarket between six and seven o'clock. Anyway, how are you getting on?'

'I haven't found anything yet,' he muttered.

'Well, keep looking.'

Half an hour passed. Sunita was studying a map of the Balsall Common area when Dawson gave a shout.

'Hey, come and have a look at this Sarge,' he said, ruffling his spiky hair with his hand.

She stepped over to where he was sitting and peered at his monitor. There was an image on his screen of a man with a motorcycle helmet and black leathers. He was walking out of a food shop carrying a pizza in a box. He stepped over to a motorbike and began eating the pizza.

'Could be the same guy we saw on your screen,' he observed.

'What's the time at the foot of the screen, Brett? I can't quite read it,' she said.

'It's 6.30 p.m., Sarge.'

'How long do you reckon it takes to make a pizza?'

'Fifteen minutes?' he suggested.

'So is it conceivable this is the guy we're looking for? Let's consider what might've happened. He sets off for Balsall Common with his package. But he hasn't eaten and he's hungry.'

'Yeah,' Dawson murmured.

'He knows there's a shop that sells pizzas in the village. So he rides past Whitstone Drive at around 6.10 p.m. and calls at the food shop down the road. He orders a pizza and waits for it. He spends a while eating the pizza and then goes off to deliver the package in Whitstone Drive.'

'That's all possible, but you're forgetting one thing. There are no other sightings of him entering Whitstone Drive on camera. How come the supermarket camera doesn't pick him up a second time?'

The sergeant shrugged her shoulders. 'I've been looking at a street map. There's more than one way of getting into Whitstone Drive. He could've come out of the pizza shop and gone along Station Road to get there.'

'OK, so it's starting to make sense.'

'We've got no choice, Brett. It's the only lead we've got. Can we look and see if there's any footage of him riding away from the food shop?'

Dawson spent a few minutes scanning through the video and eventually found a sequence showing the rider heading for a roundabout near the shop and then roaring off into the night.

'The clearest images are by the shop,' said Sunita. 'Can we zoom in and see if we can read the registration?'

Dawson pressed some keys and enhanced the images with a region of interest filter.

'Here we are, Sarge,' he said with a note of excitement as the yellow number plate loomed up in the middle of the screen.

'Right, can you do a PNC check on the number while I print off some of these images?'

Chapter 35

That same Thursday morning, the chief inspector, concerned about the attack on Liam Clancy, made the seven-mile journey from his office to Heartlands Hospital in Birmingham.

The young man had been rushed to its accident department at four o'clock the previous afternoon after being found bleeding on a street pavement in Edgbaston.

Liam's grandfather, Pat, had only known the barest of details when he phoned the DCI. He said Liam had been on his way to meet members of the 101 Crew when a group of youths burst round a street corner and swarmed towards him.

He was stabbed in the back and stomach by two of the youths, who then ran off. Liam was left gasping for breath and battling for his life.

'A couple of cars stopped, and people got out to help him,' Pat told Roscoe on the phone. 'If they hadn't done that, the poor lad might not be with us today. One of the paramedics managed to get a few words out of him. He said he recognised one of the lads as being "from the West Side".'

Roscoe expressed deep regret that Liam, who had played such a crucial role in their investigation, had been attacked so viciously – just a few days after fellow gang member Danny Nelson had been stabbed in a park and taken to a different hospital.

He had ended the phone conversation by saying, 'I'm so awfully sorry, Pat. That boy's been such a tremendous help to us. It's so shocking he should've been assaulted like that. Please let me know if there's anything – at any time – that I can do for you.'

Roscoe remained contrite as he drove to the hospital. He had placed his main informant's grandson in jeopardy by encouraging him to join a criminal gang. How could he look his old friend in the eyes again? How would Pat ever forgive him?

He parked in the main hospital car park and walked through the glass-fronted entrance, clutching grapes, a bouquet of flowers and a get-well card. He climbed the stairs to the first floor, where he understood Liam was being cared for in the intensive care ward. He spotted Pat Clancy standing by a reception desk.

'Pat!' Roscoe exclaimed, putting his gifts down on the desk. He warmly shook his friend's hand. 'How's Liam?'

'He's still on the critical list, I'm afraid, and they won't let me see him,' said Pat.

'What about the other members of the family?'

'They're all over in Ireland at the moment, which is just as well in the circumstances. Of course, I haven't mentioned he's been working for you. I've just said he's in hospital. His dad's travelling back today.'

'How did you explain the stabbing to them?'

'I just said he was on his own and got attacked by a group of youths. I didn't say he's been running a candy stall for the Old Bill.'

'Shush!' said Roscoe, as a young nurse arrived at reception and established herself behind the counter. 'Look, I've got these flowers and grapes. I don't know if the nurses will give them to him when he perks up.'

'I think you mean if he perks up,' said Pat, sobbing.

Roscoe put his hand round his friend's shoulder.

'Come on, Pat. He's a young lad,' said Roscoe. 'They're very resilient. I'm sure he'll be OK.'

'There was a hell of a lot of blood on the pavement, Mr R. One of the people who found him followed the ambulance in his car and visited the hospital to see if he was OK. I had a few brief words with the fellow last night.'

At that moment, a nurse came along the corridor from Liam's ward. She asked Pat, 'Are you Liam's grandfather?'

'Yes,' he said.

'The doctors will be coming to see you in a minute.'

'Oh, thank you, love.'

While she spoke to him, Roscoe remembered he had to phone Tom Vickers and explain what had happened to Liam. The stabbing had operational implications since officers from the West Midlands force would at some point wish to interview Liam about the incident.

Pat sat down on a red seat in a nearby waiting area. Roscoe joined him, making small talk in an attempt to lift the old man's spirits. Eventually, he couldn't think of anything else to say and the two men sat together for several minutes in silence.

Roscoe began thinking about crooked detectives Trent and Bains and their links to the drugs gang that Liam had infiltrated. He recalled how doggedly Trent had pursued Vickers' car and the threats made against the inspector. His CID team had all the evidence they needed now. The time was approaching when justice would finally catch them up and bring their criminal operations to an end.

These thoughts were passing through his mind when a bearded doctor in a white coat unexpectedly walked up to them.

'I'm Dr Ahmed,' he said. 'Mr Clancy?'

Roscoe's friend looked up. For the first time, the detective observed his eyes were red from all his tears.

'Yes?' said Pat.

'I've got some good news for you. Your grandson's a little better and he's asking to see you,' the doctor said. 'He's still very weak and he's not out of the woods yet, but we've taken him off the critical list.'

'Oh, that's tremendous, doctor. Thank you!'

'He was stabbed twice – once in the abdomen and once in the back. By a stroke of luck, the blades are thought to have missed the major blood vessels. But he's in a lot of pain.'

'Can I come into see him now, doctor?'

'Yes, follow me.'

Pat picked up Roscoe's gifts and card. He hovered beside the detective for a moment.

'It's all right, Pat. You go on,' said Roscoe. 'I'll be all right here. Give the lad my best wishes.'

Roscoe walked to a quiet part of the waiting area. Ignoring a notice requiring mobile phones to be switched off, he called Tom Vickers at the Operation Temple office.

'Tom,' said Roscoe in hushed tones, 'that young lad who's been helping us – he's been stabbed. Looks like it may've been the rival outfit, the West Side Gang.'

'When did this happen?' Vickers asked.

'Yesterday afternoon,' said Roscoe. 'It looks as if he'll be OK. But the West Midlands force will want to question him. That's going to be tricky. Trent and his friends will be counting on him refusing to cooperate and, in a way for the moment, that suits us as well.'

'Leave that to me,' said the inspector. 'I've got one really good contact at West Mids – someone whose integrity is rock solid. I'm sure we can sort something out, so our investigation isn't compromised.'

'All right. As soon as I'm finished here supporting Pat, I'll be calling in to see you.'

Chapter 36

Nelson Road in Smethwick was an unremarkable street of small, terraced houses on the eastern side of the town, nestling beneath a network of telephone cables. Each house had a ground-floor bow window overlooking a modest front garden.

Sunita Roy found a parking space close to the courier's home, number twenty-nine, and cut the engine.

'There's a good chance he's in,' she told Dawson as she clambered out and felt the chill midday air on her face. 'There's a motorbike next to the bins.'

'Who do you think could've arranged such a deadly delivery, Sarge?' he asked as they crossed the street.

'I wouldn't like to guess. I believe in following the evidence,' she said as they approached the courier's garden gate.

'My money's on Tyrone Blake. I think he arranged the delivery and then went back three nights later to make certain they were dead. The only other key suspect is Mike Gainsby. He's linked to an address in Handsworth and must've had a grudge against Filipowski after his tyres were shot.'

'But he was on a course on the 16th, wasn't he?'

'Yes, unless he took some time off from it.'

Dawson followed as she pushed open the black metal gate and strode to the grimy, wooden front door. After pressing the bell, she peered through the window into a sparsely furnished living-room.

After more than a minute, a short, tousle-haired man in his twenties came to the door looking as though he had only just been roused from his bed.

'If you want Ricky, you've just missed him,' he told Sunita.

She ignored the question. 'Are you Simon Archer?' she asked.

'Who wants to know?'

She showed her warrant card. 'Heart of England Police.'

A sign of alarm crept across his face. 'I know the insurance has run out. I've had problems getting hold of my broker,' he said.

Dawson interrupted. 'We're not here about that,' he said.

'We can leave that for another day,' Sunita agreed as she glanced past him into the dingy hall. 'We're making inquiries about a delivery. You work as a courier. Is that right?'

'Yeah,' he said, leaning against the doorpost.

'Who do you work for?'

'Soho Express in Soho Road. Look, you'd need to talk to them if it's about deliveries.'

Sunita shook her head. 'We need to know about your trip to Balsall Common on Wednesday evening last week.'

'I really think you should speak to the office. I don't want to upset my boss.'

She was finding his attitude galling but managed to keep her temper.

'Look, we just want a little cooperation,' she insisted.

'Yes,' said Dawson. 'Of course, we could always return to the matter of your insurance.'

That remark seemed to melt the ice.

'All right. You'd better come in,' he said.

He led them into the front room, where the two detectives settled themselves down on a dark-green settee.

'What do you want to know?' he asked while standing near the doorway.

'You delivered a small package to a house in Whitstone Drive at about a quarter to seven,' Sunita said.

'That's right. The woman told me it was urgently needed medicine.'

The sergeant looked bemused. 'A woman?'

'Yeah, she said it was insulin for a diabetic.'

'Do you remember what number it was in Whitstone Drive?'

'I think it was forty-seven. Why? What's the problem?'

'You haven't heard, mate, have you?' said Dawson. 'Two people were found dead a few days later.'

Archer took a few steps backwards and slumped down into a chair.

'Oh my God,' he said, before clamping his hand to his mouth. 'And that package had something to do with it?'

Sunita shrugged her shoulders. 'Maybe. We're not sure. The main thing we need to know is who arranged the delivery. What was the woman's name and what address?'

'The office got a call at four o'clock from the woman and they called me. Do you know the Global Mart supermarket in Soho Road?'

She nodded. 'Vaguely.'

'There's a little place a few doors away called The Windmill Café. She said she'd be sitting in the window and she'd look out for me. I was due to be there at half past five, but she messaged me to say she'd been called away and was leaving the parcel with Imran, the cafe owner.'

'So you didn't get to see her at all?' said Sunita.

'That's right.'

Dawson interrupted to say, 'Looks like we'll have to have a word with the cafe man, Sarge.'

Ignoring him, Sunita asked Simon, 'How did the woman pay for the delivery?'

'Debit card over the phone.'

'So when you arrived at the cafe, what happened?'

'Imran shouted out to me that he'd got a package for me. I told him I knew all about it. I thanked him and rode off to Balsall Common.'

Dawson glanced at his sergeant and shrugged. 'What happened when you delivered the parcel? What was the fella like?'

'He came to the door straight away, signed for it and went back inside.'

'What did he look like?'

'Just an average bloke in checked shirt and jeans. One thing I remember is he'd got very short hair. So this was the guy who died, was it?'

The pair nodded together silently.

Then Sunita said, 'The woman must've given a name so you could collect from her. What name did she give?'

'She just called herself Tina.'

* * *

A bell rang as Sunita Roy pushed open the door of The Windmill Café half an hour later. She walked past a handful of customers who were nursing a cup of tea or tucking into a late breakfast. Brett Dawson followed a few steps behind her.

'Seems fairly quiet in here,' he remarked. 'Must be the lull before everyone rushes in for their lunch.'

They found the owner, Imran Haq, making a sandwich for a customer.

'Can I help?' he asked.

Sunita produced her warrant card. 'Heart of England Police,' she said. 'Can we have a chat somewhere?'

'I hope this won't take long,' he said. 'It's nearly lunch time.'

He led the pair into a storage room, next to the cafe's toilets.

'Now, what can I do for you?'

'On Wednesday of last week, a woman left a package here for a courier,' said Sunita. 'We've just been to see the courier from Soho Express. He says the package was left with you and you handed it to him.'

'That's right. The courier's called Simon. I've known him for years. He first came in here as a teenager. What's happened then?'

'We want to know about the woman who left the package with you,' Dawson said. 'What did she look like?'

189

Imran, a short, stocky man with grey hair, stared down at the floor and stroked his moustache.

'She was tall, quite pretty and she'd got short, blonde hair,' he said. 'She ran off as soon as she'd handed me the parcel.'

'What time did she leave it with you?' Sunita asked.

He paused to think for a moment. 'About quarter past five.'

'Had you ever seen her before?'

'I'm not sure. She looked a bit familiar, but I meet a lot of people in my job. Maybe she's been in for tea on a couple of occasions. I'm not sure.'

Sunita smiled as Dawson asked, 'Do you normally let people treat your cafe as a parcels office?'

He shrugged his shoulders. 'I've got a reputation round here as a man of the community. I try to help people where I can and, in return, I run a steady business. She was a lady in need. She explained she'd got an appointment to get to and that she'd been told the medicine in the package was urgently needed. So I didn't think twice about it.'

'And did she give a name?'

'Just gave the name Tina.'

'Do you remember anything else about her? You know, something that might make her stand out from the crowd a little?'

Again he searched the floor for an answer. Then he raised his head. 'Well, she had dangly earrings and white varnish on her fingernails.'

At that moment, a woman in an apron peered round the storeroom door.

'Imran, it's getting busy,' she said in a quiet voice.

'I'm sorry. I'm having to watch the time,' he said, holding the door open wide for them.

'It's all right. You've been very helpful,' Sunita told him as they walked back through the cafe.

'We've got what we wanted,' added Dawson.

He walked in front of the sergeant and held the street door open for her. They glanced knowingly into each other's faces. She mouthed the name 'Betina' to him.

Chapter 37

Just after nine o'clock on Friday, Heather Young rose from her chair in the CID office.

Seymour Trent watched from the corner of his eye as she straightened her long hair and then walked towards him. Her fawn skirt swished from side to side as she approached. He caught a faint whiff of her perfume. Then she leaned over the side of his desk in her low-cut, white top, showing a glimpse of cleavage.

'There's a call for you on line one, Seymour,' said the doe-eyed information analyst as she smiled at him. 'She's been waiting for more than five minutes.'

'Tell her I'll be free in just one minute,' he announced as he watched Heather sashay back to her seat.

Maybe one day, he thought to himself.

'Look, can I call you back in a few minutes?' he told the officer from the Metropolitan Police he was speaking to. 'Yes, it won't be more than a few minutes … Yes, I know you've got to go out … OK, bye!'

Trent waved at Heather to attract her attention. Then he mouthed, 'Who is it?'

Heather mouthed back, 'Polly.'

Trent sighed and shook his head. 'Put her on,' he said.

'What's going on, Seymour?' his girlfriend demanded as she came on the line.

'What d'you mean?' he said, trying to keep his voice down in front of his colleagues. He sensed this would be a difficult call.

Philip Bains glanced over at Trent and smiled. The smile was not returned. The sergeant at once returned his gaze to his computer.

'I'll call you back in two,' Trent whispered before hanging up.

Then, grabbing his mobile phone from his jacket pocket, he mumbled, 'Bit of a crisis,' and hurried to the stairwell outside the CID office.

'Why didn't you call me yesterday? I waited in all day for you,' Polly told him.

'Look, I've told you before not to call me at work. It's very busy at CID in the mornings.'

'Damn your CID. Why didn't you call me?'

'I was going to, but I had a very busy day with Stephanie's family.'

'Oh. So you were having a jolly time with bloody Stephanie and her bloody family.'

'Well, of course, it wasn't what I'd have chosen to do, but sometimes in life you have duties to perform. I'll make it up to you.'

'And while you were having your jolly time with your family, you couldn't find a minute or two to call me?'

'I was stuck there for five or six hours. It was a long drive home. I was shattered.'

'You can't think that much of me if you can't spare a couple of minutes to call me. I tried to text you, but your phone was off continuously.'

'I was doing a lot of driving and a lot of gabbing. There was a bit of a family row and I was trying to calm everybody down. I just never got round to it. I'm sorry.'

'It's not good enough, Seymour. I was alone all day. My brother's gone away with some mates. You should've phoned me.'

'Let me take you out for a meal. We could go to that new Indian that's opened.'

'No, Seymour. You've blown it,' she said, raising her voice. 'We've had some good times, but you can forget about it now. You're just a selfish, pig-headed scumbag and I never want to see you again.'

Then the line went dead. There was an awkward silence in the office among his colleagues when he stepped back to his desk. Many of them had guessed the inspector and his girlfriend had been arguing. His face had turned red and he was perspiring profusely.

He then noticed Bains was gesticulating with his hands in an attempt to attract his attention. He was also mouthing a few words the inspector failed to comprehend.

Trent pointed towards the end of the room with his thumb. Bains immediately stood up and walked to the gents' toilets. Trent remained at his desk for several minutes before joining him beside the wash basins.

'Anyone else around?' Trent asked.

No one was standing at the urinals and two cubicle doors were wide open, but the middle of the three doors was nearly shut. Bains kicked it. The door flew open. That cubicle too was unoccupied.

'I know you don't like talking business in the office,' said the sergeant. 'I thought you should know I destroyed the receiver and voice recorder at the weekend, as you suggested. So they got nothing on us. By the way, I'm really sorry about you and Polly.'

'Yes, well…' said Trent.

'You've had arguments before. She'll get over it and come running back.'

'I'm not sure she will this time,' said Trent. 'But anyway, now you're here, what are you doing at lunchtime?'

'I was going to the canteen.'

'Forget that for the moment,' Trent whispered. 'We've got a problem. Don't want to say too much, but have you heard of a taskforce codenamed Temple? I've had a tip-off that that trouble-maker Gavin Roscoe's involved. An insider's warned me that this Temple unit's been set up by the assistant chief constable with the aim of closing down our extracurricular activities. That guy in Coleshill, Michael Edwards, has turned out to be Tom Vickers. He works closely with Roscoe. But don't worry. I've got an idea to spike their guns. Shall we go to the Queen's Arms at a quarter past one? I'll tell you all about it.'

Chapter 38

Sunita Roy's car was held up in heavy traffic just before ten o'clock, as she made her way into the Birmingham district of Handsworth accompanied by Brett Dawson.

Eventually she found a side turning and parked. After they had both climbed out, Dawson yawned and stretched.

'Another late night?' she inquired while they walked together towards the main street.

'Just not getting enough sleep,' he explained. 'I get woken up every morning by the barking next door.'

'Maybe you should have a word with your neighbour,' she replied.

'I'm sure it's the dog, Sarge,' he quipped.

She shook her head and ignored his attempt at humour.

'Let's just focus on finding Betina, shall we?' she said.

'Strange that she's mixed up in the Balsall Common job,' he remarked. 'What possible motive could she have?'

'Who knows,' replied Sunita, raising her voice to compete with the Soho Road traffic noise. 'Maybe she took exception to Filipowski and Anna spending a night together. That's something we need to find out.'

Two police cars in the Heart of England livery were parked directly outside the Gold Star Agency. Four uniformed constables got out of the vehicles as the detectives approached.

'Ready when you are, Sarge,' remarked a burly officer with black-framed glasses, whom Sunita later learned was PC Josh Wilson.

'Right. Let's see if we can find the lady,' she said, as she pressed the intercom and waited.

A silky, sophisticated woman's voice asked, 'Who is it?'

'Police,' Sunita replied brusquely.

The buzzer sounded immediately. She pushed against the door and marched up the stairs, followed by Dawson and the three constables. Monika Kowalska met them on the landing with eyes as cold as a Moscow winter.

'There's such a thing as police harassment, you know,' she said. 'This is the third time this week.'

'Madam, we're in the middle of a murder investigation and every one of our visits has been relevant to our inquiry. Is Betina around?'

'Our Romanian girl, Betina Fischer? No, she isn't. Why do you want to see her?'

'It's all to do with our investigation into the deaths in Balsall Common.'

'Well, I'm sorry. She's not around. Anyway why have you brought so many people with you?'

'We believe there's some link between these premises and the two deaths, and we've brought a search warrant.'

Dawson delved into the inside pocket of his jacket and drew out the paper warrant, which he placed in Monika's hand.

'All right,' Sunita announced to the constables. 'Start searching the rooms in pairs.'

Monika looked alarmed. 'You can't do that. What about the punters?' she demanded. 'This sort of thing can have a serious effect on our business.'

'We'll give them five minutes to leave. Then we start our sweep of the premises.'

'What the hell are you expecting to find?'

Sunita shrugged. 'Well, we might find Betina. Failing that, clues to her whereabouts.'

'Oh my God. What's happening to the world?' asked Monika. 'First Tiff and Anna die. Then you think one of our best girls has some connection to it. And now you try to ruin my business. Betina isn't here. Can't you get that into your head, Sergeant?'

'Where is she exactly?'

'She's gone back to Romania to see her family. How long will this search take?'

'Not long.'

Sunita and Monika moved to the side of the landing as three men, perspiring and looking flustered, emerged from bedrooms at almost the same time. One was fastening his shirt as he walked down the corridor and, without speaking, descended the stairs.

Two scantily clad girls stepped into the corridor and glanced nervously towards Sunita. The detective recognised one of them as Sofia Kozak.

'What's going on?' asked Sofia.

'We're just looking for evidence that might tell us how Filipowski and Anna were killed,' Sunita said quietly.

'It's all right, Sofia,' said Monika. 'They say this won't take long. You girls have a break. Put your feet up for five minutes. Sergeant Roy, perhaps you'd like to come with me to my office?'

Sunita nodded, and the pair walked to the far end of the corridor. Monika took her place behind her desk after offering a chair to Sunita.

'I spoke to you a little harshly earlier this week. I think I ought to apologise,' said Monika. 'To be honest, the two deaths have knocked me sideways and I'm on anti-depressants from the doctor.'

'I'm sorry to hear that,' said the sergeant. 'It was mentioned to us that you'd taken the deaths very badly.'

'Yes. I'd known Anna for four years and she was a sweetheart. Tiff and I… well, I was very fond of him.'

'When did Betina leave Birmingham?'

'Two days ago. Her mother's been taken ill. She's very close to her mother. You know, Betina is a quiet, gentle girl. I can't imagine why you need to speak to her. She really can't have anything at all to do with your investigation.'

'We'll decide on that,' said Sunita sternly.

Monika fished about in one of her drawers and placed a mobile phone on her desk.

'We found Anna's phone in one of the bedrooms,' Monika explained, passing the handset to Sunita. 'She must have forgotten it when she was last here.'

'Thank you for that. So when did Betina last come to this building to work?'

'She was here on Tuesday. It was late on Tuesday she heard her mother was sick.'

'Have you got her Birmingham address?'

'I'm not sure. I think she's just moved.'

'Could you have a look for it?'

A shriek from along the corridor brought their conversation to a halt. Sofia was screaming, 'Monika! Come quickly!'

Monika leaped up and strode out of the room. Sunita could hear words exchanged between Sofia and Dawson, who was insisting that he should be allowed to search a bedroom wardrobe.

Sunita took advantage of Monika's absence to search her three desk drawers. The first was filled with office stationery, pens, spare lightbulbs, a bunch of keys and a phone charger. The second contained a pair of black, crotchless knickers, boxes of condoms and a sex toy.

Sunita was about to give up when she inspected the bottom drawer. She pulled out some computer printouts listing business expenditure and, underneath, discovered a small address book. For the time being, she carefully placed the typed accounts and the book inside an exhibits bag.

The office door flew open and Brett Dawson's face appeared.

'What was all the commotion about?' Sunita asked him.

'One of the women objected to me searching a cupboard,' he explained. 'Maybe she didn't like the idea of me poking around in her collection of whips, handcuffs, wigs and lingerie. Sarge, I was just glancing out of the back window and noticed some rubbish bins. One of the girls says they share a bin area with the mini market.'

'Good. I'm going to carry on speaking to Monika. Can you take one of the team and search the bins? You know what we're looking for, don't you? Any sticky tape and brown paper like those we found in Whitstone Drive.'

* * *

PC Josh Wilson agreed to help Brett Dawson search the agency's bins. He followed Dawson down the stairs, out of the building and along a nearby alley that led to a small yard behind the premises which was surrounded by brick walls.

Dawson opened a wooden gate and at once saw two large green wheelie bins. Seven clear bags filled with waste for recycling stood beside them.

'Better make a start,' Dawson muttered as he untied a knot on the first bag. 'Do you know this is the second time this week I've been asked to wade through rubbish? If I'd known I'd be spending so much time sorting through people's waste, I'd have got a job at the recycling centre at the end of my road.'

'What are we searching for exactly?' asked Wilson, untying one of the bags.

'Some brown paper and tape,' said Dawson. 'Maybe some white powder as well.'

'Drugs?'

'Yeah.'

The pair spent twenty minutes emptying the bags onto the concrete, sifting through the rubbish and then placing the contents back.

Dawson was becoming disenchanted and thought of giving up. Then, as he reached for the final bag, Wilson stood up and waved two pieces of paper at the detective.

'This what you're looking for, mate?' he asked.

Dawson stepped across and took the items from the constable. One was a small piece of brown paper resembling the packaging found at Whitstone Drive. The other was a piece of crumpled white paper which bore similarities to the written note.

'Good man,' Dawson exclaimed, patting Wilson on the back.

Leaving the constable to repack the bag, he hurried back upstairs and showed the items to his sergeant.

'Well done, Brett,' she told him. 'But forget about that for the moment. I've found an address for Betina. She lives at 132A, Windermere Road, which is only round the corner. Scoot round there with a couple of our team and see what you can find.'

* * *

Disillusioned and frustrated, Sunita finished work in the CID office six hours later and, carrying her coat, stepped towards the stairs. She was about to descend when she heard a familiar voice with a Black Country accent say, 'Do you call this a day's work?'

She spun round angrily. She was weary after an exhausting nine-hour shift without a lunchbreak and resented any suggestion of laziness.

Then she saw her colleague Tom Vickers standing there with a broad grin after emerging from his office.

'I could say the same to you,' she retorted as her grimace turned into a smile.

'What's up, Sunita?' he asked his ex-girlfriend. 'You look as much fun as a rainy Sunday in Halesowen.'

'Oh thanks for the compliment,' she said as she edged her way down the first few steps. 'It's just the case of these two deaths. We've hit another brick wall.'

The inspector walked towards her. 'I saw the guvnor earlier. He said it looks like the stuff that killed the couple was couriered down from Soho Road.'

She nodded. 'Yes, but the girl who organised it has gone to Romania. I've just heard back from the airline. They've checked the passenger lists and she flew out on Wednesday.'

'That's a bummer.'

'Yes, so everything's come to a grinding halt for the moment. It's so depressing,' she said. 'I feel I've let the boss down.'

'Don't be daft. He thinks the world of you. Did the guvnor tell you the latest about Operation Temple?'

She shook her head.

'It's all going ahead on Monday. I'll have to be up at about quarter to five in the morning because I've got to get to Hinckley, over twenty miles away.'

'Hinckley? Isn't that where Phil Bains lives?'

'That's right, Sergeant Bains. I've got three PCs coming with me. At some point, I'll be alerting the Leicestershire force – just out of courtesy. But I'm leaving that right to the last minute, just in case. The guvnor's picking up Trent. He's obtained warrants for the whole gang – eleven altogether. All their places have to be searched and they've all got to be interviewed.'

'How many of those having their collars felt are cops?'

'Four.'

'Four?'

'Yes, four rotten apples in the barrel. That's Trent and Bains, obviously. Then there's Trent's girlfriend Polly Cook from North Warwick Traffic and Dougie Mott from the drug squad. It's really exciting. We're moving into the final phase.'

Chapter 39

The genial Irishman with a receding hairline and a gentle manner was leaning on the reception desk at the entrance to the hospital's Montgomery Ward on Saturday morning.

'Tell me again what it was you actually saw,' Pat Clancy asked the nurse sitting behind the desk.

'Well, it was about half past seven last night,' said the young, blonde-haired nurse. 'A young man aged about twenty-five wandered in, asking for a man named Lee. I said we'd got a Liam and a Leanne. He said, "No, I'm pretty certain the name's Lee." I said he'd got the wrong ward and he went away.'

Clancy stroked his chin and looked her in the eye.

'And what did this young man look like, would you say?'

'He was a mixed-race lad. About average height. He had very short black hair and was wearing a red and white sweatshirt and blue denims.'

'That's a worry, I have to say,' said Clancy, stepping back from the desk.

'You don't think he was one of your grandson's friends then?'

'No, I don't.'

At that moment, Roscoe emerged from the nearby lift and walked slowly towards the desk, carrying a wicker basket laden with fruit.

'Good morning, Pat!' he said. 'How's the young man?'

'Gavin! How wonderful to see you,' said Pat, reaching over to hug his friend, nearly knocking some of the fruit out of the hamper as he did so. 'Liam's fine. The doctors say he might be allowed home early next week.'

'That's great news,' said Roscoe.

'Yes, the doctors are really pleased with him.'

'That's tremendous. Can I go into see him?'

'Of course. That's all right, isn't it, nurse?'

The young girl nodded.

'Yes. It's straight through and on the right,' she said. 'Well, you know where it is, Mr Clancy.'

Roscoe followed as his friend made his way along the corridor to Liam's bay, which he was sharing with three other patients. Liam's bed was in a far corner, next to the window.

'Mr Roscoe. This is a pleasant surprise now,' said Liam, who was sitting up in bed with a copy of a tabloid newspaper. Smiling, he said in a quieter voice, 'How's the case?'

'We've reached a critical stage,' said Roscoe, in equally hushed tones. 'There will be a lot to tell you next week.'

'It would be good to know my efforts have led somewhere,' said Liam.

'You played a really important role in the whole investigation. Don't have any doubts about that. But I'm so sorry about what happened to you. How are your injuries?'

'My back and stomach are still very painful, but I'll be fine. Just fine.'

Clancy drew up two chairs for himself and the chief inspector.

'He was in the wrong place, but it's the luck of the Irish,' said Clancy. 'It was just a couple of nicks. You've got to take the little potato with the big potato.'

'Mr Roscoe,' said Liam, 'come and sit by the window. I've got a few things to tell you. My grandad said you were asking about a woman named Polly.'

'That's right.'

'She's Trent's fancy woman. She came over from Lincolnshire, where he's from. She works in your traffic department.'

'You know Trent's married, don't you?' said Roscoe.

'Yes, she's his bit on the side,' said Liam. 'There's a couple of other people I should be telling you about. One's a guy called Dougie. He's getting the old backhanders from Trent because he works in the drug squad and he keeps tipping them off. Trent always knows exactly when any drugs raids are planned. But it works two ways, Mr Roscoe. Trent tips off Dougie about the goings-on in the other gangs – so Dougie is now highly thought of in the drugs team.'

'That's very useful information, Liam.'

'And there's more. Trent's also got an IT man – you know, a computer whizz-kid, who can hack into computers, including the main police computer.'

'That's very difficult – if not impossible – to do.'

'Well, this character claims to have done it. I haven't got his name, but he's done it. He's been trying to wipe out some of the previous convictions of Tyrone Blake and Tahir Khan.'

'You're sure about this?'

'It's what I've picked up from the 101 Crew. Afterwards, he had to uninstall his software from his computer and then burn it. If he hadn't done that, they'd have tracked him down.'

'That's very interesting.'

'There's another little thing. The lads are saying Trent arranged for Blake to shoot Tiff at his home and then put Blake in charge of the day-to-day running of the drugs business. He always trusted Blake more.'

Roscoe smiled. He had been jotting down details of the conversation in a small notebook.

'That's really useful stuff, Liam,' he said. 'I've got to go now. I can see one of the nurses looking at me. You obviously need plenty of rest. We want you out of here as soon as possible.'

'Well, it's been great to see you again, Mr Roscoe. I'm glad if I've been able to help you.'

'You've been a tremendous help,' he insisted, shaking Liam warmly by the hand. 'Just you focus on getting better.'

Clancy accompanied Roscoe as he walked back along the corridor in the direction of the lifts. The detective put his arm round his friend's right shoulder.

'Pat, your grandson's been such a great help in this really important investigation,' said Roscoe. 'I can't thank the pair of you enough.'

'Gavin, there's something I need to tell you,' said Pat, quietly. 'A young lad visited the ward last night asking for a chap called Lee.'

'Liam's gang name?'

'That's right,' said Pat, who then repeated the information the nurse had given him.

'You need to get him out of here as fast as possible, Pat,' said the detective.

'I know. I'll have a word with the doctor and maybe bring him home tomorrow. He's well enough anyway.'

'Let me know if you need any help.'

'I definitely will.'

Roscoe became stern. 'I deeply regret your grandson being placed at risk. If I'd known in advance just how dangerous it might be for him, I might've gone about things differently.'

'Don't you worry about that for one minute, Mr R. We've got a saying over in Ireland. You'll never plough a field by turning it over in your mind. The job had to be done and we had to nail those crooked coppers.'

'Take care, Pat, and thanks once again.'

'Mind how you go now, Mr R, and don't you worry about a thing. We'll be fine now.'

Chapter 40

Somehow, Gavin Roscoe had heard the early morning alarm call. He had showered, dressed and managed to make his way downstairs. Yet he still felt only half awake. He muttered to himself as he heaved his arms into his navy-blue coat.

It had just turned 5 a.m. How do farmers, milkmen and postal staff cope with rising from their beds so early? he wondered.

He draped his blue scarf round his shoulders before gazing into the lane outside. Under the orange glow of the streetlight, he could tell a cold, frosty morning awaited him. His lawn was speckled with glistening white crystals. He peered across at the ghostly shapes formed by his neighbours' trees – the skeletal trees poking their leafless branches into the sky like human fingers and arms.

Here and there, a light flickered on or off in houses in Biddington across the fields – the only signs of life in a village that slept.

The chief inspector was startled by a nearby sound. Helen was standing behind him in a white dressing gown.

'Oh, Gavin, your scarf shouldn't be like that,' she moaned.

She undid the top two buttons of his coat and wrapped the garment more neatly round his neck.

'I didn't realise you were up,' he said.

'I heard you moving about and thought I'd come down. You don't like these early starts, do you?'

'Whatever my personal feelings, this is an important day,' he said, kissing her goodbye.

He unlocked his car, started the engine and let it warm up for a minute or two before reversing along the drive and heading for the M42 motorway. After passing Birmingham Airport, he continued driving northwards before reaching the town of Coleshill at the end of his twenty-two-mile journey.

As his BMW climbed the hill towards the town, he noticed a turning on the left with the name 'Marshalls Way'. After following this street for a few hundred metres, past row upon row of modern terraced and semi-detached houses, another sign directed him to Cherry Tree Place, a gated community of modern detached houses where Seymour Trent lived with his wife, Stephanie.

It was ten minutes to six when he parked near the gates and turned off his engine. The street outside the complex was deserted. His was the only car. Then his mobile phone rang. It was Chief Superintendent Norris.

'Good morning, ma'am,' he said. 'It's a cold and frosty morning here in North Warwickshire but the sun's on its way.'

'If I want a Midlands weather report, Gavin, I'll ask for it,' she snapped. 'Where the devil is this place?'

'It's just off Marshalls Way. As you come up the hill from Stonebridge Road, it's on the left.'

'Well, I'm damned if my driver can find it. We've just seen the "Welcome to Coleshill" sign.'

'You're not far away, ma'am. Drive for a further three hundred metres and Marshalls Way's on the left.'

'Wish I'd never volunteered for this now,' the chief superintendent muttered before hanging up.

As Roscoe waited patiently in the street with the car lights off, DC Wendy Hopkirk drew up in a grey Ford Fiesta. Then four uniformed constables appeared in two separate cars, followed by forensic officers in two further vehicles. Senior forensic scientist Dr Alice Ling entered the close in a white Kia Sportage moments before the chief superintendent's blue Jaguar XF saloon drew up. He walked across to her car and she wound down the rear window.

'Right, Gavin. Let's get this over with,' said Norris. 'Never like arresting our own. But sometimes needs must. I remember when Trent first joined us. He'd got an impeccable background and was destined for the higher ranks. But something went wrong – greed, no doubt. Now it feels like amputating a festering limb. You don't want to do it, but you have to act to preserve the rest of the body.'

'Yes, ma'am. Regrettable but necessary.'

'I've also been disturbed to hear that DS Bains, Polly Cook and DC Mott are suspected of being in league with Trent.'

The chief inspector nodded.

'One thought occurred to me, Gavin,' she continued. 'There's a good chance Trent won't be at home. He's got good contacts in the force and he may well have been tipped off that we're coming.'

'I hope not, ma'am,' said Roscoe. 'Temple's a tight ship and we left it right to the last minute before briefing everyone about this morning's operation.'

Roscoe's phone rang again. It was Tom Vickers.

'Morning, Tom,' said the chief inspector. 'All set?'

'Yes, guv,' said Vickers. 'We're outside the house in Hinckley, and I've just briefed the team. We're all ready to rock 'n' roll.'

'OK. Let's do this,' said Roscoe before ending the call. One of the uniformed constables approached him.

'Sir, as it's a gated place, how do you propose we get in?'

'It's all locked up, is it?'

'Yes, sir. I think so. The handle doesn't seem to turn. It's probably been bolted from the other side. I guess the residents have all got keys.'

'You're local, aren't you? What's your suggestion?'

'I could clamber over the top and let you in.'

'OK. Go for it,' said the chief inspector, admiring the officer's spirit.

* * *

Inside 12, Cherry Tree Place, Seymour Trent was sleeping soundly in his front bedroom beside his wife. He was oblivious to the approaching footsteps and failed to hear his front doorbell ring.

But gradually, as the ringing persisted, he began to stir. Then loud knocking commenced.

He wrapped a grey dressing gown round himself before opening the blinds and peering out. Then he was overcome by shock. There were more than a dozen officers – four in uniform – gathered on the pavement outside.

'What the bloody hell…?' he shouted.

His bleary-eyed wife, who was still lying beside him, turned her head on the pillow. She raised her right hand to her eyes as she strained to focus on him in the half-light.

'What is it, dear?' she asked.

'A whole army of cops are outside,' he said.

'What on earth do they want?' she mumbled.

'How do I know?' he replied brusquely. 'But, if I don't let them in, they're going to break the bloody door down.'

He hurried onto the landing and down the stairs. He knew by now they were real police – not members of a rival gang seeking his blood while disguised as police. He had recognised Gavin Roscoe's distinctive ruddy complexion.

'What's that sneaky bastard Roscoe doing here?' he asked himself.

Although initially confused and agitated, Trent's mind leapt into overdrive. As he approached the main door, a hundred and one questions were spinning through his brain. Stephanie, who had donned a lacy white gown, stood at the head of the stairs, watching him and listening.

'What's all this?' he demanded as he flung open the door.

'Seymour Trent,' said Roscoe, 'I'm arresting you on suspicion of conspiring to pervert the course of justice and of importing and trafficking class A drugs. You don't have to say anything. But it may harm your defence if you don't mention when questioned something which you later rely on in court. Anything you do say may be given in evidence.'

'This is nonsense,' shouted Trent. 'Who's put you up to this? You've got absolutely nothing on me.'

'Go and get yourself dressed quickly,' Roscoe continued in a quiet voice. 'We're taking you for questioning.'

One of the constables was asked to accompany Trent upstairs in case he tried to destroy any evidence.

* * *

As Trent dressed, Roscoe asked Wendy Hopkirk to phone the other units and inquire about the progress with their arrests.

Ten minutes later, as the forensic officers began searching the house, Trent returned to the landing dressed in a grey suit. He had to pass his wife, who was sitting in a confused state on the top stair.

'Don't worry, love,' he assured her. 'I'll be back later. I've done nothing wrong.'

He went downstairs where he was immediately handcuffed to one of the constables. But he remained defiant, insisting, 'You're making a huge mistake here, Chief Inspector. You ought to focus on real crooks, not hard-working DIs like me. By the way, have you got a warrant?'

'Yes. It's here,' said Roscoe.

Trent snorted in disgust before stepping out of the building into the emerging daylight. Seconds later, he turned back and yelled to Stephanie, 'They've got no evidence because there is no evidence!'

On hearing this, the chief superintendent approached him in her wheelchair.

'That's where you're wrong, Inspector Trent,' she said as he towered above her. 'We've got more than enough evidence to show you've been running a criminal enterprise while at the same time masquerading as an honest police officer. You're a disgrace to the uniform and I'll make it my personal duty to ensure that you get sent down for the maximum amount of time possible.'

One of Trent's neighbours, roused by the commotion, had come to watch the proceedings. He was then persuaded to open the main vehicle gate, thereby allowing the police and forensic staff to bring their vehicles in. Trent was forced into the back of one of the police cars and driven away.

Dr Ling and her colleagues were now making steady progress with their search of the house. Team members had been briefed to look out specifically for any evidence that might link Trent to either the O'Sullivan murder, the Filipowski murder or the drugs trade. Norris was shaking her head.

'This is a sad day, Gavin,' she said as she looked up at Trent's home.

'I agree,' said Roscoe, who noticed DC Hopkirk was walking towards him. 'Will you excuse me a moment, ma'am?'

Turning to the constable, he said, 'Any news, Wendy?'

'Yes, sir. Most of the operation went to plan. Nine suspects are on their way to St James Street. But there's no sign of Tahir Khan or the two Nowak brothers. We've alerted all units.'

'Thanks. Good work, Wendy,' said Roscoe, returning to the spot on the pavement where the chief superintendent was still sitting.

'Tom has arrested Sergeant Philip Bains in Hinckley,' he informed his boss. 'All the main suspects are in the bag.'

'There were some dealers as well, weren't there?'

'That's right, ma'am. We've got all the suspects except three of them. So, all in all, not a bad morning's work.'

'Yes, Gavin. I think we can be proud of ourselves, but it's a shame if some are still outstanding.'

'We're going to get the media team to launch a press appeal,' Roscoe informed her.

The pair negotiated their way towards their cars. Then DC Hopkirk joined them.

'Sir, I wondered if you'd got a minute? I thought you might like to see what Inspector Trent keeps in his garage,' she said.

All three proceeded to the side of the yellow-bricked house. She raised the partly open garage door to reveal a silver Bentley Continental.

'It's a brand-new registration, sir,' she said.

'Good heavens!' said Norris. 'Must be worth more than a hundred and eighty thousand pounds. How can he afford that on an inspector's salary?'

Chapter 41

The chief inspector's heart began to pound in anticipation as he and Tom Vickers descended the stairs at headquarters and headed towards the custody suite three hours later.

'The moment's finally come, Tom. You've spent months gathering evidence against this corrupt copper. Now it's time to watch him squirm.'

As the pair began attending to the recording equipment in the interview room, two burly custody officers led Seymour Trent in and directed him to sit at the table in the centre.

'Morning, Inspector Trent,' said the chief inspector. 'Won't keep you long. We're waiting for your brief.'

Trent glanced at Vickers. 'Ah, Mr Edwards, the gadget man,' he exclaimed.

Roscoe looked surprised.

'It's all right, guv. The two of us have met before,' said Vickers.

'Of course,' said Roscoe with a knowing smile. 'Actually, his name's Vickers.'

A few minutes later, Trent's lawyer, Magnus Huckabee, an overweight, balding man in his early forties, arrived and sat down beside his client.

After switching on the digital recording equipment, Roscoe announced the names of those present.

'Now, Inspector Trent, I'll just remind you why we're here. You've been arrested in connection with the murder investigation you conducted into the death of Brendan O'Sullivan. To remind you, he was found dead in Sedgeworth two years ago. You face a possible charge of conspiring to pervert the course of justice. You're also suspected of being involved with the importation and trafficking of class A drugs, namely heroin and cocaine.'

'My client strongly denies all these allegations,' said Mr Huckabee. 'We've had a long conversation this morning. He can't understand why he's here.'

The chief inspector shook his head in exasperation.

'Mr Trent's here because we've had a whole team of detectives working for several weeks investigating his conduct. I can assure you we've got enough evidence to prosecute him on both charges. Now, Mr Trent, can you tell us where you were on the afternoon of 22 January two years ago? It was a Monday, if that helps.'

'I was at my desk in Summerstoke CID and I've got loads of witnesses,' said Trent.

'That afternoon two men shot Mr O'Sullivan dead at his home with four bullets. You were in charge of the joint MIT team that investigated the death. This team made a half-hearted attempt at finding witnesses and then fabricated evidence against two men, Winston Stevens and Raj Kumar. You sent a file of this fabricated evidence to the CPS.'

'We didn't fabricate anything,' said Trent. 'I can honestly say we worked tirelessly on that investigation in January and February into that terrible murder and, when the trial took place, we were convinced the right men were convicted.'

Vickers interrupted to say, 'It's our contention you faked the evidence and that, throughout this time, you were associating with two men, Tadeusz Filipowski and Tyrone Blake, who ran a notorious crime group.'

Glancing at Mr Huckabee, the accused man shrugged his shoulders.

'I'm not going to deny knowing the two guys you're talking about,' he said.

'That's good because we've got a recording of a conversation between you and one of them at a pub in Vine Hill,' said Roscoe.

Trent turned pale. He had not expected to hear that. However, he put a brave face on this setback.

'As you know, I was in the area that evening,' Vickers explained. 'I'm sorry I had to give you a false name, but it was necessary as part of our undercover investigation. We've got photographic evidence of the two of you entering the Three Gardeners pub along with your sergeant, Philip Bains.'

He removed a colour photograph from a folder and held it up for Trent and his lawyer to see.

'For the purposes of the DIR,' said Roscoe, 'Mr Trent is being shown a photograph of three men outside the Three Gardeners pub at Vine Hill.'

'Look,' said Trent, regaining his composure. 'I–'

Just as he was about to speak, Huckabee intervened. 'I'd urge you to respond by saying, "No comment."'

'No, it's OK,' Trent assured him. 'There's something Mr Roscoe and his colleague ought to know. I've been running an undercover investigation into Mr Blake and his friends. Phil Bains and I kept this confidential, but we've been infiltrating his drugs gang.'

'Don't try and con us,' said the chief inspector. 'We've got you talking about drugs on tape, and it doesn't sound as if you're investigating him. Quite the contrary. We can play parts of it to you, if necessary.'

Vickers told his superior in a low voice that he had a transcript of the pub conversation with him, but Roscoe shook his head. He was reluctant to release a transcript or play the full recording. He believed it was bad practice to reveal the full extent of their knowledge so early in the interviewing process.

'Early on in the conversation,' Roscoe went on, 'you're caught saying, "The West Siders are trying to muscle in on our trade." That doesn't sound like the words of a UCO. Sorry, Mr Huckabee, an undercover operative. Sounds more like the words of a gang member or even a gang master.'

'Don't be ridiculous, Chief Inspector,' said Trent. 'I've simply learnt some of the language used by these criminals for easier acceptance by them. They've got to trust me before they'll let me into their confidence.'

Vickers sneered. 'That's a nice try, but it won't wash. Later in the dialogue, you're heard talking about a lawyer named Giles, who happens to be the solicitor hired by Stevens and Kumar to get their case reopened. You're talking about giving him false leads. You'd hardly be talking like that to a convicted criminal like Blake if you were running an undercover police operation.'

'Good point, Tom!' said Roscoe. 'I'm afraid, Inspector Trent, you'll have to do better than that. We searched Blake's home in Handsworth and guess what we found in his loft?'

'Go on. Tell me. A portrait of my mother?'

'No. A Beretta 9000S which our ballistics team have been examining. We believe this was the weapon used to kill O'Sullivan – not the gun your CID came up with.'

Trent shook his head and looked down at the table.

'We were assured by our experts that Winston Stevens' gun was the one used to kill O'Sullivan,' he said. 'The jury accepted that. End of story.'

'No, it's not the end of the story, I'm afraid,' said the chief inspector, who was becoming tired of Trent's scornful attitude. 'The gun you're referring to was a Beretta 92 semi-automatic pistol which was labelled as Exhibit G and presented in court as the murder weapon. We'll need to review that ballistics evidence. But the gun found in Handsworth has definite links to the murder.'

'You haven't been to the storage vault and collected the four bullets to test with this new gun, have you?'

'No, we could've done, but we didn't need to,' Roscoe insisted.

'Your clumsy team only found four bullets at the scene,' Vickers said, 'but we now know five bullets were fired in total. Our investigator found a witness who heard five shots and we then discovered a bullet lodged in the ceiling of the dead man's home. Our ballistics expert at headquarters carried out tests with this fifth bullet. Markings on a trial bullet he fired with Blake's gun matched those on the ceiling bullet. They've got the same grooves and scratches.'

Trent gazed at them as coldly as a doctor might look at a leper.

'So you've been clever boys and found a flaw in the original case? So maybe there'll be a successful appeal and the two scumbags we arrested will be freed. That doesn't make me guilty of – what was it you claimed? Perverting the course of justice?'

Roscoe furiously hit back.

'Tyrone Blake, the man you've been cosying up to – while tenuously claiming to be infiltrating a drugs gang – has turned out to be the prime suspect behind the murder you were meant to have been looking into,' he said. 'You and Blake are thick as thieves. We've heard you reassuring him no one will guess you and Tahir Khan were involved in the killing. We'll have no problem at all getting the voice on the tape identified as yours. Blake even refers to you in a friendly way as "Seymour". So it's time you dropped your cocky attitude, matey.

'You'll find that, once our whole case has been presented, you won't have a chance in hell of getting off. You're likely to receive a lengthy prison sentence and it almost certainly means the end of your police career. Your days in the force are numbered. You may as well face facts. The game's up.'

'Look, Chief Inspector. I'm very misunderstood. I'm just a straight copper trying to do his job. I've only been running the CID office a couple of years. You can only work with the talent you've got. I'm sorry if our murder investigation didn't meet your high standards and my undercover methods have upset you. But I'll be honest – I just did the best I could.'

Roscoe tutted. 'Your CID department framed two innocent men. You were in charge throughout that time, and it begs the question: how many other innocent folk have you compiled false evidence against?'

'False evidence!' Trent scoffed. 'We were just doing our jobs.'

Roscoe looked him directly in the eyes.

'Inspector Trent, we've got you bang to rights. For the purposes of the DIR, the suspect is repeatedly shaking his head.'

'No one should fret about Stevens and Kumar,' Trent insisted. 'They're just vermin who've been up to their ears in crime for years. We can all sleep a lot more soundly with them off the streets of Birmingham.'

The chief inspector leaned back on his chair on hearing this.

'You're starting to know some of the streets of Birmingham pretty well yourself, Mr Trent,' Roscoe went on. 'Particularly the streets of Edgbaston and Aston, where your gang are peddling hard drugs.'

At this point, Mr Huckabee reminded his client it might be wise not to comment until he had listened to all that the detective had to relate.

'We've heard you boasting about "blow" and "smack" and how the city centre's been your best trading area,' said Roscoe.

'I was just worming my way into Blake's confidence,' he claimed. 'I'm not going to comment any further, as my brief's advised me.'

'Look, Inspector Trent,' said the chief inspector, 'your best course of action is to save us all a lot of time and to admit everything. That way the judge is more likely to take a lenient approach with you.'

'Stuff your bloody recording and stuff your bloody ballistics evidence,' said Trent angrily. 'D'you know what I think? I think I must've upset someone – perhaps some pathetic sleazeball I've arrested for breaking the law on my patch. They've made up a tale about me because they want their day of vengeance. And, for your part, you want to make it all stand up so you can boost your miserable crime figures. Well, I'm not playing your game and you won't get another word out of me.'

Chapter 42

A week after police arrested DI Seymour Trent and leading members of the 101 Crew, an enthusiastic young prison officer thumped loudly on a cell door at Ashwood Vale Prison.

'Innocent!' he called. 'Your visitor's arrived.'

'About bloody time!' a gruff voice inside responded. 'Visiting time's halfway through.'

'It's all right. As it's the police, we'll make sure you get plenty of time to talk. You know what they say, confession's good for the soul.'

Carl Innocent stood in front of a mirror, combing his lank, grey, greasy hair as a key turned and the door sprang open. He carefully put on his wire-framed glasses and gazed at the warder standing in the open doorway.

'Well, we'd better not keep an officer of the law waiting, had we?' said the sullen-faced inmate.

The warder, Daryl Johnson, led Innocent along the iron walkway in D Wing and down the stairway. They passed along several dingy corridors until they reached the visitors' hall where around fifty prisoners and relatives were deeply engrossed in conversation.

The room, about the size of a church hall, had cream-coloured walls and a brand-new carpet in startling purple. More than twenty tables were arranged across the room. These were surrounded by metal-based lounge chairs which were also furnished in the same bright colour.

Within seconds, Innocent spotted his visitor – the only person sitting alone. He was a clean-shaven, stocky man in a white shirt, blue striped tie and navy-blue trousers. He had short, brown hair and he was reading a magazine about British country houses. The visitor leaped up as soon as he noticed the two men striding towards him. He held out a podgy right hand, which Innocent declined to shake.

'I'm DS Thompson!' announced the visitor. 'Would you like to take that seat opposite me?' Then, turning to the warder, he grumbled, 'Bit surprised to see this country home magazine here – what with all the robbers and thieves you've got in here.'

'I'll pass on your comment to my manager,' said Johnson, taking a seat at the nearby table so he could overhear the conversation. He sat with his left elbow on the table and his face cupped in his hand, watching the two men.

'What's all this about then?' Innocent asked, after sitting down. 'I got a note from the governor's secretary. I suppose it's about the Dinwood case.'

'No. This is a totally separate matter,' said Thompson. 'Firstly, I have to ask you if you're happy to proceed with this interview on a voluntary basis?'

'Yes, well, I'm prepared to listen to you,' said the morose prisoner. 'Whether I'm going to tell you anything's a different matter.'

At that moment, the hubbub of conversation in the hall was interrupted by a loudspeaker announcement. 'Will Warder Johnson please go to the principal warders' office. Telephone call.'

'That's me. Won't be long,' said the prison officer as he walked off.

'Good. That's better. I can speak freely now,' said the sergeant.

'So what's all this about?' Innocent demanded.

'I've been sent here with a proposition.'

'Who by?'

'Don't interrupt. It'll become clear in a minute, but we haven't much time. The screw will be back in a minute. I've got some good news for you. My friends and I are going to get you out of here.'

'Who says I want to get out? I like it in here – free food, clean sheets, no work, no bills, no worries.'

The sergeant looked perplexed.

'If you're going to be like that…' he remarked, taking to his feet.

'No, hold on. Let me hear what you've got to say. Maybe I'll change me mind, with a little persuasion. Why would you and your friends want to help me get out?'

'We've got a common interest. A man by the name of Gavin Roscoe.'

On hearing this name, Innocent's face rapidly started to turn as purple as the carpet.

'That's the bastard who got me locked up here,' Innocent said with disgust. 'He's a nosy, bastard copper – sorry, no offence to you.'

'None taken,' said the visitor, whose real name was Philip Bains. 'That Mr Roscoe's upset me and my boss as well.'

'Come on. Who's this boss of yours? Obviously, another copper.'

'I can't tell you anything more,' replied the sergeant solemnly. 'But he's a man of some influence who's had to shut down his business for a while on account of that man. Mr Roscoe's got us into a lot of trouble and we both want to make sure he gets his just desserts.'

Innocent laughed.

'That Roscoe's definitely no friend of business. I've had to close my place down altogether. What's this mysterious proposition you've got then? You've got me a little intrigued now.'

'We've got a mutual interest in dealing with this man.'

'Too right. If I ever get out of here, one of my first priorities would be to sort him out. I know the tearooms where his wife works, you know, through my business days. I've got a definite score to settle with him. I'm doing life for things I ain't done.'

The sergeant smiled.

'We've heard you were caught bang to rights for killing your brother-in-law, a property developer and a retired teacher.'

'They never had the evidence. It was all circumstantial. If it wasn't for that bloody detective and his Asian sergeant, I'd never have been locked up. The real killer's still out there, for God's sake.'

The sergeant decided to overlook Innocent's questionable claims.

'Look, the warder will be back in a minute,' he snapped.

'That phone call – it was all arranged, wasn't it?' said Innocent.

'Couldn't possibly comment.'

'And I'll bet your real name's not Thompson.'

'My real name doesn't matter.'

'If your parents could hear you now.' He paused for a moment and glanced down at the lurid carpet. Then he added thoughtfully, 'One of my neighbours once had a cat called Thompson. He was a fat little bugger always getting into scrapes.'

'Watch your lip,' said the visitor.

'Only saying,' Innocent replied.

'Now listen,' said Bains. 'We'll spring you, get you a shooter, some cash and a motor, and set the satnav for Queensbridge. We can also provide a passport and an airline ticket for Spain. What d'you say?'

'And I just head for the tearooms in Queensbridge and do the rest?'

'Precisely.'

'I'll need fuel and clothes. And a phone would be nice.'

'I'll get you the latest iPhone with all the bells and whistles, shall I?'

'There's no need to be sarcastic. I'll definitely need fuel and clothes.'

'We'll make sure there's plenty of unleaded in the motor and we'll get you kitted out with clothes. We might not have much time before chummy gets back. So what d'you think, Carl?'

'Nice little plan you've got. But why not tackle the job yourselves?'

'The way my boss is thinking is, if someone like me does it and gets caught, we might go down for life. Doing time would be extra hard for a bloke like me, given my line of work. On the other hand, someone like yourself – who's already a lifer – what's going to happen? What's the worst they can do? The judge at your trial recommended a forty-year minimum term. They've thrown away the key already. You're more than likely going to end your days in clink.'

'Thanks for the encouraging words.'

'Like it or not, it's true, isn't it? Prosecutors said after the case they were looking into other deaths you might've been involved in. But with our little deal, you're going to walk out of here. After you've finished in Queensbridge, you're set to enjoy months of freedom – maybe years. You might dodge arrest and live out of reach of the law, like Ronnie Biggs. Even if you're caught, what then? They'll just add a few years to your sentence. So what?'

'I can see your reasoning.'

'Come on. You've got a score of three. What's one more? We're offering you a car and a shooter.'

'Aren't you worried I'd simply head straight for the airport and forget about the job?'

'We've thought about that, but, having read through your case notes and prison reports, we're pretty confident you'll want to settle your score first.'

'You've obviously been well briefed. You don't sound like any copper I've ever met. Most of 'em are preachy, sanctimonious prats – totally up their own arses.' He paused and then asked, 'A satnav set for Queensbridge?'

The sergeant nodded.

'I assume the motor's taxed and insured.'

'Insurance? That's a tough call – given your situation. Let's just say we'll make sure you're OK.'

'That's not what I asked. I won't use it if it's illegal. Has it got an MOT? You know what the cops are like round here. Or perhaps you don't. They've always been…' His voice trailed off as he noticed his visitor was becoming agitated.

'How should I know if it's got a bloody MOT?' said the sergeant. 'Look, I'll sort it. OK?'

'Your idea's got legs, that's for sure,' Innocent admitted. 'How will you get me out of here though?'

'You're due at the Crown Court in Birmingham next Monday, aren't you?'

'Yes, I'm a witness in the Dinwood case.'

'Well, something might happen on your journey. That's all I'm saying.'

'I see,' said Innocent, thoughtfully. There was a pause. Then he said, 'Mr Polkinghorne won't be very happy.'

'Who the hell's Mr Polkinghorne?'

'He's the prosecuting QC. I'm his star witness.'

Bains was about to respond but noticed Daryl Johnson hurrying back towards them.

'Quick. Have we got a deal?'

'Looks like we have,' replied Innocent as the warder resumed his seat at the next table.

'Sorry about that. Some time-waster. Had to go right to the other end of the building. So, Sergeant, has Mr Innocent been helpful?'

'Yes, I think so,' said Bains, glancing at Innocent's face for any signs of a reaction. 'There's just a couple of suspicious deaths I had to ask him about. I don't believe he's connected with either.'

'And he behaved himself, I hope?'

'Most definitely. He was very helpful, and I trust he's going to be even more helpful in the future,' he said enigmatically.

The sergeant stood up with his attention still focused on the prisoner.

'We'll be making contact with you again soon, Mr Innocent,' Bains declared. 'Thank you for your time and we trust you'll continue to cooperate with us in the future.'

'Now you've explained it all, you can bank on it,' Innocent replied. Then he added, 'Make sure it's a good runner.'

The warder was confused. 'Good runner?' he queried.

'He's very interested in cars,' Bains said quickly, 'as you probably know. I'm getting myself one of the brand-new Fords.' Frowning, he turned to the prisoner with the words, 'Yes, it'll be a very good runner.' Then he walked away.

Johnson led his prisoner back along the maze of corridors. As they clambered back up the metal stairs, the warder remained puzzled.

That's strange, he thought to himself, I never realised Innocent was keen on cars. Maybe I can get him interested in the mechanics course.

Chapter 43

Brett Dawson was queuing to buy a drink at the CID's regular drinking haunt, The Golden Fleece, when he was astonished to see Sunita Roy walk in.

'Hi, Sarge,' he yelled. 'Can I get you a drink?'

'An orange juice, please,' she said as she glanced around. 'I'm looking for the DCI. You haven't seen him, have you?'

'He's over in the corner.'

She found the chief inspector in an ebullient mood. He was drinking a double Jameson on the rocks while speaking to Tom Vickers. After a few minutes, Dawson returned from the bar. He placed another glass of whiskey in front of Roscoe and handed Sunita her drink.

'He's knocking them back,' she whispered.

'Yes,' Dawson said as they sat down a few seats from the chief inspector, 'I've noticed his intake's increased of late. Hope he's not driving home tonight.'

Roscoe waved and smiled at his sergeant.

'Good to see you,' he yelled. His voice was nearly drowned out by the sound of chatter and the pub's amplified music.

She squeezed past a group of women and settled onto the upholstered bench-seat beside her boss.

'Sir, I wanted to check we've done all we can to notify the airport police and Interpol about Betina Fischer,' she said.

'Don't worry about that now, Sergeant. It's seven o'clock,' he replied, taking a sip of whiskey. 'I can find out the latest on that tomorrow. Tom and I are celebrating. Trent's girlfriend's going to give evidence against him. Excuse me.'

The chief inspector made his way to the gents' toilet, which was at the back of the open-plan pub.

'Is the boss all right?' she asked Vickers, who leaned across the table towards her.

'He's fine.'

'I hope he's getting a taxi home.'

'He will.'

'What's all this about Polly?'

'We've had a call from her solicitor. She now wants to give evidence against Trent in return for a lighter sentence herself,' Vickers said as he took a swig of lager. 'We hope she's going to tell us about his involvement with drugs, the O'Sullivan case and the two arson attacks. She may even be able to help us nail Blake for shooting me in Sedgeworth. The other news is that, after arresting Blake and searching his house, Omar Khalid found not only the Beretta used to shoot O'Sullivan, but also a Glock 17 connected with the Filipowski shooting and a key which fits the front door in Whitstone Drive.'

'Excellent news!' she said.

'What's excellent news?' asked Dawson, who had been trying to eavesdrop on their conversation.

'Omar's found things at Blake's house linking him to the Filipowski shooting.'

Dawson shrugged his shoulders. 'We know the pair were dead before he went round there.'

'Of course,' she said, 'but we can still pin attempted murder and arson on him.'

Vickers leaned across again. 'I've had Giles Farquhar on the phone. He's very pleased with what we've achieved. He's confident he'll win an appeal on the strength of the new evidence we uncovered and will get the two wrongly convicted men out of jail. He'll then seek compensation for wrongful arrest and prosecution.'

'I hope he's successful,' she said. 'They should never have been taken to court in the first place.'

'Who shouldn't have been taken to court?' asked Roscoe as he returned to his seat.

'Stevens and Kumar,' she replied.

'Oh. I thought you meant Trent for a minute.'

'Sir, what is the latest on Trent and his gang?' asked Sunita, before sipping her orange juice.

'They've all appeared in court twice so far. Naturally, bail's been turned down for Trent and Blake. But Bains has got a clever lawyer. He was granted bail and so have all the others, including Polly Cook and Dougie Mott.'

'I take it Trent and Bains have been suspended from their posts?'

'Naturally. All four police employees have been relieved of their duties. I'm really pleased for our Tom. It's been his first major case since becoming an inspector.'

'It was important to catch Trent,' said Sunita.

'Do you know that corrupt officer was up to more tricks than you can imagine?' her boss continued. 'But he was really shocked to find we still had a copy of the pub recording. He had the audacity to claim he'd been running an undercover operation to infiltrate the drugs scene in Birmingham when we confronted him with the tape.'

Vickers laughed. 'How ridiculous. It's not his job to investigate the drugs trade – that's the job of the drug squad.'

'Exactly,' said Roscoe. 'Anyway he knows now we've got a ton of evidence. He's a desperate man, trying to find excuses.'

Vickers interrupted to say, 'He was full of invective for the guvnor. Swore he'd get his own back.'

'Yes,' said Roscoe. 'Never mind. Let's talk about more cheerful subjects. How do you rate the Blues' chances against Queen's Park Rangers tomorrow, Tom?'

'I'd better go,' said Sunita. 'Not meaning to be rude, but football's not my thing and, in any case, someone's coming round for a meal.'

'Enjoy your evening,' shouted Roscoe, while Vickers and Dawson also yelled goodbye greetings.

She turned and waved before vanishing into the night.

* * *

Sunita rushed up the stairs to the kitchen of her first floor flat in Warwick and switched on the gas hob.

Glancing at her watch, she searched the cupboards for some vital ingredients, put an apron round her waist and spent the next ten minutes cooking a spicy mushroom and broccoli stir-fry.

She was serving up the food on two heated plates and preparing to sprinkle cashew nuts on the top when her doorbell rang.

After wiping her hands and hanging up the apron, she rushed downstairs and opened the front door. She beamed at her friend Samir as he leaned forward and kissed her gently on the right cheek.

'You've arrived just at the right time,' she said. 'I've just finished cooking.'

'It's so kind of you to invite me here for a meal,' he said, following her up. 'Hey, that smells good.'

'It's just a stir-fry,' she said. 'To be honest, I only got back from work a short time ago.'

She fetched the plates from the kitchen and they both sat down at her living-room table to eat.

'I hope the mushrooms are OK,' she said.

'They look fine,' he insisted, wrapping some noodles round his fork. 'Hey, it's a lovely place you've got and it's such a lovely street. This is really tasty.'

'One of my more successful stir-fries. I'm sorry I haven't been able to see you for more than two weeks. I've been involved in a really tough case.'

He put down his fork. 'Yes, you were mentioning a little bit about it on the phone when you called me last night – the two deaths.'

'Yes. Unfortunately a key suspect is abroad, so I can't really take things forward at the moment. That's why I thought it would be a good idea to meet now.'

'Oh, Sunita, I must confess I've been worried about whether we would ever see each other again.'

Sunita put her cutlery down. 'Whyever would you think that?'

'Because of something you said when I was dropping you off here on that Sunday I last saw you.'

She looked confused. 'What was that?'

'You told me there was something you ought to tell me. But, before you could, your DCI phoned and informed you about the incident in Balsall Common.'

Sunita looked blank. Then her eyes lit up.

'Oh, I know what I was going to say. That if we were to continue to see each other, you'd have to be very understanding at times. I've got a very demanding job and it can involve very unsocial hours. Your job with computers is different – it's more nine to five. But my work is the kind that can take a toll on a relationship. I'm very ambitious, Sam, and I don't think I'll ever change.'

Samir leaned back in his chair and grinned broadly. 'Oh, is that all it was? I am concerning myself about this for more than a fortnight, thinking you were going to say you weren't wanting to see me again.'

'Of course not,' she replied. 'I think you're a wonderful person. I just wanted you to understand how difficult life can be for me at times.'

She reached across the table and clutched his hand. Then she kissed him.

Chapter 44

Welcome to the news at one. Security's been tightened around a city's crown court this afternoon where a serial killer's due to give evidence at a murder trial. Extra police have been drafted in at Birmingham Crown Court, where forty-seven-year-old Carl Innocent is appearing as a witness.

Innocent was jailed for life two years ago after being convicted of three murders in the Warwickshire village of Norton Prior. The prisoner, who recently changed his name by deed poll, has been summoned to appear by Arnold Polkinghorne QC, representing the Crown in the Francis Dinwood murder case.

Energy companies were battling to restore power to large parts of the North of England today after heavy rain and gales overnight brought down power lines and caused widespread flooding…

Detective Sergeant Bains flicked off the car radio. He glanced towards the driver sitting beside him, Tahir Khan. They had turned off the main Pershore Road in Edgbaston and were parked in a black Audi Q7, which had tinted rear and side windows, a few metres along a side road, Brunel Way, close to Calthorpe Park.

'Shouldn't be long now,' Bains remarked. 'I've got three guys on look-out and we should hear from them the minute the convoy appears.'

'Bloody cold today,' moaned Khan, who like Bains was wearing suitably dark clothing.

'Yes, but at least it's stopped raining.'

'Why did you decide we should stop here? I'd have thought it would've been easier to do this little job in a quiet country lane.'

'Well, Seymour found out the main route they usually take up from the Vale is along the A441 and then they take the inner ring road. They're mainly fast roads and, of course, there's a chance they'd be on a blue light. The only part of the journey where they're forced to slow down is here. They turn off the Pershore Road and use this street as a cut-through to Bristol Road at the other end. So this is our only chance before they hit the dual carriageway.'

'How does Seymour know they always come along here?'

'We've got an insider. The prison driver's wife used to live round here, so he's very familiar with the area. There's an added bonus for us – there aren't many shops round here, so there's not much in the way of CCTV.'

Just then Bains' mobile phone rang. It was Leroy, one of the new gang members Blake had recently taken on. The sergeant looked at his watch.

'What did you say, Leroy? … It's just coming up to twenty past one and they've just passed the zoo at Cannon Hill? … OK, thanks, mate,' said Bains as he ended the call.

'I'll just let the brothers know,' he told Khan, while pressing buttons on his phone.

'Hello, is that Gabriel? … Hi, it's Phil. They'll be here in a couple of minutes. Are you both ready? … Good. Don't forget to dispose of your phone afterwards … OK, so you know exactly what to do? … Good man!'

The minutes ticked by. The two men put black balaclavas over their heads. The sergeant, who had a Beretta pistol on his lap, was becoming nervous. The adrenalin was beginning to flow. He kept glancing over his shoulder at Khan's sawn-off shotgun on the back seat and watching in the side mirror as the traffic passed slowly along the Pershore Road behind.

Suddenly they became aware of a siren in the distance. The noise became louder until the pair spotted a glimmering blue light near the junction. Khan flashed his headlights on and off to alert Gabriel and Dominik Nowak – who were two hundred metres ahead at the entrance to the Bedford housing estate. The Nowaks started up their hired box lorry and waited in anticipation just a few metres back from Brunel Way.

Within seconds, a police motorcycle appeared at the Pershore Road junction, where its rider halted briefly to cast his eyes around. Then he set off along the cut-through.

After he had travelled at least a hundred metres up the street, two constables in a police Ford Focus with its siren blaring turned the corner, followed closely by a white prison van with blacked-out windows. A solitary officer in a police Range Rover brought up the rear.

The motorcyclist continued past the entrance on the right to the Bedford estate, but no sooner had he gone by than the eighteen-tonne lorry lurched across the road, at once separating the rider from the police car.

The lorry careered directly in front of the car driver – forcing him to slam on his brakes.

The van driver behind was compelled to do the same. The lorry, which was eleven metres long, completely blocked the road. Despite the police driver turning off his siren and hooting his horn instead, the man in the cab made no attempt to shift it.

Then, just as the constable was thinking of stepping out of the car to have words with the driver, he was stunned into shock. Part of the lorry's blue webbing was hauled back and a man in a black balaclava strode across the lorry's floor – like an actor taking to the stage in a chilling melodrama.

What really caught the attention of the two officers in the Focus was that the slim man, Dominik Nowak, was grasping a double-barrelled shotgun. He pointed his menacing weapon at the car's windscreen, ordering the constables to remain inside.

Meanwhile, at the other side of the lorry, his masked older brother Gabriel was confronting the motorcycle escort, who had spun round and driven back. Gabriel, who was stockier than his brother, was brandishing an Uzi submachine gun. He fired several shots at the outrider, striking him in the upper body and sending him crashing to the ground. Then he joined his brother on the other side of the lorry – so both their guns were trained upon the two policemen.

As soon as they felt it was safe to do so, two women rushed from a nearby house and tried to revive the stricken motorcyclist, who by now had become unconscious. The pair launched a battle to save his life.

If the two officers in the Ford Focus had looked over their shoulders, they would have seen that two more thugs – Khan and Bains – had driven up behind the Range Rover. These two masked men leaped from their car. Bains pointed his Beretta at the Range Rover's driver, while Khan threatened the man at the wheel of the prison van, demanding he wind down the window.

'Let the prisoner out!' he screamed through the open window.

The driver shook his head.

'Can't, mate. The doors are controlled,' he said defiantly.

Bains fired his Beretta into the tarmac, just below the man's door, as a warning shot.

'You'd better get him out or you're dead!' the sergeant yelled.

The burly driver quickly became compliant.

'Better do as he says,' the driver mumbled to the female colleague sitting beside him.

The woman stepped out of the van reluctantly, walked round to the rear and began fumbling with the door-lock. Khan followed her and watched as she grappled with the mechanism.

While the guard was struggling to open the van doors, Dominik Nowak jumped down from the lorry. He had noticed one of the constables in the Focus had moved his hand towards his police radio. Fearing he might set off a panic button, he angrily smashed the car's windscreen using the butt of his gun. Both constables were showered with fragments of glass.

'Just one false move and you both get this!' he announced maintaining a threatening pose with his gun.

The officer who had raised his hand quickly lowered it again.

'You're making a big mistake,' said the constable in the driving seat of the Focus. 'This whole place will be crawling with Old Bill in a matter of moments.'

'Shut your mouth!' screamed Dominik. 'And keep it shut.'

Khan began to get agitated with the prison guard. He feared she might be playing for time.

'You'd better hurry up, love!' he shouted.

But he needn't have worried. A few seconds later, looking bewildered and agitated, Carl Innocent emerged from the dark recesses of the van and stepped out onto the middle of the road, blinking.

Khan then pointed the gun at the guard's head to make her unfasten Innocent's handcuffs. Perspiration was running down the prisoner's cheeks. He straightened his new pair of glasses and swept his greasy grey hair away from his eyes.

'Took your bloody time, didn't you?' he muttered, rubbing his wrists. 'It was hell in that sweatbox.'

'Come on!' Bains ordered him. 'Get in the car!' Then, careful to avoid calling out anyone's name, he bellowed, 'Come on, everyone!'

As Khan returned to the Audi's driving seat, Dominik Nowak kept his gun trained on the hapless constables. But, once assured his brother had abandoned the lorry and had safely slipped into the back of the Audi with Innocent, he shot the front tyres on both police vehicles and the prison van.

Dominik Nowak and Bains joined their associates in the Audi, Khan turned it round and they all sped off together towards the Pershore Road.

Khan, who had removed his balaclava in order to drive, forced his way out onto the busy road, turned right and headed out of the city. The whole audacious operation had lasted barely five minutes.

'Where's this bloody motor you promised?' Innocent asked Bains as they followed the traffic along the road towards Selly Oak.

'Ungrateful bastard, aren't you?' said Bains from the front passenger seat. 'We get tooled up and risk our lives for you. I'd have at least expected some thanks.'

'Don't assume I'm not grateful. You've given me a few hours of freedom – maybe a few days if I'm lucky. But I'm an old hand at this. I'm going to get caught and they'll just add more years to my sentence.'

'Strange time to be having second thoughts, Carl,' Khan remarked, as he overtook a bus.

'I'm not having second thoughts. It's great to be out. I just want to get in the car and get going,' Innocent complained as he sat hunched up between the Nowak brothers. 'I've got too many unhappy memories of the streets around here.'

'Those coppers back there were speechless!' said Gabriel Nowak. 'They were this much away from ploughing into the lorry.'

'That police driver did have to get a bit lively with the foot-break, didn't he?' said Bains, laughing. 'It was a good idea of ours getting the lorry, wasn't it, Gab? And just as well you knew how to drive one.'

'Yeah, but I never had an HGV licence,' said Gabriel.

'You never had a licence?'

'No. Me dad drove lorries and taught me. But I've never had a licence.'

'It's never stopped you nicking them,' Khan pointed out.

Then, as the car passed the entrance to Birmingham Wildlife Conservation Park, Khan drove into a quiet, tree-lined side turning on the right.

'Here we are,' he said. 'And there's Leroy.'

'Where's me motor?' asked Innocent, anxiously. 'Oh God! What have you got me? A bloody Fiat Punto?'

'It's a really good, reliable motor,' said Bains.

Innocent walked over to the black Punto parked at the side of the road. He looked it up and down contemptuously.

'I suppose it'll have to do,' he said.

'It's a smart little motor,' said Bains. 'You're not going to the Ritz in it, are you? It'll get you where you want to go.'

'Back in the slammer probably,' Innocent muttered to himself. Then out loud he said, 'It's nicked, yeah?'

'Of course,' said Bains. 'But we haven't had time to change the plates.'

Innocent studied the registration letters and numbers. Then he opened the driver's door.

'Judging by the reg number, it's from the Highlands,' he said. 'It smells like some jock's puked up in the back of it.'

Bains ignored Innocent's flippant remark. He was losing patience with the man.

'Leroy, can you give him the keys?' Bains asked. Then, turning back to Innocent, he continued, 'There's fresh clothes in the back. There's a gun and ammo in the glovebox. Look, here's the keys and three hundred quid in cash. It's got a full tank. Have you driven one of these?'

'I'm sure I must have, a few years ago.'

'I haven't got you a phone, but to be honest, it could prove a problem anyway because it might give your location away.'

'No probs. It's got a satnav?'

'It's got a satnav.'

The words had only just left Bain's mouth when two police cars raced along the main road past them. They were heading in the direction of the incident scene with their sirens blaring and blue lights flashing. The gang members also heard the distant sound of a helicopter.

'Gotta go, Carl,' said Bains, tapping him on the arm in a gesture that was intended to be friendly. 'Good luck!'

Khan had been revving up the engine of the Audi, which had been stolen in south Birmingham two days before. He began calling out for Bains to hurry. Bains raced towards the car and jumped in. Khan at once sped off.

'Thank God for that!' said Bains. 'That man could drive you mad. Gab, you know that copper on the bike. D'you think he'll be OK?'

'He's bound to be all right,' said Gabriel. 'They've got bloody Kevlar vests these days, haven't they?'

'Up to a point. Come on,' said Bains. 'We've got to get rid of this car. Every copper in the Midlands is going to be on the look-out for it now.'

Chapter 45

Gavin Roscoe was unprepared for the bitterly cold weather when his car glided into the main car park on the bleak housing estate in the centre of Birmingham.

As he stepped onto the tarmac, which was less than two miles from the scene of the prison van escape, he was struck in the face by a blast of icy wind whipping between the tower blocks. He felt a shiver as he locked the vehicle.

Here he was, back on the Cumberland Estate – the complex of tower blocks, low-rise flats and maisonettes he had once patrolled as a young policeman during the few short years he spent with West Midlands Police.

A mother with a bawling child in a pushchair startled him by emerging out of nowhere. She scurried past, wrapped up in a thick, brown winter coat, cursing the infant beneath her breath as she passed.

Roscoe strode towards ten-storey Kenton House. He turned the corner of the building and reached the entrance. He then climbed the single step into the communal porch, pushed his way through the glass door and took the lift to the fourth floor. This time he was heading for Liam Clancy's flat.

While walking along the balcony, it dawned on him that the last time he'd visited the estate had been when Pat Clancy had first introduced him to his grandson.

How much had been achieved by Operation Temple since that time. Liam had helped them gain vital details of Seymour Trent's criminality. Both Clancys had played a pivotal role.

However, Roscoe still felt ashamed that Liam's life had been put at risk. He doubted if there was any form of compensation available and decided he would not mention the subject as he reached Liam's front door.

Two CCTV cameras had been installed on the wall above the entrance, giving the occupier clear views of any approaching visitors. Liam, who was dressed simply in a shabby white T-shirt and blue jeans, flung the door open the moment the bell was pressed.

'Mr Roscoe!' said Liam. The untidy state of his ginger hair suggested he had only just got out of bed. 'Come in, come in, come in. It's great to see you.'

He led his guest along a gloomy hallway. Thumping music was coming from the living-room at the end of the corridor.

Liam had clearly been watching some scantily clad girl gyrating to the music. He walked over and switched it off.

'How are you, Liam?' Roscoe asked.

'Oh, I'm just fine,' he replied, picking up his mobile from the end of the brown, leather settee. 'Sit yourself down. I'll call Grandad. He'll be so pleased you're here.'

'I needed to make sure you were OK,' Roscoe added.

Liam explained how his wounds were gradually healing. Altogether he had spent six days in the hospital and had been home for the past twelve. Roscoe became ill at ease when the young man confided that officers from the West Midlands force had been to see him.

'How long did they interview you for?' he asked.

'Oh it was only twenty minutes or so. It was a young constable. He seemed genuinely concerned about my injuries.'

'What did you say about the incident itself?'

'I just told him I'd been to Calthorpe Park to meet a group of friends. We'd had a drink and smoked and then split up.'

'He believed you?' Roscoe asked.

'I think so. I explained I was walking home – it's only a couple of miles or so – when this group of lads came round the corner. He asked me if I could recall any faces.

He said, "We could drive you round the area or show you some photographs." I told him it would be no good. I didn't really remember anything much of the incident.'

'You didn't see who attacked you?'

'It happened so quick, Mr Roscoe, and they came up behind me,' said Liam, as he stretched himself out across the length of the settee. 'Two or three were black guys. Two or three were white. I wouldn't know them if I saw them again, and that's the honest truth. It was just so quick. It was lucky I never had any drugs with me.'

'Yes, very lucky – or Tom Vickers and I might've had some serious explaining to do.'

'The copper also wanted to know why they'd done it,' Liam continued. 'I just said I'd no idea. "Maybe they didn't like my face," I told him.'

The pair then heard the sound of a bunch of keys rattling outside Liam's front door.

'Here's Grandad now,' he said.

Pat Clancy, who clearly had his own key to the flat, strolled into the room carrying a white supermarket carrier bag containing several bottles of spirits. Roscoe stood up to greet him.

'Gavin! Great to see you!' he exclaimed, reaching out to shake the detective's hand. 'I've read in the papers about a detective inspector who's been arrested in a corruption probe. Seems like a good reason to celebrate.'

'Any excuse will do for you, Pat!' said Roscoe.

'No, seriously now,' said Clancy, who appeared to have been drinking already. 'You and Liam have done the world proud. They should lock up bastards like that DI – excuse my language – and throw away the key.'

He lowered his burly frame onto the second armchair and removed one of the bottles from his bag.

'Look at that, Gavin!' said his old friend, who looked somewhat dishevelled in his open-neck white shirt and crumpled grey trousers. 'This is the real stuff. A Jamaican friend of mine's just brought it over from the Caribbean.'

'Rum, is it?' asked Roscoe.

Clancy screwed up his face.

'Not just rum, Gavin. This is the genuine Barbados angel-juice and the good news is it's got to be drunk.'

'Don't forget me, Grandad,' said Liam.

'Sorry, Liam. You're only getting a taster. You're still on the recovery list.'

'Look, Pat, I'll be straight with you,' said Roscoe. 'I only called round to check on how Liam was doing. It's really great to see you both, but I think I'm going to make a move. Helen's dad's got his retirement party tonight and I promised to be there.'

'Bring the old boy up here,' said Clancy. 'I'll give him a tot of this rum. It'll knock his socks off.'

'It might put the whole idea of retirement out of his head!' said Roscoe with a laugh. 'No, it's kind of you, Pat, but I'll have to say no, even though I never really got on with the old codger. I've got to drive back. I'll be in deep trouble if I miss this party.'

'Come on, Mr R,' said Clancy. 'Look, there's some fizzy Coke in the kitchen. It'll go lovely with it. I'll fetch it.'

While his grandfather was out of the room, Roscoe asked Liam about the youth who turned up at the hospital inquiring about a patient named Lee.

'Oh, it was OK in the end, Mr Roscoe,' said Liam, smiling. 'It was just someone with my wages. I bumped into him in the street the other day and it was all sorted out. So nothing to worry about.'

At that moment, Pat Clancy came back. He handed Roscoe a large glass tumbler filled with rum, Coke and ice.

'Get that down you, Gavin!' he commanded, placing the glass on a small table next to the detective's chair. 'There's plenty more where that came from.'

Roscoe rose to his feet. He smiled at his friend, patting him on the arm.

'Look, it's very kind of you, Pat, but I've really got to go. I only called in to see how Liam was. I'm so pleased he seems well on the way to recovery. Goodbye to you both! Don't worry. I'll see myself out.'

Chapter 46

The strident sound of the 1969 rock classic *I'm Free* by The Who reverberated around the Apollo Tearooms. They'd also played *My Generation* by the same group, *The Last Time* by the Rolling Stones and *Hello Goodbye* by the Beatles.

'I hadn't realised so many songs from Grandad's generation were about retirement,' Mel Roscoe remarked as she slumped down into a chair.

Her brother George, his fiancée Amanda and their friend Sean Munro smiled at one another.

George had proudly introduced Amanda to his grandparents and their friends. But as the drinks flowed and the voices of the revellers grew louder, the younger party guests had decided to repair to their quiet corner.

'George, I liked the gift your mother gave your grandad,' said Sean.

'Oh, the saucepan rack so he can hang up his saucepans for good. Yes, very apt for a retiring catering boss. But, knowing our grandad, he's not going to give up using saucepans in his retirement.'

'He's always cooked lovely meals,' said Mel. 'There were other funny gifts,' she added. 'I liked the clock that says, "Who cares what time it is?"'

'The cake was lush,' said Amanda. 'What did it say on the icing? "How can we cater without you?"'

George took a sip from a glass of beer. 'Hey, did you all hear about the escaped prisoner?'

'No. What's happened?' asked Mel.

'That psychopath that killed three people in Norton is on the loose.'

'My sarge sent me a message about it,' said Sean. 'He broke out of a prison van in Edgbaston. We've all been told to keep a look-out.'

'It's turned into a huge manhunt,' George went on. 'All the Midlands forces are on alert for him. They think he's somewhere in Brum because he's got strong ties to the city. Dad and his sergeant helped put him behind bars, you know.'

'Doesn't his wife still live in Norton Prior?' asked Sean.

'I'm not sure,' said George. 'They were both living round here at the time of the murders. If he's got any sense, he'll be as far from here and the prison as he possibly can be.'

'Actually, talking of Dad,' Mel said. 'I can't understand where he's got to. He promised Mum he'd definitely be here.'

'Perhaps he's got held up on a job,' Sean suggested. 'Maybe he's been called in to help find this prisoner.'

'It's possible,' said George. 'But I heard him promise Mum he'd be here as well.'

Mel laughed and said, 'I heard Grandad going on about it. "It's not like Gavin to miss a drink," he kept saying.'

Mel stood up and strode towards the window. She had heard the sound of a vehicle stopping close to the building.

'That might be his car now,' she announced as beams of light from headlights flickered around the drawn curtains. She knelt on a chair, pulled back one of the curtains and peered out into the murky night. A dark car was parked outside. As its driver turned the lights off, she discounted it as being her father's BMW.

'No, it's not him,' she said with a sorrowful tone to her voice.

It turned nine o'clock. Over the sound of the stereo system, George realised he could hear the phone ringing behind the counter.

'Mel, go and answer it, will you?' he said, tugging her arm. 'It might be Dad.'

'Is it ringing? Oh, it is.' Mel stood up and hurried over to the phone.

'Tearooms?' she said, picking up the handset.

* * *

The chief inspector disliked breaking promises. He had fully intended earlier in the day to arrive at the tearooms in good time for his father-in-law's party. But sometimes circumstances ruled against him. Now he had the onerous task of explaining his absence to his family.

'Mel!' he said as the strains of music echoed down the phone. 'How's the party going?'

'It's fine, Dad. Where are you?'

'Listen. I'll have to be quick because I've borrowed someone's phone,' he replied. 'I got a cab and we've broken down.'

'I'll just go and get Mum,' said Mel, placing the handset down on the counter.

She made her way into the back room where her grandfather, Dennis, and her grandmother, Carol, were still sitting at the head of the main table. Helen, looking glamorous in a mauve, patterned party dress, hurried to pick up the phone.

'Gavin? Where are you?' she asked.

'I'm so sorry, darling,' he said. 'I got a minicab back from Brum and we've broken down in the middle of nowhere.'

'What's happened to your car?'

'Nothing. It's just that you know how worried I've been about Pat's grandson, Liam. They talked me into having a couple of drinks. I didn't want to drive, so Pat arranged a cab.'

'Whereabouts are you?'

'I'm near Redditch. There's another cab on the way, so I'll be with you soon. Pass on my best wishes to your dad.'

'All right,' she said. 'Be as quick as you can.'

* * *

'Dad's been delayed, has he?' asked George, who had been sitting too far away to overhear the conversation.

'Yes,' Mel said. 'He's had a drink, so he took a cab and it's broken down.'

'It's wiser not to drive if you've had a drink,' Sean remarked.

'That's right,' said George. 'Dad would never risk his licence. I expect he'll be here shortly.'

By a quarter past eleven, the party had ended and taxis began to arrive. Helen, George and Mel ventured out into the high street so they could say goodbye to the Lloyds on the pavement.

'Wonderful meal, dear,' said Carol Lloyd. 'Don't worry about Gavin. I'm sure he did his best to get here.'

'These things happen,' said Helen.

She kissed them both on the cheek while observing a black Fiat Punto gliding to a halt across the street. Its driver seemed to be watching them. But she ignored him and turned back into the restaurant.

Shortly afterwards, most of the guests had left and Helen locked up. She drove back to her home in Woodside Way with Mel and several boxes containing leftover food. Sean Munro followed in his car with George and Amanda as passengers.

They were all back at home by half past eleven. George, Amanda and Mel had retired for the night. But Sean and Helen sat in the living-room, drinking coffee and talking. She had made up a bed for him in the spare room upstairs.

'How are you getting on at work?' she asked.

'To tell you the truth, Mrs Roscoe, I'm loving it. Both George and I have the same ideas. We want to help people and make a difference. And I've got ambitions. I want to move to Coventry or Stratford and make a name for myself. I really believe I could rise to the top – just like my dad.'

Just as he spoke these words, they were both startled to hear someone knocking loudly on the front door.

Chapter 47

Thrown off guard by the sound of a late-night visitor at the door, Helen Roscoe went to the window and peered out into the dark February night. She strained to see who could be standing outside her house at twenty minutes past twelve. But she could only see a reflection of her own face and the living-room behind her.

'It's a bit late to receive visitors,' she muttered.

Sean Munro put down the coffee he was drinking. He stood up and joined her at the window.

'It's probably your husband,' he suggested.

'No. He wouldn't knock – he's got a key,' she said.

As she spoke, the caller knocked twice more.

'Let me go and see who it is,' said Sean in a quiet voice. He strode into the hall and peered through the door's frosted glass.

'Who is it?' he demanded.

'Sorry to bother you,' a deep voice responded. 'Gavin?'

'Who are you? It's gone midnight,' Sean called back.

'Yes, I'm sorry it's late,' said the man.

Sean turned round and exchanged glances with Helen, who was standing behind him, nervously clutching her hands.

'Is Gavin there or Helen?' the man said.

'It's all right,' said Helen, her face brightening on recognising the voice. 'It's our next-door neighbour.'

She squeezed her way past Sean as she gradually regained her composure. She reached up, drew back the bolt at the top and pulled the door open.

'Ben, what on earth's wrong?' she asked as a white-haired man with clear-framed glasses stood beneath the glow of the outside light. 'You nearly gave me a heart attack.'

'So sorry, Helen,' said the neighbour, Ben Jordan. 'Someone's left their lights on. Just thought you ought to know. They could have a flat battery by the morning.'

Sean peered across the lawn at his Astra. Its headlights were shining onto the garage door.

'Oh, thank you,' he muttered, darting through the doorway and heading straight for his car.

Then, after switching the lights off, he returned and smiled at their visitor.

'Thank you so much,' he said.

'Think nothing of it,' said Mr Jordan as he walked off towards the garden gates.

'Yes, thank you, Ben,' Helen called after him. 'Well, Sean,' she continued, 'I don't know about you but it's definitely time for bed.'

∗ ∗ ∗

Helen lay in her nightdress beneath her duvet for what seemed like half an hour. But she was unused to sleeping alone and found it hard to nod off.

As she lay on the king-size bed, thoughts of her father's party were swirling round her head. Thoughts of her father unwrapping his gifts. Thoughts of the light-hearted speeches. Thoughts of the loud music and laughter.

Suddenly, these reflections were interrupted by a noise from the kitchen downstairs. It sounded like someone loudly closing a cupboard door. Earlier, Sean had turned down the offer of a snack. Had he changed his mind and gone to the kitchen? Was George down there, perhaps looking for some pills to settle an upset stomach?

Gradually, as the minutes passed, curiosity overcame her. She flicked on her bedside light, put on her dressing gown, slipped her feet into her slippers and opened the bedroom door. She gazed out into the dark corridor, half expecting to see the landing light on or the sight of someone hurriedly returning to their bed.

But the light was off and no one was there. She groped for the light switch and turned it on. Then, somewhat gingerly, she walked slowly along the landing and began to negotiate her way down the stairs.

Nearly every stair protested as she descended. At last, she reached the bottom where she was surprised to find light shining from under the kitchen door.

For a second, she wondered if she should venture inside. Perhaps Gavin had finally returned and had set his mind on a sandwich before bed? Again curiosity beckoned her in. She turned the handle. The door creaked open.

'Gavin?' she called. 'Gavin?'

She peered round the door. There was no one there. But someone had been there. A discarded crust from a sandwich lay on the table and the back door was wide open. Helen was bewildered.

She peered inside the fridge. As she had half-expected, some of the leftover sandwiches had been removed.

As she closed the fridge door, she noticed something strange. Two notes that she and her husband had left for each other had disappeared. Both had been held to the side of the fridge by magnets. One had said, 'Don't forget the 11 February party.' The other had said, 'Don't worry. I'll be there. G.'

She found them seconds later on the worktop on the far side of the room, beneath the picture window. She went to the back door. Had someone left the house for some fresh air? She peered out, shivering as she was struck by the cold winter's air. Everything was pitch black. Straining her eyes, she could faintly see the dark shapes of the distant trees. The only sound came from the wind rustling through the branches.

Then she was astonished to find a pane of glass in the back door had been smashed.

Bewildered, she walked back into the kitchen and at once began shaking with fear. A middle-aged man with wire-framed glasses and dishevelled grey hair was standing in the centre of the room, staring at her.

Escaped prisoner Carl Innocent was smirking as he stood in an ill-fitting, navy-blue windcheater jacket and jeans. The shock of finding a stranger in her kitchen at midnight caused her to gasp for breath. She grasped the edge of the kitchen table, fearing she might faint.

'Who in Christ's name are you?' she demanded.

He stood staring at her for a moment. Then he stepped unsteadily towards her.

'Thank you for the sandwiches. The bread weren't that fresh but I was hungry.'

'Who are you? What d'you want?' said Helen, as she struggled to regain her composure.

'I want to speak to your husband, my dear.'

'He's not here,' she said as her feelings of confusion were gradually replaced by a sense of outrage at a stranger's intrusion into her home.

Without giving her any warning, he suddenly grabbed both her wrists and held them tightly, pinching her skin. She squealed in pain.

'That can't be true. Look,' he insisted. He nodded towards the fridge notes on the worktop. Then he read the words out loud, 'Don't worry. I'll be there. G.'

'Well, he couldn't make it,' said Helen. 'He's not here. But the house is full of police, so you'd better leave quickly, whoever you are. And please let go of my wrists. You're hurting me.'

'A house full of police? I don't think so, my dear,' said Innocent. 'In any case, I ain't frightened of no cops.'

Helen wondered if she should change her tack. She sensed the intruder might be a criminal or a mental patient and decided it might be wiser to try to appease him.

'Are you still hungry?' she said.

'I ain't now,' he sneered, releasing her left arm and taking a black Glock 9mm handgun from his jacket pocket with his right hand. 'I'm only hungry for revenge. Now I'll ask you once more where Mr Roscoe is and then, if you still won't cooperate, I may start to lose my temper with you.'

'I swear on my mother's life he's not here,' Helen insisted. 'His car's not here. You can check the garage if you want. You'll see his car's not here.'

'I'm not bothered about his car,' said Innocent, releasing his grip on her right wrist. 'I'll wait for him. He's bound to show up sooner or later. I tell you what – let's move into your front room. It's not too comfortable in here.'

He indicated she should make her way to the living-room by waving the pistol's muzzle in that direction. Terrified of the stranger, she scurried through the hall and entered the front room. Innocent kept close behind her, from time to time pressing the gun into her back in order to keep her mind focused.

'What a pretty room,' he sneered. 'And such a big TV.'

'Look, who are you?' Helen asked. 'And how did you get in?'

'Never mind that,' said Innocent. 'You sit yourself down at that table near the window and I'll sit over here keeping my eyes on you.'

'L-Look, I'm very tired,' she continued. 'I've had a long day. Why don't you take some more food and go?'

'You're going to make me angry now,' said Innocent, who had made himself comfortable on one of the two settees. 'You don't want to do that, my dear. I've told you. I'm going to wait here for Mr Roscoe. I've waited a long time already.'

'You haven't been here long. I only went to bed half an hour ago,' Helen pointed out.

'Yes, but I've been waiting a hell of a lot longer than that to see Mr Roscoe. I've been waiting more than two years.'

A kernel of an idea was emerging in Helen's mind. Was this intruder a criminal that Gavin had once dealt with? Was it someone from Gavin's past with a score to settle? She was unsure, but it was one possible explanation for the terrifying experience she was going through.

At that moment, they both heard footsteps on the stairs. Somebody was coming down. Oh God, was one of her children going to join them? She suspected her life was at risk from the maniac sitting in front of her with a gun, but were her problems set to be compounded? Was the life of one of their children also going to be set at risk?

A voice was calling, 'Mum? Mum?' Then George appeared in the doorway. He stopped still in stunned silence. He had heard voices and had sensed that all was not well. Now he saw the man he vaguely remembered from newspaper pictures and TV images – the serial killer now calling himself Carl Innocent.

'You're the escaped prisoner!' said George, his words echoing round the room.

'That's right!' said Innocent, standing to welcome the new arrival.

'Careful, George!' warned his mother. 'He's got a gun!'

Chapter 48

Carl Innocent beckoned a startled George into the living-room.

'Come on in, Mr Clever Guy, and join our little gathering,' he said. 'Welcome to the Gavin Roscoe Reception Committee. Quite a reception he's going to get as well.'

'Dad's not coming!' George stated loudly, hoping his booming voice would rouse Sean. 'He phoned me just before midnight on his mobile. He's stuck in Brum, Mr Innocent, and he won't be back.'

'All right! There's no need to shout,' said Innocent. 'I'm not deaf. Looks like we've got a long wait. I tell you what, young man – I take it you're the son?'

'Yes.'

'Why don't you send a text message to your dear father and invite him round? Tell him I've got a gun pointing at your mother and not to bring any company.'

'I could do that if you like.'

'And you can show me the text before you send it,' Innocent insisted.

George began tapping at his phone.

'So here I am,' Innocent went on. 'In the home of Roscoe the Reptile, the bastard who got me locked away for crimes I never done.'

'He was part of a police team,' said George, who stopped pressing the keys. 'Other detectives played a similar role in your arrest.'

'Don't annoy me. This thing goes off,' said Innocent, who seemed to have forgotten about sending a text to Roscoe.

To prove his point, he fired a shot at the fireplace. Within the confines of the room, the blast sounded like thunder. The whole room shook. Innocent was at once surrounded by a cloud of red brick-dust which gradually settled on the floor.

'Powerful little thing, ain't it?' he said, as he stood up and paced around the room, toying with the Glock. 'Maybe I should just shoot you both and forget about Mr Roscoe. Maybe that would be fair punishment for what he's done to me and my life.'

As he spoke, a floorboard creaked somewhere above.

'What's that?'

'What do you mean?' Helen asked.

'There's someone up there. Maybe it's time for you and me to have a little wander around.'

'There's nobody else here,' she assured him.

The escaped man seemed to have made his mind up. It looked as if he would inspect the whole building. Perhaps he believed her husband was close by.

He became so wrapped up in his thoughts he was unaware Sean Munro, bare-chested and wearing just a pair of jeans, had quietly come down the stairway. The resourceful young officer had carefully rested his weight on the handrails either side to avoid stepping on the creaky wooden stairs and alerting the convict.

Helen, who could see all the way through the hall, noticed him tiptoeing towards them, like a panther stalking out his prey. To create a sudden distraction, Helen pretended she had heard the sound of an approaching car.

'This might be my husband now,' she cried.

As Innocent darted to the window and peered out, Sean, who was several inches taller than his adversary, sneaked into the room, crept up behind Innocent and pounced. He thrust his arms around the convict in a bear hug, taking his opponent totally off-guard.

Innocent staggered around for several seconds, gasping for breath, as the unknown assailant clung to his back, crushing his stomach and ribs.

George rushed forward simultaneously. He made two attempts to grab Innocent's right hand in an effort to wrestle the gun from his grasp but each time the convict managed to evade him.

The three men struggled together in front of the fireplace as Helen watched with concern. The two off-duty policemen seemed to Helen to be getting the better of the intruder as the trio spun round the room.

But after a couple of minutes, Innocent had regained his breath. Then, summoning up all his reserves of strength, he swung round sharply, ramming the man on his back against the edge of the door and forcing him to release his grip. Sean was sent sprawling across the carpet. As he fell, he struck his head against the fireplace.

The convict might have felt a sense of relief at having unburdened himself of his attacker. But George saw this moment as an opportunity. He grabbed a dining chair and struck Innocent across the head with it as hard as he could, knocking him to the floor.

Innocent was dazed. His head was bruised and bloody. But Helen sensed he had not come here, to the heart of Gavin Roscoe's world, to be beaten and humiliated by the man's family. He was still, somehow, holding on to his gun and now his time had come. Sean and the escaped prisoner staggered to their feet simultaneously.

Innocent pointed the gun at George, who was still holding the chair, then at Sean, who was approaching him. Then he aimed at George once more.

Desperately, in a bid to take control of events, Sean charged towards Innocent with all his might. Somehow, whether by accident or intention, the gun went off. The explosion shook the room.

253

Helen screamed and sat quivering in her chair, weeping. George took a step back in shock. Sean slumped to the floor, clutching his stomach. The fugitive grinned.

'Anyone else want some of this?' he snarled.

Just then, sirens could be heard faintly in the distance. Helen guessed that either Mel or Amanda had dialled 999 from their upstairs rooms. A feeling of relief swept over her. Shortly their ordeal should be over.

But, for the moment, Sean had been shot and was writhing on the floor in pain. She rushed to his side, opened his shirt and examined the wound.

The blaring sirens became louder. Innocent was aware of them now. The police were on their way. They might be there at any moment. He might be caught and returned to prison – thus ending his efforts to settle his score with Gavin Roscoe.

'Time to go!' he said.

He rushed to the front door, peered through the glass and then ran back into the living-room, where he squinted at George over the top of his glasses.

'You're coming with me, lad!' he told him. 'I might need you for a safe passage.'

He pointed his gun at George and ordered him to walk to the entrance. The convict eased open the front door. On the driveway, at the far side of the front lawn, stood Helen's Fiesta, Sean's Astra and his own stolen Fiat Punto.

The sound of the sirens was drawing nearer. Blue lights could be faintly seen, flickering among the trees along the main road.

'Come on, lad!' said Innocent, thrusting his gun into George's back.

George looked back anxiously at his faithful friend, Sean, who was now lying still on the floor in a pool of blood, and at his weeping mother, battling to resuscitate him.

Reluctantly, George stepped outside. Then Innocent followed him closely, still pressing the gun against his body.

Amanda, who had slipped on some clothes, appeared halfway down the stairs with Mel close behind in a pink dressing gown.

'George!' Amanda screamed. 'George!'

As Innocent and the young constable advanced together onto the lawn, the pair could make out a line of police cars in the lane. Then they became dazzled by portable lights. Firearms officers with flak jackets and peaked caps, holding Heckler and Koch sub-machine guns, were taking up positions behind their vehicles.

'The place is surrounded,' a voice boomed out. 'Throw down your weapon! Put your hands in the air!'

'Never!' Innocent screamed back. 'I've got Roscoe's lad, so you'd all better back off.'

* * *

George Roscoe was not afraid. He believed Innocent needed to keep him alive as a hostage. But in his mind, as they continued to move, step by step, towards the lane, he was devising a plan to distract the fugitive, giving himself a chance to flee and his police colleagues a clear view of their target.

'Hold your fire!' the police commander ordered his team as the pair drew nearer.

The seconds ticked by. The commander raised his megaphone. His voice crackled again through the early morning air.

'Carl Innocent! This is your last warning! Throw down your weapon!'

George gazed through gaps in the trees towards the main road and the fields beyond. Then suddenly he shouted to the convict, 'Look! My father's coming!'

Innocent stopped in his tracks. He gazed towards the main road. He pushed his glasses back towards his forehead in the hope of a clear view of Roscoe's vehicle appearing. Sure enough, the shape of a vehicle could be faintly seen in the distance. It was approaching the top of Woodside Way. It was heading towards them.

As Innocent stared, almost mesmerised, at the sight, George seized his opportunity. He leaped behind Sean's car and was, at least briefly, out of the madman's view.

Innocent fired two shots towards him, but they both missed George and struck the front of the Astra.

This was the moment the firearms team had been anticipating. Without waiting for any further order from their commander, all four marksmen opened fire.

The mystery car drove on past the lane, its driver none the wiser as to the events unfolding just a few metres away.

Innocent slumped to the ground in a hail of bullets with blood seeping from his head as Amanda screamed her fiancé's name again from within the house.

Two officers ran forward onto the lawn where Innocent lay still. One crouched down and began carrying out chest compressions on the convict. Two female paramedics joined them, using the man's jacket to support his head.

As the team continued their efforts to save Innocent's life, Amanda darted outside and raced across the lawn. Two doctors and two paramedics had gone inside and were attending to Sean on the carpet.

'George! George! Are you all right?' Amanda yelled.

She reached Sean's car. Her boyfriend was now standing up, leaning against the bonnet. She flung her arms around him, kissing him fondly.

'Yes, I'm OK,' said George quietly, as an armed officer came forward to speak to him.

'You sure you're all right, mate?' he asked. 'You're trembling a bit.'

'I'll be fine in a minute – now he's out of the way,' he said hesitantly.

'You've been very brave,' the officer said.

George simply shrugged his shoulders and tried to smile. Then, as they strolled back towards the front door, he noticed Amanda was shaking her head and crying.

'Oh my God, George,' Amanda sobbed, 'I think Sean's dead!'

Chapter 49

Despite becoming the victim of some occasional light-hearted banter among police colleagues in the past, Gavin Roscoe had never considered himself a heavy drinker.

Several friends had retired from the force over the years to run pubs or hotels and the easy access to alcohol had sometimes been the ruin of them. Only too well aware of the risks of alcoholism, he had avoided the temptation of embarking on drinking binges.

However, on this Monday in February, he had agreed to have two double rums with his close friend Pat Clancy and his grandson Liam. He had then let them arrange a minicab to take him to the tearooms.

The twenty-five-mile journey from the heart of Birmingham should have taken less than an hour. The Skoda Octavia Hatchback was only five years old and appeared to be in good working order. He should have arrived well in time for the last hour and a half of the party.

But, midway through the journey, after their satnav had directed them along a remote country lane, the engine stopped and the car spluttered to a halt.

'I don't understand what's wrong,' muttered the driver, a friend of Pat Clancy's called Connor. 'It's been going like a dream for the past month.'

He opened the bonnet and spent nearly an hour trying to fix it.

Then he gave up and spent another half an hour trying to contact his firm and arrange for another vehicle.

But they were in a rural valley, surrounded by trees, and his phone signal was poor.

Although Connor eventually got through, Roscoe had to visit a nearby farm and use the farmer's landline in order to call the tearooms.

'Are you feeling all right?' asked Connor as he climbed back into the car. 'I saw you were a little unsteady on your feet just now.'

'Bit of a headache,' Roscoe complained. 'I had a couple of rums with old Pat earlier on. I had a look at the label on the bottle before I left. Do you know it was eighty percent proof?'

'You'll be having a headache, right enough,' said Connor. 'Pat told me it was premium Bajan rum made from the finest molasses. He's promised me a bottle too. By the way, I think it must be an electrical fault.'

'Do you know how long it will be before the other cab gets here?'

'Should be here by one o'clock at the very latest,' said Connor.

'One o'clock? That's ridiculous.'

'Sorry, old pal. Can't be helped.'

The chief inspector got out of the car and walked about, trying to see if he could obtain a better phone signal. Eventually he realised that, if he walked fifty metres up the hill away from the trees and stood in the middle of the road, he could make and receive calls – even if the reception was intermittent.

He was astonished to discover DC Khalid had left him four text messages and two voicemail messages, appealing for him to call CID urgently. Mel had also been texting him. He quickly dialled Khalid's home number.

'Sir, Chief Superintendent Norris wants to speak to you urgently,' he said.

'Why? What's happened?'

'Carl Innocent escaped yesterday and he's been down in Queensbridge, looking for you.'

'Oh my God. Looking for me?'

'If you call the chief super, she can explain everything, sir.'

Roscoe immediately phoned Norris, who began the conversation by demanding, 'Where the hell have you been?'

'Long story,' he replied. 'I gather Carl Innocent has escaped from the Vale?'

'An armed gang held up his van on the way to Birmingham Crown Court and they whisked him away. It's a mystery how he managed to find your address and make his way to your house in Woodside Way.'

'Oh my God. Is everyone OK? Is my wife all right?'

'Your whole family's safe, Gavin, but your son's friend, PC Sean Munro, has been shot and he's in a critical condition in hospital. Innocent was taken out by the firearms squad and he's also critical. Neither is expected to live.'

'Oh, Jesus, you can't be serious. I'll have to get home straight away.'

'Where are you at the moment, Gavin?'

'I took a cab and we've broken down just north of Redditch,' he said.

'I'll send a squad car over there to pick you up and take you home,' she said. 'Just give me your location. West Midlands Police and the Home Office have already set up a joint investigation as to how the hell Innocent got out. I've been asked to play my part, so I'll be down with you later in the morning.'

'Has Sean's dad been informed?'

'I've sent DS Roy to the family home in Warwick. She'll be breaking the news to the parents.'

'Sean's mother died. It's just the father, Vincent, who worked for the Met.'

'Oh, OK. She'll find that out when she gets there. It's a terrible business, Gavin.'

'How the hell did that maniac get out of the Vale?' Roscoe shouted down the phone.

'Masked men with guns held up the prison van in Edgbaston,' said Norris. 'They blocked the road with a lorry.'

'Any idea yet who's behind it?'

'Not yet. Innocent's wife and her boyfriend were taken to a safe house yesterday as a precaution. But, judging by the latest news from the hospital, I think we can safely allow them home now.'

'Oh, for God's sake, ma'am. The guy's crazy. He should never have got out.'

'Well, it's all over for him now. About four bullets in him, from what I've heard. He was lying on your lawn for a time because the IOPC were alerted and had to call experts in. The shooting is all over the news. The word is Trent's gang might be behind the escape.'

Chapter 50

Scenes of crime officers were hard at work at the Roscoes' home, The Willows, when the chief inspector arrived there just before two o'clock on Tuesday morning.

He felt guilty that he had been away from his family in their hour of need. Guilty that his son's best friend had been gunned down at his house. Guilty that his own son had nearly been killed. And he felt guilty that his wife had witnessed a night of terror. All apparently on his account.

Tears had begun to well up inside him from the moment he had learnt of the tragedy.

But now, as he approached his home, his thoughts were being tempered by reality. It was the killer Carl Innocent – not him, Gavin Roscoe – who had brought fear and grief to Woodside Way. He himself was as much a victim as Helen, George or Sean, he told himself.

He was obliged to park a short distance away along the main road because the whole of Woodside Way had been cordoned off. A uniformed constable was standing guard at the lane's entrance, preventing anyone except residents and police from passing down it.

As he approached the cordon, he was besieged by the press, who bombarded him with questions.

'What was your reaction when you heard PC Munro had been shot?' asked Jim Trissenden from the *Queensbridge Gazette*.

'Should there be a public inquiry into Carl Innocent's escape?' a reporter from a tabloid newspaper asked.

John Singleton from Midlands TV thrust a microphone in his face. 'Have you got a message for the family of PC Munro?'

Roscoe peered towards his driveway gates, where a second constable was on duty.

'Gentlemen and ladies,' he said. 'I know you've all got a job to do, but you've got to appreciate I've been away and haven't had a chance to speak to my family. My thoughts and, I'm sure, my family's thoughts are with the victim's family at this tragic time. One of our senior officers, Chief Superintendent Norris, has told me she's coming down this morning and I think you should reserve your questions for her. Now, if you'll forgive me, I'm going in to see my family.'

He nodded at the constable, who raised a police tape so Roscoe could pass through. Unable to use the front door because of forensic work being conducted, a second constable had to escort him to his own back door. A light rain began to fall as he turned the handle and pushed the door.

Helen was in the kitchen. She threw her arms around him without saying a word. The pair hugged each other for what seemed to Roscoe like several minutes. Her annoyance at his failure to make it to the retirement party was forgotten. Instead, she felt a sense of relief that all members of their family were safe.

'I'm so sorry I wasn't here,' Roscoe said.

They were the only words he spoke as they stood silently together in the kitchen.

Then, as their initial joy at being reconciled had passed, Helen said, 'You heard what's happened?'

'Well, I've got some of the details,' said Roscoe. 'But I've not heard the full story.'

After sitting down together at the kitchen table, Helen recounted the night's distressing events. She told of the terror at finding the escaped prisoner in their kitchen – in the exact spot where they were sitting now. She told of the attempts by George and Sean to snatch the fugitive's gun and the horrific moment when Sean was shot and collapsed on the carpet.

She told of the moment George was taken hostage and ordered out of the house at gunpoint. And of George's bravery at distracting the killer while on the lawn and how Innocent fell to the ground in a hail of bullets. When she had finished, she broke down in tears.

'I was sitting with Sean for nearly an hour before bedtime,' she sobbed. 'He was telling me about his ambitions. He wanted to work in a busy town or city and planned to rise to the top, like his father. An hour later, he was lying in a pool of blood.'

'Must've been a tremendous shock for you to see him shot before your eyes,' said Roscoe, putting his right arm round her shoulder. 'Try not to upset yourself. We're going to have to think about what to say to his father and sister. They should be in the forefront of our thoughts now.'

'The paramedics said they thought he would be all right, Gavin,' she said.

'Let's hope they're right.'

He stopped talking for a moment and looked away. He recognised that, in the same way he had devoted time to help Liam recover from his wounds, he might now have to devote time to help Sean and his family overcome their ordeal. He glanced back at Helen.

'How did this maniac find our house?'

'I've been wondering about that myself. You know the black Fiat Punto parked in the lane?'

'The one the forensic people are examining?'

She nodded. 'Yes, I noticed it outside the tearooms when I was saying goodbye to Mum and Dad. He must've followed us when we came home.'

'How's George?' he asked.

'He's taken it very badly, as you can imagine. He's upstairs in his room, talking to Amanda.'

'And Mel?'

'She's gone for a long walk with her boyfriend. Obviously, she is very shaken up. The crime scene manager's been very good. He thinks they'll be finished here late this afternoon.'

'What's happened to Sean?'

'They took him to Queensbridge General.'

'I'm very worried for him,' said Roscoe. 'Most victims shot in the stomach don't make it.'

'How on earth was a serial killer like that able to escape?' said Helen. 'That's what I can't get my head round.'

'I don't know, but there'll be a full inquiry. Norris will be here later on. She's heavily involved in the investigation, and she can update us.'

'D'you want a coffee, darling?'

'That would be terrific. I need something to pep me up.'

While waiting for the kettle to boil, she looked into her husband's eyes. Her own eyes were red and stained with tears. She looked pale and drained of energy.

'Gavin, I have to ask you something,' she said. 'What happened last night came about because of your work for the police. It comes after Tom was shot in Sedgeworth. I really think it's time you decided how you want to spend the rest of your life, because we can't carry on like this.'

'Helen, this will never happen again. Carl Innocent's life is over.'

'Gavin, Carl Innocent may be on his deathbed, but there are other evil people out there. I really think you should give up your police work. Maybe you could help me run the tearooms.'

'I hear what you're saying, darling. I can imagine how awful you must feel right now. I promise you I'll give the subject some serious thought.'

'Please do, Gavin,' said Helen, as she poured him a strong coffee and handed it to him. 'The children and I have suffered enough.'

* * *

After drinking his coffee, Roscoe climbed the stairs. He stepped across the landing to George's bedroom at the front of the house and knocked gently.

'Who is it?' asked George.

'It's your father.'

'Come in, Dad,' said George, who was sitting on his bed. 'Where have you been?'

'I'm so sorry, George,' said his father, giving him a hug. 'I was in a cab and it broke down.'

'You should have been here,' George continued.

'I know and I really regret not being around.'

'We were just watching the rolling news on the BBC,' said George.

Amanda was standing by the window, holding a paper tissue in her hand.

'Good morning, Mr Roscoe,' she said.

'Hello, Amanda. Are you all right?'

'Yes. Would you like me to…' she began.

'No, it's OK. Stay right there. I just wanted to see how you both were.'

'We're fine now, Dad,' said George. 'I was meant to be back at work this morning, but the sergeant said I could take a few days off. Amanda's not due back at work until tomorrow. Dad, I feel so awful about Sean. He was such a good friend to us. He didn't know Grandad and Grandma, but he took time off to pick me and Amanda up and drive us over here for the party.

'That bullet was meant for me. It should've been me lying in a pool of blood by the fireplace.'

His father sat down on the bed next to him.

'George, you have to understand it's not your fault Sean has been seriously hurt.'

'I've been trying to explain that to him, Mr Roscoe,' Amanda said. 'But he just won't listen.'

Roscoe shook his head. He leaned forward, staring at the floor.

'You mustn't think like that, George,' he insisted. 'Sean is close to death because Carl Innocent was a selfish, blood-thirsty maniac, not because he was a lousy shot and had intended to shoot you.'

'Dad, it seems to me the whole reason he was here was to get back at you – either to kill you or a member of our family.'

'George, from what I've heard, he had ample opportunity to kill either your mother or yourself, but he didn't. He was only really interested in killing me.'

'I suppose you're right, Dad.'

'You know he's right,' Amanda added. 'Sean wouldn't want you taking the blame.'

Chapter 51

The chief inspector collected his car from the Cumberland Estate in Birmingham early on Wednesday morning and then made the eight-mile journey to St James Street.

He had taken Tuesday off in order to spend time with his family. Now he had to face once again the challenges of his job and, in particular, assume charge of the investigation into Innocent's escape and the aftermath.

Later in the week, he, Helen and George hoped to visit Sean in hospital if he had been released from the intensive care ward by then.

Facing the Munros would prove an onerous task. Vincent's dearly-beloved son had been seriously hurt while a visitor to their home. He'd had surgery for his stomach injury and now seemed to be recovering. He and his family were all hoping he would pull through.

Sean had acted in the finest traditions of the British police force – trying to protect the Roscoe family from a deranged gunman.

Roscoe could not help wondering how it would have been if George had been the one who had been badly injured.

He was in a subdued mood as he unlocked his room in CID and placed his navy-blue coat on a hanger. He turned round to find Sunita Roy hovering in the doorway.

'What is it, Sergeant?' he asked brusquely. 'I've got an appointment with the chief super.'

A heavy silence hung in the air. Then she said, 'I just wanted to say how sorry I was to hear what happened to your family, sir. I was devastated to hear of Sean Munro's injury…' Her voice trailed off.

'That's greatly appreciated. Thank you,' he said. 'There is something you can do. Later this week I want you to come with me to the prison where Innocent was being held. We need to look into all the circumstances that led to the escape.'

'I'd be happy to help, sir,' she said before returning to her desk.

Shortly afterwards, Roscoe climbed the stairs to the second floor and approached the chief superintendent's office door, which had been left partly open.

'Come in, Gavin,' yelled Norris. She was hunched over her desk, writing an email as he walked in solemnly.

'You look shattered, Gavin. These events have clearly taken their toll.'

He nodded as he drew up a chair from beside the door and sat down.

'Yes, ma'am. I didn't get much sleep last night,' he said in a low voice.

She pushed a pile of that morning's national newspapers across the desk.

'Have you seen these, Gavin?' she asked, peering towards him over the top of her glasses.

Roscoe glanced at the front pages. One tabloid headline said, 'Escaped convict shot by police.' Another banner headline screamed, 'Fiend of Queensbridge fights for life.'

But it was the headline in that morning's Birmingham regional newspaper that stood out for the chief inspector. He picked it up. Dark-haired Sean Munro's smiling face covered most of the front page. Emblazoned across the top, it said simply, 'PC Courage.'

'I like this one, ma'am,' said Roscoe.

'Yes, very apt,' said Norris, leaning back in her chair. 'I've just heard the Dinwood trial is likely to be abandoned as, without Innocent, there wasn't enough evidence to place before the jury. A waste of thousands of pounds.

Anyway, I had a word with the press yesterday when I was down in Queensbridge.'

'I know. I just hope that, as a result of all the publicity, we get some information coming in. I kept in touch with DS Roy and DC Khalid by phone yesterday. West Midlands have already had a few calls that might lead them to the hired lorry used in the escape.'

'Gavin, I gather you've got a team examining Innocent's phone and all the staff computers and laptops at Ashwood Vale?'

'That's right, ma'am.'

'We believe part of the reason he wanted to escape was because his wife had sent a "Dear John" letter to him in prison, telling him the marriage was over and she'd found someone else. He went berserk, injuring two warders and nearly strangling a doctor. When his wife saw on the news he'd escaped, she was terrified. Gavin, do we know exactly how he discovered your home address?'

'We believe he knew our family connection to the tearooms. He went there first and then must've followed the family's cars to Woodside Way.'

'Yes, as I thought. There's speculation about that in the press. I gather your son, George, has taken it all rather badly.'

He nodded. 'Yes. He was close to Sean Munro. They were at Ryton together.'

'Did you know Sean's being put up for a bravery award?'

'I'd heard murmurings, ma'am. I can't think of a better candidate.'

Chapter 52

Sunita Roy waited patiently in the car park outside police headquarters on Thursday, as her boss manoeuvred his way out of a tight parking space.

Then she jumped in and they drove off towards the market town of Evesham.

'How are you feeling now, sir?' she asked as the BMW headed through the suburban streets in the direction of the M42 motorway.

'A little better this morning, thank you, Sergeant,' he replied. 'The news about Sean Munro is a bit more positive. The doctors expect him to survive, so I've got a new impetus about me now. I really want to find out as much as I can about Innocent's escape. I owe it to myself and the two families.'

Within a few minutes, the car was travelling south along country roads into Worcestershire. Roscoe described how his family were gradually coming to terms with the terrible events three days earlier. Helen had closed the Apollo Tearooms for the week. The family had ordered a new living-room carpet and the bullet discharged into the fireplace had been removed.

'Helen's been badly affected by what happened. She may need counselling,' he explained. 'We may even have to move house if she finds it hard to cope. We'll just have to see how things pan out.'

After about twenty-five minutes, they found themselves travelling down a country lane and caught their first glimpses through the trees of the grey walls surrounding Ashwood Vale Prison.

They quickly found a parking space outside the maximum-security, male-only prison and entered the two-storey entrance block, which always reminded Roscoe of a library built in the sixties. The chief inspector approached a guard sitting behind the long counter inside the reception room. He produced his warrant card from his pocket.

'You DCI Roscoe?' the official asked curtly. 'Can you both sign in? Then, if you go through that door, someone will take you up to see the governor.'

Fifteen minutes later, a smartly dressed blonde secretary ushered the two detectives into the first-floor office of prison governor, Emlyn Griffiths-Jones.

'Good morning,' he said as he rose from behind his double-pedestal mahogany desk to greet them. 'I'm sorry we're meeting in such unfortunate circumstances. Would you both like to sit down?'

The pair seated themselves on two wooden, ladder-back chairs in the room, which reminded Roscoe of the chief superintendent's office at St James Street. A portrait of Queen Elizabeth II was hanging on the wall behind the governor.

'You know, this is the first time in living memory that one of our prisoners has escaped and we have more than six hundred men here,' he revealed. 'The only consolation for me is that it happened while he was on escort and didn't break out of these walls.'

Sunita leaned forward. 'We gather an internal investigation is under way,' she said.

'Yes, of course, as always happens in these situations. It just seems this gang of men took the police by surprise. It couldn't have been foreseen. I was told this morning Innocent's now on a life support machine, so it's looking unlikely he'll pull through.'

'We hadn't heard that,' the chief inspector admitted.

'We'd like to talk to the prison officers who dealt with Carl Innocent, if that's possible,' Sunita said. 'We'd also like to take a look at his cell.'

'Well, of course,' Griffiths-Jones said. 'We'd be glad to help in any way. There wasn't really any one officer who had responsibility for Innocent. You know, he was a very difficult man to deal with. Did you know he had to be put in solitary confinement for a short time last month? He'd received a letter from his wife about a divorce. He went ballistic. He nearly strangled the doctor.'

'There was a brief report about it in one of the tabloid newspapers,' said Roscoe.

'All right. I'll arrange for one of our senior officers to take you down to the main warders' room and you can have a chat with some of them.'

A heavily built prison officer, who gave his surname as Warner, led the pair down to the ground floor office where fellow warders relaxed during their break times.

It was modestly furnished with two white tables, wooden chairs, a blue sofa and a wide-screen TV. Three warders were sitting at a table by the door, readings newspapers and magazines. Warner beckoned them over.

'Right, guys,' he said. 'These are two detectives from Heart of England Police. They want to know about Innocent. Who wants to start us off?'

Two other warders immediately walked out of the room without making any comment.

'I'll be honest,' said one of the remaining men, putting his newspaper down. 'He was as crafty as a cartload of monkeys. You couldn't turn your back on him.'

'Had warders been checking his emails and phone calls recently?' Sunita asked.

'Yes, but he didn't have much contact with the outside world,' said a second man. 'The only thing is he had a letter from his wife in January. He went mental that day. I think that put the idea of an escape in his mind.'

'So do I,' said the first man. 'I'm sure he wanted to sort out the boyfriend. God knows how he got diverted to Queensbridge. Maybe he broke in because he was hungry. That's all I can think.'

'No,' said the second man. 'I read he'd got a grudge against the main detective who put him away.'

Roscoe said nothing to reveal it was his home that had been the scene of the shooting.

While listening to the conversation, Sunita watched the third warder, an earnest man in his late twenties who had been following every word.

'What about you?' she said suddenly. 'Did you have much to do with Innocent?'

'I'm Warder Johnson. I got to see him from time to time,' he said. 'I've been trying to get him on a training course for the past six weeks. He got thrown off the last one.'

'And did you notice anything different about him of late?' she asked. 'I mean, apart from the letter from his wife, was he in communication with anyone else outside?'

'No, he was a loner,' said Johnson. 'Spent most of his time doing the crossword. Sometimes he went to the gym. That's it.'

Sunita persisted. 'Did he have any visitors?' she asked Johnson.

'No. He used to get a few visitors when he first came here, but he'd sometimes refuse to see them. As a result, most of them stopped coming.'

'I see.'

'I can show you his cell if you like. All his belongings are there. We've got to send them to his wife, but we haven't had a chance to pack them up.'

'We're extremely short-staffed at present,' Senior Officer Warner explained.

'I think it would be worthwhile to take a quick look at the cell, don't you, Sergeant?' said the chief inspector. 'That's if Mr Johnson's got the time?'

'I can spare him for ten minutes,' said Warner. 'Show them the cell, Daryl.'

Johnson escorted the two visitors across the bright purple carpet in the visitors' hall and along several corridors. Eventually, they reached the entrance to D Wing, where a fellow officer checked their identities. Their footsteps echoed around the vast Victorian chamber as Johnson led them up the iron stairs to the first landing. They followed him for a few metres until they reached the open door of cell 5.

'Everything's just as he left it,' the warder explained helpfully as he showed the pair inside Innocent's cell.

Beside the bed was Innocent's broken television and stereo and his damaged bookcase containing dozens of books about the Midlands, motor racing and horse racing. There were travel guides, puzzle books, biographies, dictionaries and novels.

'He seems to have been well-read,' the sergeant remarked as she inspected Innocent's book collection. 'I'd have thought that was unusual among prisoners.'

'He was fanatical about *The Times* crossword,' said Johnson. Then he added, 'I've just had a message. I'll be back in five minutes.'

'Not much here,' the chief inspector remarked. 'I think it's time to go, Sergeant.'

'Hold on! What's this?' asked Sunita, pulling a blue toiletry bag from beneath the bed.

'Probably just his soap and toothbrush.' Then he realised she was studying an electric toothbrush she had found in the bag.

'That's unusual,' she said, holding the brush towards the window to take advantage of the daylight.

'What is it, Sergeant?' Roscoe asked as he sat down on the bed.

'It looks as if the bottom of the battery compartment may've been removed several times. Look! It's scuffed and pitted.'

'I see what you mean, but that's how it is with electric toothbrushes. After replacing the battery a few times, the plastic can get a bit worn.'

'Not with these. This model is rechargeable and there's no need to get access to the lower part of the gadget. You don't normally have to remove the base at all.'

'It's possible he had a problem with it,' her boss suggested. 'But I'm impressed by your thorough approach to this. You've reminded me of the time I was at training college, Sergeant. It was drummed into us the importance of even the most trivial matter in an investigation. Having a mania for minute detail is at the heart of a detective's craft.'

She wrenched the bottom part off the toothbrush and four small rolls of paper fell out. She stooped to pick them up.

'What's that, Sergeant?' he asked as he sat down on the bed and watched her.

'Well, this is a pencil map of Queensbridge,' she replied. 'And these pages wrapped around it look like the months of January, February and March, torn from a calendar. The inner workings of the gadget have been removed to create a secret compartment. Let's see what we've got here.'

'You've done well, Sergeant.'

Sunita discovered three dates on the calendar pages had been circled in black pen. Next to each one were some words in tiny, spidery handwriting.

'He's marked off some key events in his life,' she said in a low voice. 'There's 16 January.'

'That's the day he got the letter from his wife,' said Roscoe.

'That's right. He's written, "D Letter". Maybe that's D for Divorce. Then he's circled 5 February and written, "DS Thompson".'

'Who the hell's that?' the chief inspector asked.

'Maybe someone from West Midlands CID? He's put a ring round Monday's date of 11 February and written, "Vengeance Day". And he also circled 12 February and scrawled, "Disposal". I wonder why he's done that? Oh, hang on! Don't you remember from three years ago, sir? Innocent had an obsession with tidying up after each murder.'

'Yes, that was one of the gruesome aspects of that investigation,' Roscoe recalled. 'I wonder what he'd got in mind for my body?'

'Luckily, we'll never know,' Sunita assured him.

'Well, we've got an idea now that his visit to Queensbridge was part of a careful plan,' Roscoe remarked. 'But it's this DS Thompson that intrigues me.'

Just at that moment, Daryl Johnson reappeared in the doorway.

'Everything all right?' he asked.

'It's time for you to come clean and tell us about DS Thompson,' said Roscoe. 'Where was he from and what was he doing here on Tuesday of last week?'

'Oh him,' said Johnson. 'I didn't mention that guy because I thought you knew all about him – since he's in the same force as yourselves.'

Johnson spent the next few minutes explaining how the man calling himself Thompson had sent an official-looking email from the Heart of England Police email server requesting an interview with Innocent.

He described the visitor as a tall, stocky man. He was clean-shaven, Caucasian and had short brown hair. He spoke with a faint northern accent.

'Did he have podgy fingers?' Roscoe asked.

'Now you come to mention it, yes.'

'Sounds like Bains.'

Sunita nodded. 'Yes, it does.'

'Can we have a look at all the CCTV footage around visiting time on 5 February?' Roscoe asked. 'We'll also need to take a statement from you, Mr Johnson. All this could prove to be vital evidence.'

Chapter 53

After his painful visit to the Munro family on Friday morning, the chief inspector set off for his office. During the journey, he took a hands-free call on his car phone from Tom Vickers.

'Morning, guv. Any news about Sean Munro?'

'Yes. Things are looking up,' said Roscoe. 'His condition is now stable and he might be transferred to a general ward in a few days.'

'That's brilliant,' said Vickers. 'I thought you ought to know DS Roy's gone off to the airport. She received a call to say that Betina Fischer had arrived on a flight from Warsaw this morning and been arrested.'

'So they're bringing the woman back to St James Street?'

'Yes, guv. She and Dawson.'

'Good. I'm looking forward to interviewing that woman.'

'Guv, while I'm speaking to you, we've found the black Audi used by the gang in Edgbaston in the prison van escape. They'd set it on fire near Solihull, but the dashboard's undamaged and Tahir Khan's dabs have been found. We've also got details of the company that hired the lorry to the Nowak brothers. There's CCTV of Gabriel Nowak paying cash at the counter, so he's been arrested and questioned along with his younger brother. You know the rogue warder at the Vale that we discussed yesterday? Our computer guy found emails that he sent to Seymour Trent. Efforts had been made to remove them from the computer but they failed and the warder involved has now been arrested.'

Roscoe smiled. 'That's great work,' he said.

'On top of that, we've had a trawl through the CCTV at the Vale and found it was Bains masquerading under the name DS Thompson. He set up a meet with Innocent, where they must've arranged the break-out.'

Roscoe scowled. 'He's a cunning bastard, that Bains.'

'Yes. He's been arrested again, along with Tahir Khan. Omar and I will be quizzing them this afternoon.'

'Who exactly is the warder who was passing information to Trent?'

'We're not sure but we think he could be Trent's brother-in-law.'

'That would make sense. How's the motorcycle cop who was shot in Edgbaston?'

'He's been lucky,' said Vickers. 'The bullets missed vital organs and he's on the mend. The ballistics team are hoping to link the bullets and cartridges to Gabriel Nowak's gun if they can find the weapon. They found a shoeprint in traces of coffee waste in the lorry which has been linked to a shoe worn by his brother, Dominik.'

'So it's all starting to come together,' said Roscoe, breaking into a smile for the first time in several days.

'I also had a call from the chief super,' Vickers added. 'She's been informed that Nisa Shah is prepared after all to give evidence about the two men who fled Brendan O'Sullivan's house. Along with the support of Norris's goddaughter Heather Young, who works in Summerstoke CID, and Trent's girlfriend, Polly, there's a good chance now of a retrial in the "body in the bath" case and getting the false outcome overturned.'

'That's brilliant news,' said Roscoe.

* * *

As soon as he arrived at work, Sunita Roy briefed Roscoe on the arrest of Betina Fischer and they decided to question her together.

Half an hour later, she was brought into Interview Room 1.

'You realise why you've been arrested, don't you?' said the sergeant as she stared across the table into the woman's anxious, blue eyes.

'No,' Betina Fischer replied curtly, shrugging her shoulders. 'The policeman at the airport said I was being held in connection with a murder investigation. I assume it's something to do with the deaths of Mr Filipowski and Anna.'

Sunita nodded. 'Yes, it is,' she said.

Betina's solicitor, Roger Sims, who was sitting beside her, whispered in her ear. Sunita frowned.

'We want you to cast your mind back to Wednesday, 16 January,' Sunita said. 'Where were you on that day?'

The white fingernails on Betina's right hand flashed before them as she stroked her blonde hair.

'I don't remember,' she said as Roscoe took a seat beside his sergeant.

'Would you have been at your place of work, the Gold Star Agency?'

'I suppose so.'

'Well, whether you were there or not, do you remember paying a courier to deliver a package to someone's address?'

Betina shook her head. 'Don't remember that.'

The sergeant and her boss shared a similar exasperated expression.

'Look, if I can be of help here,' he said, 'we've carried out checks on your debit card statement and you paid £75 to the firm Soho Express on that afternoon.'

She looked blank. 'Did I?'

She noticed he had a folder of documents in front of him. He opened it and drew out a sheet of paper.

'Here we are,' he said as he pushed it towards her and she started reading it.

'All right,' she said. 'I owe you an explanation. Perhaps, if I tell you this, you'll let me go home. I've got nothing to do with the terrible deaths of the two people. Mr Filipowski's been ill for the past two years. He got worse and worse. Finally, they said he'd got diabetes and would need insulin injections. That afternoon, he found himself without his insulin. So I sent some to his home in Balsall Common by courier.'

Sunita shook her head. 'You went about it in a very strange way. Instead of leaving the package for collection at the agency, you left it a few metres down the street at The Windmill Café. And you gave your name as Tina.'

'That's right,' she snapped back. 'Tina is short for Betina. There's nothing strange about that. And I didn't want the courier coming to the agency because… well, you know. It's a business offering personal services to gentlemen. Things can get embarrassing.'

'Of course, it wasn't insulin in the package, was it, Miss Fischer?' said Roscoe. 'It was a parcel containing drugs, along with an extra special ingredient.'

Betina shrugged her shoulders. 'Don't know what you mean.'

'Our pathologist found the main content of the delivery was cocaine.'

'No,' she said. 'You must be joking. Everyone who knows Mr Filipowski knows he was one of the main cocaine suppliers for the Midlands. Why am I sending cocaine to him?'

'It's what killed him,' Sunita interjected in a low voice. 'Because it was laced with fentanyl.'

Betina clasped her hands to her face. 'Oh God.'

'So why did you send it?' Roscoe demanded.

'I'm honestly believing it was insulin,' she insisted, glancing towards Mr Sims.

'Look, two people died after sampling the contents of your package, Miss Fischer,' said Roscoe. 'So this is an extremely serious matter for which you could go to prison for a very long time.'

She glanced at Mr Sims again. He whispered in her ear, and she nodded.

'My client would like a brief adjournment,' said the lawyer.

'Of course,' said Roscoe. 'We'll leave you both here for a few minutes.'

* * *

While waiting for Betina Fischer and Roger Sims to confer about the case, Roscoe switched off the video recorder and the two detectives walked up to Roscoe's room in CID.

'Betina's going to find it hard to wriggle out of this,' he said as he settled into the chair behind his desk. 'I can't understand really why she came back to Britain. I'm pretty sure she's responsible for those deaths, although her motive escapes me for the moment. She'd have been better off staying in Romania with her family, from her point of view. She'd have been unlikely to have been extradited to the UK because of Brexit.'

'I know,' Sunita replied, as she took a chair by the door. 'Unless her willingness to return here points to her innocence.'

'By the way,' said Roscoe, 'I forgot to mention that I was having a chat on the phone with Liam Clancy yesterday. He mentioned to me that one of the drug pushers was a motorbike fanatic from Smethwick. That reminded me of your courier guy, Simon. So I emailed him Simon's picture and, sure enough, Liam recognised him. Looks like your Simon was, at one time, operating on the fringe of the Birmingham drugs world.'

'Oh my goodness!' said Sunita. 'Sir, do you think Betina honestly thought she was doing a good deed and sending medicine to a diabetic but that Simon Archer, the courier, for some reason removed the insulin and replaced it with the drugs?'

He laughed. 'I don't know what to think. Tiff Filipowski had a lot of enemies. Maybe one of them got Simon to switch the parcels. I've no idea. I just thought I'd mention it to you. We've got to be aware of all kinds of possibilities in cases like this.'

Sunita shook her head. 'Perhaps we should show Miss Fischer the brown paper and get her to identify it as the packaging she sent.'

'Yes. Then we can watch her face for her reaction,' he said.

* * *

As soon as the interview with Betina resumed, Mr Sims said he had an announcement.

'My client wishes to make it clear she wasn't involved at all in the tragic deaths at Balsall Common,' he said. 'As a result, she wants to tell you exactly what happened. I think you'll see that, as far as the serious events of 16 January are concerned, my client's got a completely clear conscience.'

'Before we go any further, can I just show you the packaging that was found at Mr Filipowski's house?' said Sunita.

She had brought an exhibits bag with her containing the brown paper retrieved from Filipowski's refuse bin. Some of the sticky tape was still attached to it. Betina glanced down and nodded.

'Yes, that's my handwriting,' she admitted. 'Look, someone asked me to send the package to 47, Whitstone Drive and they assured me it was insulin. Obviously, I didn't open it to make sure. I just took their word.'

'Well, you'd better tell us who it was,' said Roscoe.

She glanced across at her solicitor before turning back nervously and looking into the detectives' inquiring faces.

'It was Monika Kowalska,' she said.

Chapter 54

The sun was fading from the sky as Sunita Roy's car reached Handsworth a few hours later. The weekend was approaching. Home-bound commuters, late-night shoppers and Friday night revellers were swarming through the suburb. Soho Road was choked with traffic.

The sergeant, accompanied by Brett Dawson, parked in a side road and they walked round the corner to the Gold Star Agency.

Three uniformed constables in a police car, who had been parked a short distance away while awaiting their arrival, drew forward and stopped outside the building.

'You all set?' Sunita asked as they joined her and Dawson on the pavement.

'Yes,' they chorused.

Sunita pointed to a burly officer with glasses. 'You assisted us three weeks ago when we came searching for Betina Fischer,' she told him.

'That's right, Sarge. Glutton for punishment, aren't I? Josh Wilson's the name. We've been watching the building,' he said. 'There's been no one coming in or out.'

'All right. Brett, I want you round the back just in case. You guys can come with me.'

Sunita strode to the door and pressed the buzzer. Within seconds, Monika Kowalska's voice purred down the intercom, 'Who is it, please?'

'Police. DS Roy,' the sergeant replied.

'Just give me a few minutes. I'll be right down.'

The officers waited patiently for a while, exchanging banter with one another, and trying to involve the sergeant in their conversation. Her mind was focused on the task in hand. She was becoming uneasy and phoned Dawson on his mobile.

'Monika hasn't left through the back, has she?' she asked her colleague.

'No, Sarge. Only one person's come out and gone through the gate. That was a woman with dark hair and glasses who looked like she came from the Global Mart shop.'

'You dope! That's probably her. What time did she go past you?'

'Only a minute ago.'

'What was she wearing?'

'She'd got shiny black leather trousers and a dark jacket. I didn't think it could be our suspect because Monika's got curly, blonde hair.'

'Get after her!' Sunita demanded. Then, turning to the three constables, she shouted, 'Looks like our woman may've done a runner. Dark coat, leather trousers and dark hair, probably a wig.'

She and PC Wilson ran into the side street where her Peugeot was parked while their two colleagues set off to search the next side road along in the opposite direction.

A narrow alley called Factory Lane ran parallel with Soho Road, behind the row of shops that included The Windmill Café and Global Mart. Sunita raced along it with PC Wilson panting behind.

'It's no good. The bloody woman's vanished,' she said as she came to a halt at the end of the lane.

'Could she have driven away?' asked Wilson.

'It's possible. We've got her car on file as a blue Vauxhall Corsa, but that may've changed,' she replied.

Then, as she glanced up the road they had just entered, she noticed a blue car emerging from a car park and heading towards them.

'That's her!' shouted Sunita as the car approached them and joined a line of traffic. The sergeant ran into the road and thumped on the driver's window, ordering the woman to stop.

But Monika, although blocked in by cars which were now queuing behind her, was reluctant to surrender to the police too easily. She began trying to perform a U-turn. However, PC Wilson grabbed the passenger door handle, thrust the door open, reached in and switched off the ignition.

'This is where your journey ends,' he informed her.

* * *

Two hours later, the chief inspector and his sergeant peered through the one-way glass into the interview room where Monika Kowalska was sitting.

'This isn't going to be easy,' he said. 'We haven't got much in the way of evidence, except for the testimony of her employee, Betina.'

'She hasn't seen the top team in action yet, sir.'

He smiled. 'That's true. Where are they?' he joked as they walked down the stairs.

Monika Kowalska, now with her curly, blonde hair on display, was sitting beside her solicitor, Dipak Sharma, a stout, middle-aged man wearing glasses.

Roscoe sat down opposite her in the ground-floor room after switching on the video recorder and Sunita quickly joined him at the table.

'Now, just to remind you, Miss Kowalska,' the chief inspector said, 'you've been charged with distribution of the potent painkiller fentanyl, resulting in the deaths of Mr Filipowski and Miss Borowka. Further charges may follow. We've been speaking to your employee, Betina Fischer, who's informed us that you asked her to arrange for a package to be sent to Mr Filipowski's home in Balsall Common on 16 January. She was told it contained insulin, but this was a lie. The package contained some high-quality cocaine laced with fentanyl, didn't it?'

'There's no point you denying it,' said Sunita. 'Over the last two hours, our computer expert, John Hepworth, has gone through your computer and found you'd been searching online how to obtain fentanyl.'

'All right,' said Monika as she leaned back in her chair. 'It was me that sent the parcel. I loved him, you see.'

Roscoe frowned. 'Filipowski?'

'Yes. I know he was no angel, but there was a charm about him. He was amazing. He came from nothing and built up a huge business…'

'Based on illegal drugs,' snapped Roscoe.

'That was only part of his business. He'd got a vast range of businesses. He was about to move into a mansion with grounds.'

'So why send him that evil concoction by courier?' he asked.

'Because he'd cheated on me yet again. He'd promised I was the one he loved, and we were going to settle down. He promised me he was going to stop his philandering ways and be faithful to me. But he couldn't leave women alone, could he? He had to play with the affections of sweet Anna, who was young enough to be his daughter.'

She leaned forward and thrust her face into her hands. After a few seconds, the detectives could see she had tears in her eyes.

Mr Sharma was becoming concerned. 'Would you like to have a break for a minute?' he asked.

She shook her head. 'No. I'm OK,' she said. 'All my hopes and dreams were being destroyed in front of me and, as soon as I realised he'd taken her down to his house, I started to behave irrationally. I just thought, if I arranged for him to receive this mixture of drugs, he wouldn't be able to resist trying it. He'd share it with her. They'd be sick and wouldn't want to make love.'

Sunita had been listening carefully to every word. 'You wrote in a message sent with the package "Try this. It's brilliant. Tyrone", to make it appear to Filipowski that the drug had been sent there by Tyrone Blake and to encourage him to take it.'

Monika nodded.

'You also wanted to throw police off the scent and cast blame on Blake.'

'I did what I thought was best at the time,' Monika said in a whisper.

Roscoe raised an eyebrow. 'It's nonsense for you to claim you thought the pair would simply become ill,' he said. 'The Home Office pathologist, Dr Reynolds, has told us Mr Filipowski had 26 micrograms per litre of fentanyl in his blood and Anna had 24 micrograms. That was a huge amount and virtually guaranteed to cause death.'

'You try to paint a picture of a wronged woman seeking redress after these two people did you an injustice,' Sunita said, 'but the truth of the matter is the man was under no obligations to you and the woman, who was unlucky enough to work in your dubious business, was in the prime of her life. You knew the consequences of lacing cocaine with high levels of this potent drug. You sent them to their deaths without batting an eyelid.'

Chapter 55

'It's been a long day, Tom,' said the chief inspector as he took the first sip from his pint of QB Bitter, a medium-strength beer produced by the Queensbridge Brewery Company.

He leaned back on his bench seat amid the clamour of voices and clinking glasses in the crowded Golden Fleece pub and stretched his legs out. He felt exhausted.

Vickers took a seat beside him clutching a pint of lager.

'So you're not drinking shorts anymore, guv?' he asked as he sat beside him.

'No. I'm sticking to bitter in future after all the trouble that rum-drinking session got me into. And I'm only having one of these, mind. I've got to drive home in a minute.'

Vickers took a swig from his glass of lager. 'I hear the Kowalska woman's been formally charged.'

'Yes. DS Roy's done a sterling job. All the bin searching and door-knocking finally paid off. You know the bloody woman nearly escaped when our team went to arrest her, don't you? Up to that point she'd probably been thinking Betina would be in our sights for the murder and would remain in Romania. She probably never thought Betina would come back and point the finger at her. But when she realised they'd come to arrest her, she did a quick changing act. Of course, poor old Dawson paid her no attention when she strolled calmly out of a rear entrance. It was only when the sergeant questioned him thoroughly she realized Kowalska must have left in disguise. She raced round the corner with a constable and they nabbed the woman.'

Vickers grinned. 'Good for her. Is she coming over?'

'Yes. She said she'd join us as soon as she'd finished some paperwork. Ah, here she is now.'

Roscoe, who was seated close to the pub door, watched as his sergeant, smiling broadly, approached them.

'I won't stay long,' she remarked as the inspector went to the bar to buy her an orange juice.

'You've done a first-rate job with the double deaths, Sergeant.'

'I just did my best, sir.'

'I was watching you in the interview room through the two-way glass after I left. You were taking down a statement from the Kowalska woman. You've got great attention to detail. If you still wanted to apply for promotion, I can't see that you'd have any problem.'

'Thank you, sir.'

As Vickers returned from the bar with her drink, her phone rang.

'I'd better take this,' she mumbled. 'I've been waiting for this call.'

She stepped outside and stood beneath the glow of an orange streetlight. A group of high-spirited revellers on the far side of the road were waiting to cross while, in the distance, she could see the lights shining from the police headquarters.

'Hi, John,' she said as she answered the call from digital forensic analyst John Hepworth. 'What have you found?'

'I've finished examining Miss Kowalska's mobile phone and computer,' he said in a mellow, educated voice. 'You'll be pleased to know I've managed to save all the emails she thought she'd deleted.'

'That's tremendous, John,' she exclaimed.

'Monika Kowalska received four emails from someone calling themselves "AM" and she's got a phone contact with the same initials. After liaising with the email server and phone company, we've come up with an address in Hanover Drive, Sutton Coldfield, the home of a Mr Axel Makepeace.'

'Makepeace?' said Sunita excitedly. 'That's the guy alleged to run the West Side Gang.'

'That's right,' said Hepworth. 'There are emails about some painkiller. The very last email ends with the words, "Didn't we give them a lovely send-off?"'

'You've been a great help, John,' she said. 'I'll let the DCI know how hard you've worked on this.'

'No problem,' said John as he ended the call.

Sunita pushed open the pub door and glanced at the chief inspector.

'Sir, there's something you ought to know,' she said.

THE END

If you enjoyed this book, please let others know by leaving a quick review on Amazon. Also, if you spot anything untoward in the paperback, get in touch. We strive for the best quality and appreciate reader feedback.

editor@thebookfolks.com

www.thebookfolks.com

More fiction in this series

MURDER ON OXFORD LANE (Book 1)

A budding chorister doesn't return home from practice but his wife doesn't appear concerned. DS Sunita Roy becomes convinced he has been murdered but she has her own problems in the form of an ex-boyfriend who won't take no for an answer. Will she keep her eye on the ball when all expect her to fail?

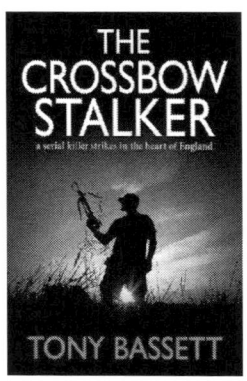

THE CROSSBOW STALKER (Book 2)

When a serial killer armed with a crossbow terrorises the
West Midlands, Chief Inspector Gavin Roscoe suspects a
motive of jealousy and revenge. But as the number of
victims increases, the connection initially established
between them wears thin. DS Sunita Roy has a different
theory and resolves to pursue her own instincts, come
what may.

MURDER OF A DOCTOR (Book 3)

Police search for the identities of people seen near the scene of a doctor's murder. And it seems like an open and shut case when a father with a grievance against him can be placed nearby. But DS Sunita Roy wants to dig deeper, and with an internal affairs investigation ongoing, she'll have to tread carefully.

All FREE with Kindle Unlimited and available in paperback.

Other titles of interest

LAST TRAIN FOR MURDER by Traude Ailinger

An investigative journalist who made a career out of sticking it to the man dies on a train to Edinburgh, having been poisoned. DI Russell McCord struggles in the investigation after getting banned from contacting helpful but self-serving reporter Amy Thornton. But the latter is ready to go in, all guns blazing. After the smoke has cleared, what will remain standing?

THE GIRL IN THE MEADOW by John Dean

When the body of a young woman is discovered under the
floorboards of an isolated house during its renovation,
questions are raised about DCI Jack Harris' own potential
connection to the site. Will he clear his name or will his
reputation be forever besmirched in the rural Pennine
community?

All FREE with Kindle Unlimited and available in paperback.

www.thebookfolks.com